Tekoa

Joe Herrington

PublishAmerica

Baltimore

First printing

ISBN: 1-59129-864-4
PUBLISHED BY PUBLISHAMERICA BOOK PUBLISHERS
www.publishamerica.com
Baltimore

Printed in the United States of America

To Mom and Dad who raised me in the way I should go.
Proverbs 22:6

Acknowledgements

Many people cross our paths and influence what we become and how we get there. Chief among them are family members...loving, trusting, and encouraging. They are the foundation upon which we build. Some are numbered as friends. They offer their support, trust and a hand to help. Some become those kindred spirits that make us blossom and draw us closer to God. My life has been richly blessed with scores of these kind souls.

There have been many that have moved this book forward. Some were the Boy Scouts in my troop that insisted I publish my stories. Some read and encouraged my meager efforts. Some worked hard hours with a red pencil helping to mold the manuscript. And then there were those who unknowingly lived the book with me. Their personalities inspired the characters. Our adventures together became the seed for the story. I fear to name them all for I would surely take too much time, and even then leave someone out. One, however, I will mention. He was my boyhood companion and fellow adventurer. David Kerr's unassuming humility, integrity, and love for rugged backcountry, inspired the David Carson character in this story.

Chapter 1

The soft, southern breeze moved easy across the prairie grass and whispered in the mesquite. The windmill creaked, a meadowlark called, and I daydreamed. Spring break was finally here, and it was time for adventure. I lay still in the tall grass planning just what it might be.

David would be riding up soon on an old motorbike that had almost killed us both more than once. We were best friends who shared many common interests. Rough-edged country boys, but well educated by the books and the land, we considered ourselves to be inventors and explorers. And naturally we had dreams of a great discovery we might someday make.

Today we were to decide what our last spring break trip would be. We were seniors at A & M, and this was our last chance for a big adventure before we had to go out into the world and make our mark. Our financial resources had narrowed it down to two things... looking for fossils along the Concho Ridge, or exploring the rugged Palo Duro Canyon.

I lay quietly, twitching a sprig of grass in my teeth and watching the puffy white cumulus clouds float across the endless prairie sky. How many times I had raced barefooted across the pasture trying to outrun their shadows. As slow and graceful as they seemed, I was no match for them.

In the distance I heard the sputtering drone of David's old bike. It sounded like a big, drunk mosquito and looked like something from the junkyard. I could see a wisp of dust rise along the horizon, tailing his route on the old dirt road. Moments later he rounded the corner post and sailed through the gate, scattering chickens and bringing worry to the old milk cow.

As soon as his infernal machine jerked to a stop, he jumped off in a dead run, leaving it to drop in the dirt. He landed beside me and thrust a newspaper clipping in my face. "This is it! This is what we gotta do!"

I studied the article. It was written by the town's local science writer and was about a recent sighting of the Marfa lights…mysterious lights that play out a ghostly dance along a ridge of mountains outside the small town of Marfa, Texas.

The lights had long been a mystery and topic of conversation among the folks of these parts. The old timers had their explanations, and the college boys had theirs. The exegesis ranged from clusters of insects emitting their natural light in a rhythmic, unified manner, to plain old ghosts. Whatever the mystery lights were, they always seemed to stir up the local conversation about this time of the year.

"This is great, David!" I said jumping to my feet. "I've always wanted to see this."

"Well, we could get our stuff together and be there by the week-end. I know old man Remes would let us set up in his pasture. His ranch borders a good twelve miles of those mountains."

Mr. Remes was a crusty old cowboy who owned half the country down there. He had raised his eyebrows at us last summer when we rode in there asking for permission to look for dinosaur tracks on his place. We had found an old survey map with some sketches and notes about tracks that hadn't been documented yet.

"What do you boys have for brains?" he'd said, thinking we were quacks. After a week of searching and crosschecking old maps and survey documents, we located the tracks, right where we expected to find them. He was tickled, and the state of Texas was appreciative. Well, that had begun a good friendship with the old man.

We went into the house and telephoned him. "Sure," he said, "you boys come on down and do your science stuff. It'll make for good talk down at the feed store."

We spent the next day collecting essentials and doing what little research we could before loading up David's '56 Chevy truck and taking to the road. The two-lane highway to Marfa was a straight line to the horizon, uninteresting and uneventful. Only during the last hour of the drive did the road begin to take on personality.

While I drove, David sat absorbed in an agriculture magazine. He was so focused that I leaned over for a glimpse. "What's got you glued to that journal?"

"Oh, one of my professors wrote this article on hybrid grains. Do you want me to read it to you?"

8

"No thanks. You keep your kind of science, and I'll stick to my kind of science."

"Say, Shelby, did you ever think about how strange we are? I mean in the things we like. There you sit, a cowboy all your life, and loving it, too. But you're a physics major. And me, a city kid most of my life, 'till I moved out here, and I'm an agriculture major. How do you figure it?"

"Well, I guess you don't. We're just lucky enough to live in a place and time where a boy doesn't have to follow the path of his dad. He can make his own. That's all we've done, and I like it that way."

"Does your dad like it that way, or would he rather have you take over the ranch?"

"My dad wants all five of his sons to find their own ways. Early on I showed an interest in technical things, and he supported me in it. I remember he would bring home old electric motors and radios for me to take apart or try to fix. Then he helped me build my little lab out back by the barn. Now don't get me wrong, he taught me to love the ranch too. I figure one of my brothers is bound to want to take over the place."

"I wish my dad saw it that way. He thinks I won't amount to much in agriculture. He always says that banking should be my future. I used to think that, too, until I moved out here and learned to grow things. Now all I want to do is develop new crops and grasses, improve land management techniques… things like that. I'll do it too. Did I tell you I've got an offer to work for a seed company in Waco after graduation?"

"That's more than I've got. I don't have any responses yet." I was pleased about David's offer. He seldom seemed to get any lucky breaks, but he worked harder than anyone else I knew, and he sure deserved some. He sat quietly looking out the window at the passing mesquite. I often wondered about his thoughts, as I did now. He was a serious young man with a heart as big as these West Texas skies. Nothing was too much trouble for him when it came to helping out a friend. But his heart wasn't all that was big. He stood every bit of six feet tall with broad shoulders and curly blond hair. He would be a real catch for some girl, but he didn't think he had anything to offer the fairer sex.

With little else said, we reached the turnoff to the Remes' ranch and drove through the stone archway that marked his property line. The country was rugged and magnificent and recent rains had left it covered with wild flowers and blooming cactus. Many of the flowers near the road were Indian paintbrushes and bluebonnets, but other wild flowers painted huge patches of rich color that stretched to the horizon. The land was unusually green and lush for this part of the country. That was good to see because there had been a drought for the past several years, and it had really been rough on these ranchers. Now, though, it was starting to look like we were finally pulling out of it.

The dirt road wound through the pasture and over several cattle guards. Green grass grew right up to the tight, four-strand, barbed-wire fence. You could always tell a lot about a rancher by the kind of fences he maintained, and it was easy to see that the Remes' ranch was well cared for. That ole man Remes knew how to care for the land and not exploit it was evident even to a casual observer.

We had to stop several times for cattle that had bedded down in the middle of the road. They would bawl and look like they expected you to go around them, then they would slowly get up, hind end first, and move out of the way. The calves would look curiously for a minute and then bounce off to their mamas.

As we topped the hill we could see the ranch house in the distance. It was a large but simple place with a porch all around it. A few other buildings were clustered nearby, bordered by stock pens and corrals. A small pond glistened in the sunlight while several horses grazed around its edge. It all sat picture perfect against a backdrop of the blue-hazed Chinati mountains. The lush green pastures purpled with distance as they stretched to reach the distant sky. Black and brown specks scattered the countryside as they moved and grazed beneath the white puffy clouds.

Old Mr. Remes was on the front porch with his wife of fifty-two years when we drove in the gate. He stood up, waved, and walked briskly to the car. A powerful gent for eighty…his lean swarthy features and brown hair belonged to a man twenty years younger. He silvered a bit at the temples, but his eyes sparkled and his step was quick.

He offered his thick, powerful hand like an eager child. "Howdy, boys, we're real happy you came. My, you're both some taller than last I eyed you. Better lookin' too. I don't mind tellin' you, Shelby, I was afeared you was a little too lean, but look at you now. Looks like you're better'n six feet and fillin' out like a real man. What do you weigh?"

"About a hundred and seventy, I reckon. I guess it was finally my time to start growin'." I responded rather sheepishly.

"Maybe so, son, maybe so. Just look at these boys, Ma. You ever seen a finer specimen of what an American boy ought to be?"

10

"No, Pa. Now hush, you're embarrassin' 'em." He seemed unusually happy to see us, and the dear lady couldn't wait to feed us.

There was a girl there, too…a plain, but pretty, blue-eyed girl, maybe a year older than we were. Bein' healthy, American boys, she caught our interest right off. Her light-brown hair blew gently in the breeze and came to rest on the shoulders of her blue gingham dress. She was introduced as Polly, their daughter-in-law. That quickly cleared things up, but it seemed strange since we hadn't even known they had a son. No more explanation was given, and we didn't ask.

They were gentle folks, but they had lived a life that would fill a library. As we ate around a big oak table, in a kitchen that could have been a museum, they talked. Into the night they talked, and we sat spellbound. It was as if we had stepped back in time, for the stories they told were of Indian raids, wagon trains, cattle drives, and stagecoaches. They told us of men they had met, like Buffalo Bill and Geronimo. They talked about the first car they had ever seen, the first telephone, the first airplane.

Polly sat quietly through all the talk. She was pleasant enough, but she seemed kind of sad, or to have a lot on her mind. Finally, the old man said, "Well boys, I have to feed at sun up. Gotta get some sleep." He and his wife got up to leave the room, but Mrs. Remes turned, reluctant to go.

"You go on Pa, I'll be in later." She seemed to enjoy our company and wanted to stay. "You boys don't look tired. I'll make some hot chocolate." Then turning to Polly she said, "Why don't you stay up with us, child?"

"No, Ma, I'm kinda' done in." She walked quietly out of the room.

As Mrs. Remes busied around the stove she said, "You boys remind me of my son, Robby."

David said curiously, "We didn't know you had a son."

"Yes, Robby was away in the Army when you boys were here last summer. Pa and I adopted him in June of '43. He was our joy. He would be twenty-one next month. He and Polly were married early last year." I could see a tear in her eye, and her voice quivered a bit.

"Ma'am, if you don't mind me asking," I said. "What happened to him?"

"Strange thing, that boy just up and disappeared one day. He went out to count calves and check for screwworms one morning and never came back. His horse wandered in about noon without him, and we started an immediate search. The sheriff had fifty men out there. They found nothin' but his tracks. They could tell where he had gotten down off his horse, but then they lost the trail. The sheriff said it was like the boy took wings or somethin'.

"He's been gone six months now, and that poor girl in there is a total wreck. I tell you somethin', Pa was real anxious for you boys to come. I think he kinda' needed you. He seems to think you'll find somethin' out there. Somethin' the sheriff missed. He says you boys have the right kind of mind for this kind of mystery."

I swallowed hard and looked at David. What a tragedy. But the spirit of my youth, and my overconfidence in our ability, told me that we just might. "Where were his tracks found? In fact," I said, "Tell us everything. Start at the beginning, and don't leave out anything!" I was excited now, and I felt that we had a mission.

She touched her lips with the tips of her fingers, and I saw a twinkle of hope in her eyes. "Let me show you boys somethin'." She walked over to a bookcase, picked up a small, stone-like statuette and brought it to the table. "Robby brought this home the day before he disappeared. Now, this old woman don't know much, but I've never seen anything like it before. He was a mighty excited boy and said he had discovered somethin'. Pa got on to him about some work needed doin', so he didn't tell me any more. The sheriff looked at it but said it was nothin' but some old glass art or somethin'. Robby may have told Polly more. You could ask her."

David was already knocking on Polly's door. When she came out we asked her if Robby had told her anything at all about the statue. "Yes, he told me he had discovered something out there, but he was afraid to tell anyone because folks would call him crazy. He gave me some little trinkets, made from the same colored glass, I think. Here, I'll show you." She went back into the room and came out with a hand full of small glass-like objects.

"David, look at this stuff. This is obsidian."

"How could obsidian be formed like that?"

"I can't imagine, but somebody is a remarkable craftsman."

Mrs. Remes interrupted. "What did you boys call that stuff?"

"Obsidian, Ma'am. It's a shiny volcanic glass. Generally, you see it ground and polished into shape, but this looks molded somehow."

Our conversation with the two women became more excited as they told all about Robby's last few days at home. David wrote everything down in his notebook as I quizzed them for details. Finally, they were talked out and went to bed. We went out to the barn loft and unrolled our soogans. We crawled in for the night, but we were still awake with excitement. An old barn owl kept us company as we talked and planned what we would do. Talk slowly quieted, and the barn owl stood a curious night watch over two very excited adventurers.

The morning was fresh, clear, and filled with the smell of frying bacon. Not wanting to impose any further, we tried to leave, but they wouldn't hear of it. Mrs. Remes served a big breakfast on a red-checkered tablecloth. That stirred a fond memory of sitting in my grandmother's farmhouse kitchen at another table with a red-checkered tablecloth.

Mr. Remes had been up before the sun and was somewhere outside doing the ranch work that seemed to never end. No matter how many hours you gave the day or how much sweat you wiped from your brow, tomorrow would arrive as if nothing had been done. Mrs. Remes had been up with him and already had a half-day's work behind her. With her silver hair pinned up in a bun, the twinkle in her eyes and her warm, radiant smile, she appeared the classic grandmother icon. The years of hard work on this ranch had been good to her. They had taken some of her physical beauty, but had given her something more… something much more that cannot be explained. These two old folks were what role models are made of. They were honest, hard working, gentle people who had a love for each other that kinda' made you a little misty eyed. I hoped I could grow old as nobly as he, with a wife as devout as this gracious lady.

As we drove off to the campsite, she said, " If you boys get tired of your own cookin' out there, then you come on up to the house."

Chapter 2

We got started early that morning. We set up camp on some high ground just north of the jagged mountain ridge we had picked out on our map. Intentionally, we picked the same area where Robby had disappeared. Our camp was far enough back that we could survey a good fifteen mile stretch of the Chinati ridge without moving. It would also serve as a good central location in our search for clues.

By noon we had two transits set up and the distance between them carefully measured. We ran a homemade telephone between them and then back to camp. We had radios, but they were for emergencies, not the all-night chatter that would surely take place. Our tents were up and all our supplies stowed. We were ready. This spot would allow us to search for clues of Robby's disappearance. It was also a location that would offer a good view of the mysterious lights, if they appeared.

The rest of the day was spent resting and just taking it easy, for we planned to be up all night. I started supper, baked some sourdough bread, and scouted around for arrowheads and possible clues. David wrote in his journal and restlessly re-checked our equipment. We talked some until sundown, but then we both went off by ourselves to watch it set. Sunset is a private time for most Western men, and we wanted it alone.

The night was beautiful but uneventful. The stars in that high, dry country could almost be touched. They were crisp and clear, right down to the horizon. Bats dipped and darted as they caught their evening meal. We watched the night pass with the turn of the Big Dipper and measured its temperature with the chirps of the crickets. No lights in the mountains, but no matter, this was only the first night.

The next night was turning out the same way, and I decided to take a walk. I rang David on the phone and told him where I would be, just in case anything came up. "I'll stay within hollerin' distance," I told him. And I walked off into the starlit blackness.

The night brings wonderment to those who grow up on the land. It called to me like an old friend, and I wanted to be out there in it, away from our buzzing contraptions and blinking lights. Science has its place, but I wasn't in the mood.

I circled the camp and dark-adapted my eyes. I liked using my night vision, a technique taught to me by my dad. "When you do it right," he would say, "you can see as well as most animals." I slipped around quietly, hoping to sneak up on a rabbit or something. The few times I had been successful at that fulfilled a strange need within me to outwit these critters. Still, I was in awe of the night and its creatures. For me, as an observer, all was peaceful and still, but for those animals that must survive the night, this was a deadly place and time. To err was to die, and to be clumsy was to starve. Dad would often remind me of that. "Respect these creatures and what it is to live." I did. With great admiration, I did.

For most of a half-hour I sat without a move or a sound. Something out there had caught my attention and was getting closer. I couldn't see it or even hear it, but I knew it was slowly approaching. I often wondered about other senses that we must have but don't know much about. Occasionally, I've felt watched or followed. I've sensed the presence of something or someone, just as I could sense this creature out there now, approaching. But how, could he feel it as I did? He must, for his approach was cautious. The game would soon be over for both of us, and no doubt the little critter would get quite a scare.

I began to notice a strange smell... a disgusting, filthy odor that made me uncomfortable. Suddenly, there was a flash of light from David's outpost. He must have dropped his flashlight, and the red lens came off. The beam of light slashed through the night like a saber and came to rest shining in my direction. Immediately there was a flurry of activity all around me. Something ran past, something large. Instinctively, I stood up, and what looked to be a man came to a sudden halt in front of me, stared for a second, and took off into the night. I turned on my flashlight and swept the area. My light beam caught several man-like figures running away and all disappearing near a clump of mesquite some fifty yards away.

My heart was pounding. I was expecting a rabbit or some other small animal. I had never expected a man. But wait was it really a man? It had the shape of a man, it stood about 6'5", but its features, what little I could see of them, looked wild. And come to think of it, the creature seemed to be wrapped in something rather than dressed in regular clothes. I replayed it in my mind. The smell was his, or theirs. There had been several of them, and they had been startled by David's light.

I called to David and began running toward his outpost. He was as excited as I was and began to exclaim, "Did you see them, Shelby? They were magnificent!"

Sensing that we weren't talking about the same thing, I said. "What do you mean?"

"The lights, I saw them. They were like bright stars that just seemed to drift above the horizon and change color. They were right over there somewhere," he said as he pointed to where I had been. I called for you and tried to signal you, but I dropped my flashlight. By the time I got my red lens back on they were gone."

"No, I didn't see them, but you're not going to believe what I did see." Meticulously, I told him every detail, just like I would describe a science experiment.

"Shelby Ferris, you're pullin' my leg!"

"No, David, honest! I even saw where they disappeared, and I think we should have a look." My story sounded wild, and even though David had an open and curious mind, he was also cautious.

"I think we should go back to town and report this."

"There is no time for that now. Anyway, I'm only suggesting we look around and gather a few facts. Then, if this is too big for us, we can report it."

Within minutes we were carefully searching for tracks and finding them plentiful. The spot where I had been sitting was surrounded by six sets of tracks, all human. Strange thing though, they wore moccasins instead of shoes. We continued the search and found them all around our camp.

"Hey, Shel, you suppose they were just watching us, or had something else on their minds?"

"I don't know, but it's kinda' creepy to think we were surrounded like that and didn't even know it." We split up to cover more ground and talked constantly, just as much to keep track of each other as to calm our nerves. The chatter went on as we searched the area following the general direction of the tracks.

Suddenly, the tracks I followed ended. They had all converged at one spot and just disappeared. Where could they have gone? I searched around for some possible explanation, but there was none.

I looked around toward David to signal him, and as I turned, the ground beneath me gave way. I went down. It was like being swallowed up by the ground. Instinctively, I threw out my arms and stopped my descent. As the dust settled, I realized I had lost my flashlight, and I was pushing with all my might to keep from falling through the hole. My feet swung free, and I used them to search for something to stand on or brace against. There was nothing. For all I knew this pit could be hundreds of feet deep or mere inches beyond my reach.

"David! Quick, I need help!" He was already on his way, and I could see his light.

"I heard all the racket. What happened?"

"Stop! The rest of this may cave in!" David pulled off his belt and sprawled out on the ground. He threw me its end and pulled me out. We both lay still in the dirt. It had happened so fast that I needed to sort through it again.

I rolled over on my back and took a deep breath. "The ground just caved in! I followed their tracks to this spot, and I fell through."

"Look at that! There is a light down in there."

"I dropped my flashlight. That's probably it." I said, as David eased back toward the hole and looked in.

"You know this thing is only about six feet deep. If you had fallen in, you wouldn't have gone anywhere." He kinda' had a sarcastic chuckle to his voice.

"I had no way of knowing that. For all I knew it might have been an abandoned well or something."

"Yeah, I know, I was just proddin' you some. Come on, let's check this out." David jumped into the hole, and I followed. I picked up my flashlight and shined it around.

"A tunnel! Let's see where it goes."

"Man, it's cold down here... break out the P-kit." Each of us always carried a *Possibles kit,* a small belt pack dating back to the early mountain men. It is easily concealed under a long shirt. Ours contained various items we might need in any scientific adventure, as well as necessities like duct tape and toilet paper. From it I pulled out a thermometer, and we sat for a moment watching the mercury drop.

David snapped his fingers a few times and broke the strange silence.

"Notice how quiet it is down here, no echo like most caves."

"Yeah, it's almost like the sound is being sucked out of here. If you listen you can hear your heart beat." Then, after a minute or so I said, "Thirty-six."

"Man that's cold. How can it be that cold down here and so warm up there?"

"You know, I bet this is a lava tube. I read about one over near Tucson. They say the cold air settles down in these caves during the cold of winter, and the lava, being full of millions of air pockets, acts like a Thermos."

As I spoke, David poked around at the walls. "That would also explain the sound absorption, wouldn't it? Let's get movin' before we freeze."

We got up and walked on through the tube. In a few spots we found ice flows on the walls. We stopped to examine, and marvel at, this strange site.

David stopped. "Listen! Do you hear that?"

"What?"

"That low rumble. It sounds like about thirty cycles or so." I didn't hear it, so he waved his hand, motioning us on. He stopped again. "How about now?"

"I hear it. I feel it, too, but I can't tell where it's coming from."

"Yeah, the frequency is too low. If it were a little higher we could tell. Come on, let's find out what it is." As we walked, the sound slowly got so intense that I could feel it in my chest.

My light caught a reflection, and we moved closer, discovering two obsidian boulders the size of car tires. They were half buried in the sand on each side of the trail. David pointed to the sand between them. It was dancing like water on a hot skillet. He reached down and touched one of the rocks. "This is the source." He yelled.

Our minds were racing through possible explanations, but it was simply too loud and uncomfortable here to discuss anything. I moved on across the vibrating sand. The sensation was strange, and for a moment I felt as if I were in slow motion. I had felt like that in dreams before, but this was no dream.

As we crossed the sand, I began to feel somewhat claustrophobic. The air seemed too thick to breathe. There was no particular smell, but it was as if we had walked into some kind of cloud. I turned to David, and he, too, was gasping for air. Without saying a word, we both ran back across the sand where the air had seemed fine. David coughed a bit and spoke loudly over the rumble, "Seems like we walked into a pocket of bad air."

"I think it's firedamp."

"Methane? I bet you're right! We'd better be very careful, that stuff is explosive."

"Funny how it's just right over there...like walking through a door. I wonder how far it goes?" I shined my light down the tunnel. "David, look at that!" As my flashlight beam crossed the vibrating sand, it bent to the left a few degrees like it had bounced off a mirror.

"Wow, now that is really strange." He turned his light on and shined it around. Our lights seemed to bend at the same place in the tunnel. We sat playing with our lights for several minutes, trying to figure out what was happening. This was definitely beyond our understanding.

My light beam fell to the tunnel floor beyond the vibrating sand, and I saw our tracks. It was plain to see where we had turned around and come back. But it was just as plain to see other tracks that went on beyond ours. I turned to David. He was looking at them too. Somebody had gone through here before us. He said. "Well, that must mean that the air gets better on the other side."

Without saying more, David walked back across the vibrating sand, and I followed. Again the strange, slow motion feeling. When I caught up to David, he was stopped for a moment, holding his breath, and pointing to the tracks. Moccasins. We moved on, and after about twenty yards the air was good and the rumble had subsided enough to talk easily again. "David," I said kinda' casual, "did you notice anything unusual as you crossed that patch of vibrating sand?"

"Yeah, I felt like I was wading through neck deep water."

"Me too. I'd say that's a pretty weird spot back there." We stood there looking back into the dark tunnel, neither of us willing to be the first with a stupid explanation. Finally, I turned and walked on, but my mind was playing with some strange notions about that place... notions I wasn't ready to talk about yet.

Chapter 3

The young adventurers walked another five minutes before something hit the wall beside them and bounced to the floor. Instinctively they knelt down, waiting. Again it happened. David pointed to a small rock as it rolled to a stop, and Shelby nodded in understanding. Someone was throwing rocks at them. After a few more had hit in their general area, Shelby got to thinking that maybe they weren't the intended target. He motioned for David to stay, and he eased forward to take a look. As he rounded the next bend he could see a pile of boulders silhouetted against a dull, faint glow. A few more rocks came over the boulders and scattered in a wide area. He concluded that whoever was throwing them didn't have anything in particular he wanted to hit.

Shelby motioned for his companion to move up, and David was soon beside him whispering, "See anything?"

"Not yet." They moved up nearer the pile and slowly peeked around a large boulder. They could see someone silhouetted against an opening in the tunnel. He wasn't very big, and as they watched, he picked up another rock and chunked it over the boulder pile.

David leaned over and whispered. "It's a boy, I think." Shelby looked again and nodded in agreement. Standing in the dim light of the entrance was a scruffy, Tom Sawyer-like boy. He wore moccasins, a ragged early pioneer style shirt with suspenders and trousers he had long outgrown. Back home they'd call them high water pants.

If they walked out there they might scare the kid, and he would run away. Shelby said as much, and David responded. "I have an idea." He reached into his pocket and came out with a handful of hard candy. The next time the kid threw a rock, David threw a piece of candy back at him. At first the kid didn't notice, but after a few more times he became aware of something landing near him. Then slowly, systematically, he would throw a rock, and David would throw a piece of candy. He picked a piece up and looked at it, turning it in his hand and holding it up to the light. After a time, he called out something they didn't understand.

"Indian? It isn't Spanish." Shelby quizzed. David just shrugged, then he stood up and called to the boy. The kid looked startled and ready to escape if need be, but didn't run away. David held out a piece of candy and unwrapped it. He turned it in his fingers for the kid to see, then put it in his mouth. "Mmm good."

"Boy, that was original," Shelby said, "couldn't you come up with something better than that?" The boy watched them cautiously as they walked up to him. He stood like a young deer poised for a quick retreat.

David began to try to communicate with the boy. "We friend...Me David...You name?"

"Good grief, David, what kind of talk is that?" (It had always amazed Shelby that Americans seemed to think that if they spoke slowly and left out enough words anyone could understand them.) "Hi, kid. Do you understand me?"

"Yes, but he sure talks funny. For a moment I thought you were somebody else." Shelby looked over at David with a don't you feel stupid look. He just shrugged and returned a sheepish grin. Then he asked the boy, his name. "Bon," the lad replied.

"Hi, Bon," Shelby said, "this is David Carson, and I'm Shelby Ferris. Sometimes they just call me Shel and him DC." He seemed friendly, but he still appeared rather cautious, and his large, dark eyes showed curiosity. Shelby continued, "Did you see anyone else come through here?"

"Yes, several Nephilim. I thought you were with them."

"Nephilim? Uh, no, but we were following them," David said sternly. "Did they see you? I mean, did you hide when they came?"

"No, they wouldn't harm me. They're my friends."

"Well, why were they out there trying to...?" David cut his friend off with a quick hand motion hidden from the boy. Shelby knew he was right of course; they needed to be cautious and glean some more information.

"What are you doing here in this place, Bon?" David asked.

"Oh, I come out here to these lava beds all the time. I like this cave, and I come here often to play. I haven't been back very far, though, because I can't see back there and Grandfather warned me against using a torch in any of these caves. They can be very dangerous, you know."

"Yeah, we know," Shelby replied, "but, how do the Ne...philim...see back there?"

"I think they can see in the dark pretty well… at least that's what I'm told. How do you see back there?"

"With my flashlight." Shelby flicked it on and shined it around.

"Where are the wires?"

"There aren't any. It uses batteries."

"I don't know anything about that. All of our lights have wires on them. The wires don't work out here."

David got back on track with his questioning. "Where do you live, Bon?"

"Oh, my village is just a short way from here. I live there with my Mom and crabby old sister. We live with my grandfather. Maybe you would like to come to my village and meet Grandfather. He would like to see your light with no wires."

"That's a good idea." David moved toward the entrance as he spoke.

"Wait! I think the Cartok soldiers are still out there somewhere. I was waiting in here for the pigs to leave the area. I don't want them to discover this place. They consider me nothing and usually don't bother us. But you're different. I think maybe they would capture or kill you."

This situation was getting more confusing by the moment, and Shelby wondered, *Who are these Cartok soldiers? Where do they come from? And why such a vile hatred from the boy? The night had been peaceful and quiet until those strange creatures appeared, and Bon said they were "Nephilim."*

The boy went out for a look, and when he disappeared, the two started to compare notes. "David, can you figure this?"

"What time is it?"

"It's about 2:15 AM."

"Right. Now look at the light coming in that entrance. That's daylight. I can name ten things that haven't been right since you fell through that cave ceiling."

"Yeah, and did you notice, Bon said his village was near here? There isn't anything around here but cows and miles of pasture."

"It seems like a dream, but I know better. I keep pinching myself to see if I am asleep, and I'm not!"

"I know, I feel the same way. But it is kinda' neat."

"This is some kind of incredible mystery, and we need to figure it out. Let's just play along and learn what we can." Shelby nodded in agreement as

Bon raced playfully back through the entrance. They might not have him figured out yet, but he was all boy.

"I think they have moved on to the west. That's the way back to their camp. Come on. Let's go." Bon led them back outside, but it was not the outside they had come from only minutes ago. That outside had been the dark of night in the warmth of spring. They had camped in the middle of a grassy pasture with a mountain range to the south. Here, it appeared to be an overcast day, and from the orange tint in the sky, it looked to be late afternoon. It was totally unexplainable. So for now, they stopped trying to explain it. They just gathered the facts, strange as they were, and took careful note of the cave entrance so they could find it again. Shelby took his compass and shot a back azimuth from two dominant peaks. David wrote down the two sets of numbers and quickly made a sketch map in his journal. The boy watched with interest, but said nothing. When they appeared to be finished, he walked on.

After a moment Bon quizzed, "What are you guys? Arasians? Gedoians? You sure don't come from around here." David and Shelby exchanged glances. What could they say and still not give away too much? Shelby shrugged at David and indicated that he give some kind of answer.

"We're Texans."

"Never heard of Texans." For now he let it drop.

As they followed Bon along a faint game trail, Shelby noticed the black rock on which they walked… a lava field, like those he had seen in Arizona and New Mexico. The little vegetation that managed to grow in this bleak, basalt landscape was well-established mesquite, greasewood, prickly pear and Spanish dagger, nothing unusual about that. The pieces of this puzzle weren't out of the ordinary. It was how they went together that had him baffled.

Shelby noticed that David was looking at the mountains. These were not the Chinati Mountains of southwest Texas; these were more like the mountains of northern California. They were huge, rugged and magnificent.

David turned and pointed back to their left. There stood a magnificent shield volcano, perhaps two thousand feet high with a steam cloud gently rising from its vent. Bon noticed their interest in the restless mountain. "Tekoa," he said proudly, "the namesake of my people. To the Cartokians, it's the god of new life."

David's eyes locked on Bon. "What do you mean? I thought civilization had outgrown that kind of superstition."

"Not the Cartokians. They're strange people. They even sacrifice to that mountain." The Texans stopped dead in their tracks.

"What do they sacrifice?" Shelby asked, almost whispering.

"Usually Gedor war prisoners, but they sacrifice their own too. They even take my people from time to time. It doesn't really matter to them. They consider us all to be dogs."

"But you don't seem to fear them." David said. "You play out here where they patrol."

"I fear them; but they're not very smart. They're like snakes. If you know their habits, you can avoid their bite."

Bon turned and walked on. They hesitated, exchanging glances, then followed.

"Be careful where you step," the boy said. "In some places the rock is thin like an eggshell. If you fall through, it's very nasty." Shelby studiously picked up a stick and used it to strike the black rock and check for soundness where he walked. David followed closely, trusting his companion. Cautiously, Shelby walked on; but he found himself checking their back trail and avoiding spots that collected sand and might leave a track. The boy was a picture of confidence and raced on playfully. He was either very good at this or profoundly naive. They hoped for the former.

When they had walked about a mile, they left the lava field and came to a beautiful green valley. Lush fields could be seen surrounding a small village. Beyond was rugged wilderness with jagged outcroppings of rock reaching up to scratch the sky. In the distance, a river meandered like a long glistening snake across the land. They paused to take in the beauty of it, only to fire the impatience of the boy.

"You coming or not?" They answered his question with movement and followed him into the village. People were busy, dogs were barking, and smoke lifted from chimneys atop plaster houses.

Many questions entered Shelby's mind, but he asked Bon the one that concerned him most. "Don't the Cartokians know about this place?"

"Sure, but we are no longer their threat. The Gedors are. They never bother us here. They only take those who wander from the village. That way their disappearance can go unexplained."

The place looked like a small village in New England around 1800. Farmland came right up to its edge, and the roads were narrow, mostly populated with horses and wagons. It was all very well kept and clean, but it was old...like something from a history book. The boys were lost in the moment and marveled at what each turn in the hard-packed, dirt street unveiled. Their senses touched it all, from the clatter of harness chains to the smell of fresh bread drifting on the faint breeze.

The people were dressed with the look of turn-of-century pioneers. The mark of hard work and strong character showed on their curious, yet friendly faces. They seemed, however, to be a mixture of European and the American Indian with the heavier percentage going to the Indian.

Positioned around the village stood three peculiar iron towers. They looked like big, inefficient, low band radio antennas. "What do you reckon, DC?"

"Low band stuff is all I can figure, but it looks like something from the 40's." He pointed with his chin. "Hey, Bon, what are those for?"

"What?" He looked around puzzled, then noticed David's fix on the antennas. "Oh, the Ether electric antennas." He paused, looking confused. "Don't you know?"

"No, I don't know, I never saw anything quite like it."

"You guys sure must live out in the sticks."

The boys exchanged puzzled glances. A possible explanation came to Shelby's mind, but he considered it too ridiculous to express aloud. So, he filed it away for later use, but the way things were going, he just might need it sooner than later.

All of the sudden, the puzzling questions of this mystery vanished, and the scenery got a lot more pleasant. Walking toward them, and noticing them, was a girl about their age. Shelby poked David, but he didn't need proddin'. His radar was working just fine. "Will you look at that!" David was in a trance, but he whispered like he thought Shelby hadn't noticed her.

"What? Do you think I'm blind? Now shape up, she's coming right at us." Shelby quickly removed his hat, and David followed suit. She walked up to them and smiled. Shelby started to speak, but nothing came out. He felt foolish for the effect she had on him. She looked Indian with large, dark eyes and waist length hair as black and shiny as a raven's wing.

She spoke first. "Bon, who are your friends?"

"My friends? Yes, friends I've brought to meet Grandfather. Shelby. David. This is my sister, Vishti."

Finally, Shelby managed words, but David was hopeless. "Hi. Bon told us about you...but he kinda' left out some details." She blushed a bit in a timid, sort of Southern way. Hands down, this was about the prettiest girl they'd ever laid eyes on.

After a moment, David finally managed words. "Howdy, ma'am." He fell silent and back into his trance. She looked a bit puzzled, so Shelby started conversation to pull the attention away from David's inability to cope. He thought people only acted like that in the movies, but this ole boy was struck.

David never did talk much about girls; he was mighty shy. Shelby had tried to get him to go out on dates, but he always had some excuse and never did. Once, the year before, Shelby did get him to double date. David provided his old '56 pickup and Shelby provided the dates. The girl Shelby was sweet on had a cousin visiting, and they wanted to go to the traveling carnival show. It was one of those dirty old run down outfits that traveled through West Texas bringing a little excitement and a shade of corruption for a stiff price. They spent two days' wages on those girls and ended up getting sick on the rides. They got them home all right, but then raced around the corner to a vacant lot and upchucked their insides. It didn't set well with David, and Shelby had never gotten him to go out with a girl again. Afraid that he would do something stupid around them, he had seemed to just give up on them... until now.

"Nice place." Shelby said, trying to make intelligent conversation, but not doing very well. The young lady was having her affect on him too. "What do you call it?"

"Tekoa, after the fire mountain. My family has lived here for more generations than I know. The fire mountain belches its ash and rock from time to time, but we always stay."

"But aren't you afraid of the volcano? It doesn't look very tame." He turned and pointed to the smoking mountain. "If a fissure were to open on this side or if the eruption happened to be strong enough it could bury everything as far as you can see."

"I know. The village of Valwon perished about thirty years ago. It was a few miles from the north slope. Surely you heard about that."

"Uh, no I didn't know that."

"Tekoa makes the soil rich. There is no better land anywhere, and the minerals here are abundant. We mine sulfur and several metals. We use the power of the mountain to run our industry." She spoke with great pride and love for her land. Unusual, he thought, for one so young. The teenagers where he had come from certainly didn't show any.

A sparkle against her buckskin vest caught Shelby's eye. A clear amber teardrop hung there from a pendant of garnet. It was magnificent, and Shelby commented on its uncommon beauty and added, "Is that amber?"

"I don't know... amber," she said as she touched it with her hand. "We call it flace. What is amber?"

"Oh, uh, it's just fossilized tree sap… resin. But that sounds so dull. Amber or flace sounds much better. Who made it?"

"I did. I make lots of these. I pick up the stones in a canyon east of here."

"What you have done is remarkable."

David had come out of it now. He was shuffling his feet and trying to look casual and interested. *Too late*, Shelby thought. He had come off as awkward as a newborn calf trying to stand for the first time. *I wish I could get it through his thick head that girls are normal people*, Shelby thought. David was his best friend, and he wanted more for him, but he couldn't catch his girls, especially if he had a conflict of interest.

Bon was growing impatient with his sister's intrusion and wanted to be off. He remained polite and respectful, but he wanted no grass growing under his feet. "Hey guys, let's go to the house."

"You coming, Vishti?" Shelby asked.

"Not yet, I have to pick up something from the store." She smiled a smile that would have warmed the heart of a statue. "Will I see you later?"

"Absolutely!" Shelby turned to follow Bon, and she walked down the street.

David stood watching Vishti for a moment. She moved with the grace of a princess. Her style and class radiated in a warm, pleasant way. As he watched, he noticed a man in his mid thirties come out of the shadows of a doorway and follow her. When she stopped to look in a store window, he stopped and waited, moving only when she did. "Hey, Shelby, there is a guy following her, I'm going to check this out."

A protective instinct surged in both of them and they took off half running. Bon was quick to catch up. "What are you guys doing?" Quickly, in as few words as possible Shelby told him. "What? No it's not what you think. Shelby…"

"Later, Bon. Okay?"

"You guys are in for a big surprise!" He called after them, but they weren't listening.

The man was coming up behind her now and was far too close. They were closing the gap on the guy, and adrenaline was fueling their fire. David tackled him, and they rolled in the dirt. Like a cat, the stranger was on his feet, and in a blur of movement David was flat on his back, and the guy was heading for Shelby. Shelby lunged at him and caught his shirt. Somehow he was rolled off but didn't let go. They hit the ground hard, and the stranger came up on top. Somewhere in all this Shelby kept hearing Bon yell at them. The stranger pinned him to the ground, and Shelby saw his open hand poised for a smashing blow to his nose.

"Your intentions may be good, but your judgment stinks, young man," the stranger said calmly as he pinned Shelby in the dirt. "You and your friend there should ask questions before you gamble your lives." Shelby could see David slowly getting to his feet, looking wary of this stranger and trying to decide if he should attack or not.

Bon burst in an explosion of laughter. "Are all Texans crazy like you?"

The stranger got up quickly as if he had been disturbed by what Bon said. "You are Texans?"

"Yeah! What are you besides a low down, sneaking skunk?"

"I am Vishti's protector." He pointed with his chin toward the girl still walking down the street. As he watched her, his figure straightened, and he looked proud to have said it.

"You mean, like her bodyguard?" Shelby followed his eyes to the girl. If she had seen this foolishness, she didn't show it. She just walked on. "Hombre, we didn't know, we thought..."

He held up his hand, indicating Shelby had said enough. He gave them both a good looking over and a smile cracked his lips. "Perhaps my job will be easy while you are here. Please pardon me, but I must go with her now."

"Yeah, sure...Real sorry about this." Shelby thrust out his hand sheepishly. "I'm Shelby, yonder's David." He shook their hands with a proud dignity that was still intact. Theirs was trashed.

"Sorek." He said, then quickly left to resume his duties with Vishti.

Bon was grinning like a fat coon. "Come on guys, let's get going. Grandfather will like this."

David glared at him. "You could have said something."

"I did, but you fellas weren't listening."

Chapter 4

Bon's house was a big place on the other side of the village. Trees lined the roadway toward the main house and met at the top, forming a canopy. Several horses grazed lazily on grass near the road. The place looked too well kept to be a working ranch; it looked more for show than anything else. The corrals were big, and the horse barns would rival some of Kentucky's finest.

Towering Sycamore trees rimmed a pasture of knee high rye grass, and several large oaks stood in a grove at its center. This was as pretty a place as Shelby had ever seen, and he said as much. Bon grinned and led them up a flower-lined walk to a raised porch that encircled the house like one of those southern mansions. They hesitated, but Bon motioned for them to follow. Somehow this scruffy little boy with worn out pants and ragged shirt just didn't fit these surroundings.

"Well, Bon, what did you drag up today?" An old man sat in a rocking chair with a twinkle in his eye that was warm and friendly. Instantly, Shelby liked him. Whatever made him feel that way was a mystery, but this was the kind of old man he hoped he would someday become.

"Grandfather, these are Texans. We met in my cave." The boy ran up the steps and hugged the old man with deep affection. For a second they saw a glimpse of alarm in the old man's eyes, but he covered it with a hardy laugh, turned Bon over his knee, and gave him a good tickle.

"You boys stay for supper? We'd sure like that, wouldn't we Bon?"

"You bet." Bon fell to the porch giggling and squirming. When he caught his breath he got up and ran into the house, letting the screen door slam behind him. The old man's eyes followed in admiration. For a moment his mind was elsewhere, but he blinked and turned back to his young guests.

"Bon says you are Texans. I don't think I've ever seen a Texan before. I've heard about them, but I never saw one." He studied them for a moment. "So, what are you doing here?" *Well now how do you even start to answer a question like that?* Shelby thought, as he stood there, awkwardly trying to be polite, but not wanting to answer. "Now boys, I'm nobody's fool. I know where you came from, and how you got here. What I don't know, is why you came and how you figured it out."

Their faces showed nothing but confusion, and he sensed it. "You didn't figure it out, did you? You don't even know what I'm talking about. 'Course not…you look to be pretty fine boys caught up in something you don't understand. Well, tell this old man what did happen, and satisfy his curiosity."

Whatever reservations they had were disappearing fast. This old man was easy to trust, and they were aching for some answers to this mystery. "Well, sir, will you answer some of our questions too?" David politely asked.

"It's a deal. Now, Bon said he met you in his cave. Let's start with that. How did you get in there?" As concisely as possible they explained about the Marfa lights, their expedition to study them, and the strange creatures that came into their camp. He listened quietly for a good twenty minutes, nodding from time to time like he understood the strange turn of events.

A large woman wearing an apron came to the screen door. "Sardisai, dinner is ready. You boys go around back and wash up. You look a fright." They hadn't thought about it before, but now they realized they must look a real mess after that fight.

They washed at an old concrete washstand, complete with a hand pump. Shelby had seen several in his life but had never actually used one, and he savored the moment. They found a can of lye soap and washed off any evidence of the earlier scuffle.

Entering the house was like stepping back in time almost eighty years. Beautiful antique furniture and fixtures adorned the place with a rich, elegant feel. Even the old, authentic looking light bulbs looked like they belonged in a museum. As they walked toward the dining room they noticed that most of what they saw belonged in a museum. Strange though, none of it looked aged, it just looked to be from another time. The place was well kept and clean. Delicate, ornate objects decorated tables and bookshelves.

Bookshelves! Shelby thought. He walked over and ran his fingers along the books, trying to recognize something, anything. Most were written in some other language. A few were English, but he recognized nothing. *Well, no clues here,* he thought.

Suddenly, he paused as his finger came to rest on a bookend. He picked it up and examined it. *Obsidian*! And it had been formed like the statues that he had seen back at the ranch. He handed it to David. "Look DC, just like the stuff Polly had."

"Yeah," David rolled it in his hand, then looked around the room. "Look, there's more!" He pointed to a small table where several beautiful obsidian objects were on display. "I have to know how they do this."

Vishti met them in the dining room, she had returned and put on a full length, blue lace dress for dinner. A different and even more spectacular amber pendant adorned her neck.

"Did you make that, too?" Shelby asked as he gestured toward the pendant.

"Yes. Do you like it?"

"Absolutely. Do you have more?"

Bon interrupted. "She makes lots of 'em for a shop in the village. What does a guy care about that stuff for anyway?"

"It's the craftsmanship I admire, Bon. This is the second time I have seen something here that was hand-crafted with a skill beyond what I have seen before."

Bon stood for a moment with a blank look on his face then said flatly, "I think you guys just like my sister."

The little varmint had also cleaned up and changed clothes. David and Shelby looked each other over and sighed. They looked like two range hands after a day of branding; they didn't fit in and knew it. As it turned out, no one seemed to care how they were dressed. The hospitality was warm and friendly, and soon the boys forgot their inappropriate appearance.

A lady in her mid-forties came to the dining room and was introduced as Vishti's and Bon's mother. She was truly elegant, and they could see where Vishti got her style and beauty. David wondered about her husband but was afraid to ask. Perhaps he was away on business.

Once the ladies were seated the boys found their places, Shelby next to Bon and David next to Vishti. *I hope he can pull this off gracefully,* Shelby thought. The old man offered thanks, and they found it comforting. It was good to find out that in spite of all the things that were different, they believed in the same God. Shelby had somehow expected them to have some strange volcano deity or something.

The dinner conversation was easy, and no prying questions were asked. Bon did manage to insert something about their earlier rumble with Sorek. Vishti giggled slightly, but was enough of a lady to let it drop. Sardisai tactfully covered his amusement.

Wishing to change the subject, David asked about the fire mountain. Sardisai proudly told its history and the lineage of his people named after the mountain. "The Tekoa people have lived here for four thousand years. Technology has changed, but our hearts have not. We have seen many wars, but now we fight no more.

"We love knowledge, and we've always been great builders. Once we had power and we built great things, but the Cartoks changed all of that. They destroyed our technology, killed our people and destroyed our towns. Now, to survive, we supply things they need. Things that we build and things we mine. We do this, and they leave us alone... usually." His eyes were a little misty. Old Sardisai had pain in his heart, perhaps some hatred too. "There are only about five thousand of my people left. They have scattered in several other villages like this one. Still, we proudly work with our hands, but we are watchful of our secrets, and one day we will again be strong."

"Grandfather, is it wise to say these things?" Vishti spoke almost reverently.

"It is good that you are concerned child, but these boys will bring us no harm." He continued to speak of the land and his people, and Shelby saw in him the qualities of the great chiefs of the Plains Indians. He told his stories well past the mealtime, and the boys grew more and more fond of this amazing old man.

They lost track of time, but must have been sitting there for two hours. They would have at least expected Bon to become restless or his mother to be bored, but they hung on Sardisai's every word. This family had a tremendous respect and love for him, and Shelby began to sense that he was more than just a simple old man.

After dinner they sat on the front porch, and Vishti and her mother sang some lively folk tunes. They could have been professional performers for all the enjoyment they brought. Their warm voices melted into Shelby's soul and stirred pleasant thoughts of his past. *It's a real shame that the TV has replaced the front porch,* he thought. *This is the way to close out a day.*

After a time, as if by some unseen signal, everybody started to get up and go into the house. Shelby looked around for a moment trying to figure what set it off. Whatever it was, he missed it. Vishti stood, straightened her dress, then asked if anyone would like to walk. Shelby started to say yes. He wanted to say yes; but thinking of David, he changed his mind. *Say yes, David, yes, yes, yes!* he thought.

He was sure that David couldn't read his mind, and looking at him, Shelby thought he had stopped breathing, so he brought him out of it with his elbow. "Uh, sure. I'd like that ma'am!" David blurted.

"Vishti. If you please, I'm not ma'am."

"Uh, yes ma'am."

She twitched her nose and gave him a sideways smile. To that, David just shrugged, and they walked off down the lantern-lit pathway in front of the house. Sorek fell in behind them, at a respectable distance. He had appeared out of the shadows, like a ghost. Shelby supposed he had been there the entire time, but he hadn't seen him.

Sardisai raised his hand and motioned with his fingers for Shelby to sit back down. "Shelby, let's finish our little talk." The young man sat back down, and together they watched David and Vishti walk off down the lighted path. "Looks like my granddaughter has taken a shine to your friend," he mused, as he ran his fingers through his white beard, "and I don't think he's figured it out yet."

"No sir, he's a little slow when it comes to girls. He doesn't think he has much they like. But he is a fine man, sir, and as honorable as they come."

"Well, humility never hurt anyone, son. It's a fine quality; I wish more people had it. But, we're not here to talk about that, now are we?"

"No sir, we're not."

"Tell me, Shelby, what do you and David plan to do?"

"We were sort of taking it as it came. We don't really have a plan, we're just trying to figure out what has happened to us. You seem so much like people we know, yet you are all... this is all, so different.

"We're just rough-edged ranch boys, and we haven't seen much, but we both have a love for science and exploration. All this is fascinating, but we can't explain any of it, and that rides pretty hard on our minds."

"That's understandable, and I think you deserve some explanation. What would you like to ask me?" The old man leaned back and smiled gently. His rocker creaked quietly, punctuating his statement.

"Well, I'm not sure where to start. How about with the men who were in our camp, the ones we followed? Bon called them Nephilim."

"They are harmless, at least they are now. Many years ago they were a race of giants descended from Anak. They were the greatest warriors in the land. Most of them stood taller than nine feet. Strange thing, though, legend has it that they had five fingers plus a thumb on each hand. Of course that was a few thousand years ago, back when they first came through.

"Today, they are simply a pathetic people that have inner-bred to the point that they have all but destroyed their race. There are less than five hundred of them now. They are gentle people, but not very intelligent. We give them work watching the gateways." Sardisai paused and lifted an eyebrow, wondering if Shelby caught his comment. He did.

"What do you mean, gateways?"

"Now that is the quick of it, son. The gateways." He paused for a moment staring off into the sky and rubbing his chin. "The gateways are what connect our worlds, yours and mine. They have always been there, and our people have used them to migrate from one to the other several times in our past. When conditions got so bad that their existence was threatened, they moved. The Nephilim, for example, came from your world about four thousand years ago. They were a race of giants that lived in your middle east.

"We, also, came from your world. And we may have to go back if the Cartoks push us any harder. That is why my people know your language. We have seen this coming for generations and started to prepare our people for the possible migration. Many years ago we sent several of our pedagogues to this Texas of yours. They learned your ways and now teach it in our schools. As you will see, we have your language, your slang, and many of your customs. We are a bilingual nation now, and while that often weakens the societal bond of a people, it is safer for us. We have also had a few of your people come here from time to time."

"Do all of your people know of the gateways?"

"No, of course not. The gateways have been a closely guarded secret. They have even been lost for hundreds of years at a time. No other people in our world know of the gateways. The Gatekeepers, the Nephilim, that is, do of course, and also a select few of our religious leaders.

"Once in a while someone will stumble upon them as you have, but that is very rare indeed. The Nephilim patrol them for us because they are not always open and sometimes they move. Most of them open once or twice a year; some every hundred years or so; and a few, like the one you came through, usually open three or four times a week. But then you can't always count on that. If the time should come for us to leave, we must know which gateways to use."

A shot of fear went through Shelby. "What do you mean, 'they are not always open'? Are you telling me that we could get trapped here?"

"Well, of course that is possible, but we keep a pretty close watch on them. I don't think they would all close. Shelby, you must guard our secret...if the Cartoks knew of this, we would be trapped and at their mercy.

"You must also think of your world and what evil they could bring to you. Their leaders are deadly, greedy, and will stop at nothing to satisfy their hunger for power. If it becomes necessary, you must agree to die with that secret. Do you understand?"

Shelby swallowed hard. What a thought. They had really stumbled into a big one this time. "Yes sir, I believe I do."

Sardisai labored to get out of his rocker. He stood and hunched his back a little, discomfort showing in his eyes. "If I'd known I was going to live so long I'd have taken better care of this old carcass." He turned and started for the screen door. "Too late for you boys to go off somewhere. Better stay here tonight. We have guest quarters out back."

"Thank you, sir. That's mighty kind."

Shelby remained on the front porch enjoying the quiet solitude. He had a lot to think about and no time to waste. He figured the most logical and safest thing to do was leave in the morning and try to return through the gateway. But to leave, when there was so much to learn, so much to do, would be against everything they had set out to do. They were explorers and should not be frightened into abandoning what would surely become the greatest adventure of their lives.

Later in bed, he told David what Sardisai had said about the gateways and the possibility of getting trapped in this world. He explained his feelings about continuing with the adventure regardless of the immediate risk.

David was silent, and in the darkness Shelby couldn't see his face, so he asked for a response. David offered little of value. He said, "What do you think of Vishti?"

"David!" Shelby got up and turned on the light. "I am talking serious stuff here. What are we going to do?"

"I know. I'm sorry. This does sound serious. But it also sounds extremely interesting, and I wouldn't mind staying around a while to check it out. Besides, I have other interests now."

"Yeah, I know. But just suppose we got stuck here. We've got family back there, and I've got a girl! That thought doesn't set well with me." As Shelby talked, he walked around the room and unconsciously picked up a small obsidian statuette and worked it in his hand.

"Hey, Shelby, that hunk of glass you've got there, we have sure seen a lot of that stuff around here. I don't suppose you would be thinking what I'm thinking."

Shelby focused on the object and realization hit him. "The Remes boy! What was his name?"

"Robby."

"Yeah, that's it, Robby. He probably came through just like we did. That means he is here someplace, maybe lost or something."

"We sure can't go back now without at least trying to find him. You know that don't you?"

"Of course I know that. What do you take me for?"

Well, risky or not, they were staying. Deep inside, Shelby was glad of it. He had wanted to stay, but the risk had him concerned. Now they had a real reason, and that made the decision easy.

At breakfast they mentioned Robby, and when they thought he might have been there. No one knew anything, but they all agreed to ask around. Bon got up from the table and slowly walked to the door. "If he has been around, my friends will know." He said quietly as he walked out.

"He doesn't seem real happy today. I wonder what's the matter?" David spoke with concern in his voice.

"Today is Dad's birthday," Vishti whispered sadly. "It is hard on all of us, but especially Bon."

Shelby hated to be nosy, but there it was, so he asked. "Where is he?"

"Dad was captured about a year ago on some trumped up charge. I think he is a political prisoner. Grandfather says they keep him so the rest of us will not resist. Dad is next in line for Grandfather's position as Chief among our people. He is much more outspoken than Grandfather and therefore more dangerous to them. With Dad out of the way things are easier for the Cartokians. They know Grandfather won't do anything that might endanger him."

"How do you know he is all right?" David asked.

"Grandfather says that they would be fools to harm him because they know the Tekoans would immediately revolt. But we're afraid that if we don't do what they ask, they will have nothing to lose and will kill him anyway."

"Is that why Sorek follows you everywhere?" David asked.

"Yes. I'm afraid it is." She blushed a bit. "Grandfather says I am also too outspoken and may stir something up. He says they may come after me next."

"They must be a rough bunch." Shelby mused.

"Not really. They just have a bad leader. His name is Croseus. A power-hungry, vicious man." She almost bit the words. "He is a supreme religious leader, a god to his people. I suppose Bon told you that he actually sacrifices their prisoners. It's not really sacrifice, even though he calls it that. He just uses his religious position to commit murder and gain power over his people."

"How did he get to be so powerful?"

"I don't know, but he is and has been for about twenty years or so. He doesn't even look like a Cartok; he's lighter in complexion, and he is certainly evil."

Vishti left them, and Shelby marveled at the hatred in one so young. He had no way to relate to what she felt. Never had his home been threatened, and never had he been without his dad. He had grown up in his dad's love and security and had always expected him to be there. Suddenly, he realized his immaturity. He was a young adult now, but he took his dad for granted like some small child. That was a situation he determined that he would rectify as quickly as possible.

Chapter 5

David and Shelby spent the day asking around about Robby. Their luck was running sour. They didn't even have a very good description of him. Polly had only said he was "tall, dark and handsome. Right out of a movie." That grief stricken girl hadn't given them much to go on, and they couldn't exactly look another man in the face and offer that description.

Suddenly, David stopped in his tracks. "We're going about this all wrong. We are ignoring everything we have learned. I'm so embarrassed." He turned to his friend. "Don't you feel stupid?"

"Well, no, but I'm sure you're going to change that."

"Look Shelby, what did Robby bring back to his wife and mother?"

"Obsidian statues."

"Exactly! And we have seen a few around here. We have to find out who makes them. That's our trailhead."

"You're right, and I do feel a little stupid."

They had asked only three people before they found the source of the statues- a family of craftsmen at the edge of town. Kadian, the father, was the man to see. Without hesitation they went to his house and found it to be something out of a storybook. The family made almost everything imaginable, and examples of their work were all over the yard.

A boy about Bon's age appeared and asked if he could help them. They told him what they were looking for, and he motioned for them to follow. Looking over his shoulder he asked, "You're Bon's friends aren't you?"

"You know Bon?" David quizzed.

"Sure, we're friends. You must be the Texans."

David and Shelby exchanged a sheepish glance. They really felt amateur now. If they ever intended to solve anything they had better shape up. "Yeah,"

Shelby said, "we're Bon's friends."

They turned through a passage of wisteria vines. The blue and white pea-like flowers hung beautifully, attracting several small bees. Beyond was a work shed with someone inside. "Dad, these are the Texans Bon was telling us about."

A huge man sat at a workbench gently working a small glass object with hands the size of shovels. He turned toward them and stood up. And up. When he stopped getting up, he was all of seven feet tall and the most impressive man they had ever seen. Wide, powerful shoulders with arms the size of most men's legs. His chest was as large as a molasses barrel. But his smile was kind and sincere.

He offered his hand. Shelby shook it with the kind of firmness his dad had always taught. "Don't ever offer a man a dead fish, son," he would say, "look 'im in the eye, and let 'im know he's important to you."

"You got quite a grip, Texan. I like that in a man...Name's Kadian."

"Shelby, sir. This is David. Comes from milking cows, I guess." Shelby felt a little embarrassed, but impressed that such a man had noticed.

"What brings you boys here?" He moved a few things off of a bench and motioned for them to sit. "Sprout, go ask your mamma to bring some iced tea for these fellas." Respectfully, the boy replied and left.

"Well sir," Shelby began, "we're looking for a man that you may have seen about six months back." Together, they described everything they could remember Polly saying, being careful not to use her exact words. The big man listened carefully, then reached over and picked up an old leather notebook. He began thumbing through the dog-eared, worn pages.

"Robby, you say? Could be here." His big finger searched the page. "Yes, I think I remember your man, nice young fellow. Said he wanted this stuff for his wife. He didn't have any money, so he worked for old man Jore across the way, building a fence." He pointed with his chin to the place across the street. "After a week he bought a few things and left. He said he would be back, but he never came."

His wife came out with the iced tea. She was introduced as Lorina, and the boy as Fricher. The Texans made small talk, but they really wanted to know about Kadian's work and asked if he would show them around. He seemed eager to show them his workshop and some of the things he had made. Excitedly they watched as he demonstrated different things and told how his father had taught him and passed on secrets. They were impressed and said as much.

Lorina spoke jokingly. "You boys are gonna make my man's head swell up so big he won't be able to work for a week if you don't stop that."

"Well, ma'am, we've never seen anyone with this kind of skill. It's kinda' hard not to be excited." David spoke with genuine awe of the man. She obviously saw it and smiled. Kadian seemed pleased at their admiration and gave them each a small obsidian locket on a gold chain.

"You boys fancy any special girls?" Somewhat embarrassed they nodded. "Well, give 'em these. You've done a tired, simple man a lot of good today."

They thanked them for their hospitality and crossed the street to ask Mr. Jore about Robby. It was a dry hole. Mr. Jore remembered Robby, had liked his work, but said the young man just disappeared. They were back where they had started, out of leads and discouraged.

As they walked out of the village Shelby looked across the fences and pastures dotted with cattle. In the distance, towering above the trees, was a tower with a shiny, copper colored ball on top. "Look at that! What do you suppose it is?"

"Maybe a radio tower or something. Reckon these folks have radio?"

"I don't know. David, pull out your radio." He turned it on and got a steady buzz of static on each channel he switched to.

"Let's check this out." As they approached the tower, the radio's buzz grew to an irritating squeal, so they turned it off. A fascinating crackle of corona excited the air and caused the hair on their arms to stand. Shelby noticed as he moved his foot around in the dirt that particles of sand were repelled by his boot and small fire-like hairs of spark arced to the ground. The pungent smell of ozone filled the air and reminded him of exciting nights in his laboratory where his own experiments with high voltage electricity charged him with a love for this stuff.

Many a time his family thought him crazy as he worked into the night in his small laboratory out back by the barn. It was loosely constructed of used lumber and bent tin, leaving cracks and holes in the walls for the winter wind to race and bite. Late at night the blue-white surging glow from arching electrodes would penetrate those cracks and give the little shack an ominous signature of its own among the dark outlines of the other barnyard buildings.

"You'll kill yourself someday!" his friends would say, as they watched in amazement at a couple of million volts of finger-like streamers and harassing brush discharges dance and envelope every square inch of the little place. But from among all the shocks and burns he got over the years, emerged only wonder and a hunger for knowledge. Now, here, this strange place drew him like a lamp on a dark night.

"Let's get out of here, Shelby. This is too weird."

"Where is your curiosity, David? This is awesome. Look at that tower. It must be a hundred feet tall, and that sphere…it must be fifty feet across."

"I have plenty of curiosity for things that don't shock and make my hair stand up. This stuff gives me the creeps." He hung back as his companion continued to survey the place and its affect on the surroundings.

"You know, David, I think this thing is geothermal powered. Look at those vents up there on top."

"That's pretty advanced stuff if it is. But I think you're right."

"Did you notice there are no birds or insects around here?"

"Can you blame 'em?" David walked around nervously. He was a great lover of technology, but he never liked electricity that got outside the confines of its wires. And he never understood his friend's infatuation with it. Shelby looked over and saw him standing in front of a sign that he had been too preoccupied to notice.

"What's it say?" Shelby yelled.

"War-den-clyffe Magnifying Transmitter Station." David stumbled through the word.

"What? I can't believe it!" Shelby wheeled and ran to the sign. That's what it said all right. Wardenclyffe.

"What's the matter, Shelby? You act like you know what this means."

"I do. At least, I think I do." His eyes lifted to the huge copper sphere, then back toward the village where he could see the three crude metal ether antennas above the village. "This is really strange, David, but let me call it as I see it. Almost a hundred years ago, Nikola Tesla performed an experiment in which he transmitted electricity, without wires, over twenty-five miles. He used what he called "Terrestrial stationary waves" and was able to light up two hundred lights at that distance."

"Wow! What a breakthrough. What happened?"

"Nothing. The project never went anywhere. He attempted to build a "Magnifying Transmitter" station at a place he called "Wardenclyffe," an industrial utopian city, but he ran out of money. I thought it had all died with him. I didn't think anybody ever figured out how he did it."

"Looks like somebody did."

"It sure does. Unless…Do you reckon he found a gateway like we did?"

"Now that's something to ponder. He sure could have done it. I have always read that he was a brilliant man who was criticized and misunderstood by the people of his time. He surely would have found understanding in these gentle folks around here. What a thought."

"It would also explain something that has been bothering me since we arrived."

"What?" David quizzed.

"Well, have you noticed that they have the most rudimentary forms of electricity, yet no basic appliances and what must be the original style of light bulbs. It is like none of their other technology has caught up yet. I mean…they all still have outdoor privies."

"That's strange all right. It's almost like somebody came in here and dropped this bit of technology on a culture that wasn't even ready for knickers and bloomers."

"Yeah. Like an experiment to prove that the concept was valid before subjecting it to a technology war like the one we had around 1900."

Later that evening in their room, David and Shelby were making notes on what they had learned and whom they still needed to talk to. Suddenly there was a frantic knock on their door. It was Vishti. Bon had not come home for dinner, and everyone was worried. Could they join the search?

They grabbed their stuff and ran to the main house where several people had already gathered. Sardisai saw them. "Did you boys see Bon at all today?"

"No sir, not since breakfast. Remember he was mighty low."

"I remember it well, and that is why I worry. Vishti, go to town, to Fricher's house. Maybe he has seen him."

Eagerly Shelby spoke. "Let us go, we know Fricher. Vishti will be needed here."

"Yes, go! Please hurry!" There was an uncommon worry in the old man's voice. In fact, everyone seemed overly excited about Bon absence at dinner. Shelby was puzzled, for he had missed a lot of dinners when he was younger. A boy just naturally gets sidetracked now and then. It was no big deal. This seemed a little strange. Something was missing besides a ten-year-old boy.

They found their way through the dark streets to the home of the master craftsman. No sooner had they entered the yard when the big man burst through the door and down the steps. Seeing them, he stopped suddenly. Definitely frightened by his suddenness they stammered, "W…we were looking for Bon…He didn't come home."

"It's true then. The fool headed boy did go." He muttered quietly to himself, almost biting the words. Seeing the question in their eyes, Kadian said, "Fricher just came home. He was exhausted from running for miles evading a Cartok patrol. The boys went after Bon's dad. Fricher got away, but he said Bon got caught. The boy just told us, and I was headed for Sardisai's place."

"What can we do?" Shelby asked.

"I don't know yet, son, but I've got to tell Sardisai." He ran off into the night.

Fricher came to the door with his mom. David spoke gently to the boy. "Fricher, where did this happen?" After a few moments of questioning, they had the information they wanted and took off for the spot Fricher had described.

There was a fine moon starting to rise, and the lightly overcast sky spread its silver light. The trail was easy to follow to the jagged outcropping of volcanic rock where Fricher had said the camp was. For an hour they alternated running and walking to conserve strength and gain time. It was very unlikely that the soldiers would expect them, for the Tekoans had so long been in subjection to these Cartok animals that the Cartokians didn't even consider them a threat. And certainly no Tekoan would brave the night to engage a Cartok patrol.

Well, they weren't Tekoans…they were Texans, and the Cartoks were in for a surprise. About the time they could make out the jagged silhouette against the sky, they could see a campfire glow against the rocks. Stopping, they both fell to the ground and Shelby said, "Okay, David, we are in it now. Let's talk plan."

They were excited now and running on adrenaline, and their minds were quick. They devised a plan and moved in carefully to survey their opponent's strength. They pulled their radios from the pack and used earphones so they wouldn't be heard. Then they separated and proceeded with the reconnaissance. Most of the time was spent lying still and watching. Shelby had observed no outposts or sentinels, and he radioed that to David. David replied that he had seen none either. Both pondered the lack of guards, the lack of anything military. These men were poor excuses for soldiers. They all seemed to be in camp, gorging on food and drink.

"I count twelve, David. Three at the wagon, six at the fire, two on the rock closest to you, and one walking out of the brush toward the fire."

"Right, I count the same. Where is Bon? Wait, I think I see another one. Yes, standing by the pine, fifty feet to your left. He is talking to someone in the brush."

"I can't see him. I'll move in that direction, so keep an eye on him, and let me know if he gets suspicious." Shelby crawled slowly along the ground, careful not to make a sound. He heard them before he saw them. It was Bon's voice and that of a man speaking a language he didn't understand. Now that he had them located, he moved closer for a better look.

Shelby could see Bon sitting down tied to a tree. He looked unharmed, but the man stood over him yelling something. He called David to report that Bon appeared unharmed. "Let's hold our position for an hour, David. We don't want any surprises."

As they watched, the men ate, drank, and got rowdy. They were a poor excuse for a military outfit. They looked more like a bunch of rejects out here doing someone's dirty work. Over the course of the hour Shelby became convinced that this was the extent of their strength. They didn't need to worry about any other men out in the brush.

He called David on the radio. "Hey, Dave, are you ready?"

"Coiled like a snake."

"Okay. I'll slip around behind Bon and let you know when I'm in position."

Carefully, Shelby moved around behind the tree. The man was still near enough that he could not risk warning Bon for fear that the lad might react in some way that might be detected. "Okay, DC. I'm ready, it's your show."

Shelby began to hear a low, eerie, rumbling drone. As it grew louder the men got quiet and concerned. Their conversation grew tense, and he sensed fear in it. This, he thought, was going to be easier than they had imagined. After a minute or so of this growing tension, the sky lit up as a glowing red fireball shot through the sky. The men jumped to their feet yelling, and David hefted a small sack of flash powder and sulfur into their campfire.

The blinding flash sent men running and screaming for their lives. Shelby put his knife to Bon's ropes and grabbed his hand. The kid was frightened, but he recognized his friend and quickly got in step with the escape plan.

They took care to avoid leaving a trail as they moved out of the area. After twenty minutes and a couple of miles behind them, they stopped at a prearranged spot. Shelby called David on the radio. Bon stared in amazement at the little black box that talked like David. Shelby let him speak into it. "Ask him where he is, Bon."

He did, and David replied, "I'm just a couple of minutes behind you guys." Bon was ecstatic with the radio, and Shelby enjoyed his excitement. He had so many questions to ask and was talking a mile a minute when David walked up.

"We better move on, guys. We have a lot of ground to cover and some real worried folks at home."

"That was a fine show you put on, David. I guess you know Bon's folks will have a million questions."

"They won't have as many as those boys back there do. They'll never figure it out." They laughed and walked on back toward town.

After a while Bon said, "I bet you Texans could get my dad just like you got me."

David was still feeling a little cocky and said, "We just might at that." Shelby thought otherwise, but said nothing.

They arrived to the welcome of a dozen women. They had assembled to try to bring some comfort to Bon's family while their men folk searched the surrounding area. Bon was the center of attention, and the Texans became instant heroes. The ladies made it very clear that these boys had the keys to their little town.

During the course of excitement, Bon burst out. "...And they said they would go after Dad." Suddenly, it got awfully quiet, and they all stared at the two in amazement. Shelby felt like he was standing there in his underwear. Words wouldn't come. They *had* said that, sort of. But, could they actually do it?

Sardisai broke the silence. "You told the boy this? Do you know what you're saying?"

David had been shocked into realization, and he wasn't talking. So Shelby responded. "We said that, and we are men of honor. We would never mislead the boy."

"Grandfather, they can do it. The Texans have great power over the Cartoks."

"The Texans have great knowledge, Bon, but it's carried in the pride of youth. That is no substitute for wisdom, and this is a difficult thing that they plan to do. Perhaps it is an impossible thing."

The happy mood of the gathering never returned. Instead, the people said their goodnights, expressed their gratitude and concern for the Texans' safety, and left.

"These folks act like we're already dead." David muttered.

"Yeah," Shelby whispered, "I hope we haven't roped something we can't hold."

Later in their room, they sat quietly. David was writing in his journal as he always did at the end of each day, and Shelby was somberly thinking about their situation. "David, why did you say that? You know, that stuff about goin' after Bon's dad."

"Man, I don't know. My mouth was working before I could rein it in. You won't back out, will you?"

"Come on, you know me better than that." Shelby squirmed in his chair and gazed out the window into the night.

The knock on the door went unnoticed at first. Then Shelby realized what it was and got up to answer it. Bon stood there with tears in his eyes. "They said you would be killed."

David got up, walked over and placed his hand on Bon's shoulder. "Now, Bon, that's just not the way me an' Shelby got it figured. We are not used to folks talking like we can't do something. We're doers, and pretty good ones at that. Now, we were just talking about a plan right before you came in. We'll get your daddy back here, and then we'll all be laughing about it, just like we were tonight. Right, Shelby?"

"Sure. Come on, Bon, what we need more than a sad face is a little support. Look here, ever seen one of these?" He held a roughly carved, flat stick with a string attached to one end.

"What is it?" Bon's question was punctuated by his obvious interest.

"It's a thunder stick." David said proudly. "I made it to scare the britches off those poor devils tonight. Take it outside and whirl it over your head."

They followed Bon out into the yard, and David worked to show him what to do. As Bon whirled the stick, its distinctive low rumble began to penetrate the night and hush the crickets.

"This is great! Did you make it up?" Bon yelled as he whirled the stick.

"Oh no." David responded, "This goes back several thousand years."

"You sure scared 'em with it." Bon began to laugh and shout mockingly, "Houy! Et ba Kadon nish! Houy! Houy! Et ba Kadon nish!"

"Say, that's what those guys were screaming tonight." Shelby mused, "What does it mean?"

"Run! The great god, Kadon is angry."

"You hear that, Shelby? They thought their gods did all that stuff tonight! What could be more perfect? This could work to our advantage. Bon, you keep that stick. And thanks for making us feel a whole lot better."

Over the next few days Shelby found opportunity to spend time with Sardisai and ask about the Cartokians. He showed great concern over the Texans' intent to rescue his son. "You boys can't know how ruthless this Croseus can be. He has people killed for entertainment. His power is absolute. You see, his people consider him a god with great powers."

"But he is just a man."

46

"Yes, to us he is just a man, but to his brainwashed people, he is the supreme deity. They'll do whatever he commands."

"But, what of the people? Are they truly wicked or are they merely puppets?"

"They're puppets to be sure. None of them are really bad people. I think we could probably live in harmony if it were not for him."

"What about his staff or council or whatever they're called? Do they have the power to go on without him?"

"Perhaps only one, the high sorcerer. The people fear him because he's the one who performs the sacrifices. He's the true butcher. Every life taken adds strength to his power over the people. He walks among the people and decides who lives and who dies."

"I thought they only sacrificed their prisoners?"

"Oh no, the prisoners are sacrificed, that is true; but that only brings fear to their enemies. To exercise the religious control over their own people, other sacrifices must be made. Their own people must atone for things like no rain, poor crops or bad economic times. No one crosses the high sorcerer and lives. He is all-powerful. That fear keeps them both in control."

"I heard of this sorcerer from several men in town. Is it true that a giant creature bit off the sorcerer's ear in a great battle and he killed the beast with his bare hands?"

Sardisai roared in laughter. "Son, don't always believe what legend brings to your young ears. Stories like that cover the real truth and propel such men to power." The comment stirred Shelby's inquisitive mind and sparked new questions. Sardisai patiently supplied the answers and unfolded a fascinating story of the land and its people.

They were quiet for a while, then Shelby asked, "What about the army? Are they very powerful?"

Sardisai leaned forward and rested his elbow on his knee. "You saw their army, son. They have no discipline. They are successful only because they are many. They have not met their match in generations and have become sloppy, arrogant and soft. They are merely a mob of bullies, but they are also a mob of many."

"Why then, do you live like this and tolerate them? Your people are great people. They are strong, skilled, intelligent. I've never seen a finer race, unless it would have been the Plains Indians of my world."

"We've been beaten down by their sheer numbers, Shelby. This does not make us feel much like men. There are times we can't face our own women, but there is little we can do except die, and then where would our families be? With what you did the other night I could see envy in the eyes of the men. But when they realized you planned to go to the garrison after my son, that envy turned color. They wish to act, but against such odds it is futile."

"Surely some would take a stand if others lead. What about Sorek...or Kadian? You must know others."

"Sorek. Yes, he surely would. And after what almost happened to Fricher, Kadian might be ripe for some kind of action as well. I don't know, Shelby, you are asking to change a way of life for these people."

"That's exactly right, Sardisai. Listen to your own wise words."

He left the old man there, deep in thought and brooding over his position. His people looked to him for leadership and protection through his wisdom. It was a heavy weight on his shoulders, and Shelby had just reminded him that it was there. He and David were committed out of nothing more than honor and compassion. These people had to find a strength that had lain dormant for generations. Sardisai could give them that strength if he wanted to, but he also knew he might give them the hand of death.

Chapter 6

Later that day, several men from town were called to talk with Sardisai. Most, Shelby recognized, but there were some he had not seen before. He watched them approach from his shady spot under an oak tree in the front pasture. He nodded courteously, touching the brim of his hat with his thumb. They did likewise and walked toward the house.

David was off somewhere with Vishti. Then it hit him. David was probably alone with Vishti, because Sorek was just with the men from town. *Good for them!* he thought.

He sat enjoying the clear day. It had rained yesterday and washed much of the volcanic dust from the sky. The stuff made for gorgeous sunsets, but it sure caused overcast days. He knew it wouldn't take long for Tekoa to put it back, but for now it was a beautiful day.

He watched a little dung beetle go about his dirty task of cleaning up the pasture and marveled at his tremendous strength and endurance. If an elephant could do as well he could carry a freight train. There were some insects here that he hadn't seen in his world, but most were familiar. The same could be said for the birds.

He twitched a twig of rye grass in his teeth and lay back for a nap. Pleasant thoughts of home eased into his mind and he slept.

The meeting with Sardisai was stressful for the old man. But the younger men who had come to meet with him were energetic and full of fire. He laid out for them the danger, the risk to their way of life, the *chance* for their way of life. They listened with a long learned respect, wishing to speak, but holding their tongues until he finished.

Kadian was the first to speak. The big man possessed no thread of pride or arrogance that might be expected from someone of his size. "Sardisai. You are wise beyond words and not a man among us would doubt you. The time has come, as you so wisely say, for us to take a stand. Fear runs among us, but it is controlled. We will stand by the Texans. We will stand for Tekoa. When we finish, the Cartoks will bother us no more."

The old man smiled and sighed in relief. "This warms my heart and makes me wish for my youth again. If only long enough to make the difference you surely will make. Thank you, my friends."

Shelby opened his eyes to see the men sitting around him. He was embarrassed that he had not heard them approach and said as much.

"You sell us short my friend, and don't be embarrassed." Sorek teased. "We could sneak up on you in broad daylight while you were looking. No better woodsmen exist. And Deccan here is the best tracker alive."

"Well, then, I'm glad you called me your friend. What's going on?"

Kadian spoke seriously. "We've just spoken with Sardisai. He suggested we help you, and we want to do that very much. We're ashamed we've done nothing before now, but we had no means…and no confidence that we could do very much. You're only young men, but you have great knowledge, and your spirit runs with the wind. We're great woodsmen, but we know little of battle. We'll do what we can if you will lead us." His huge hand motioned to the little group of five men. "We'll get as many men as you need."

"Wow! You guys are serious."

Kadian grasped Shelby's shoulder firmly. "Indeed. The time has finally come, and I'm glad to see it."

" I don't know what to say. I really need to talk this over with David."

"Why don't we meet later this evening and talk this out?" Sorek spoke practically. "How about your place, Kadian? Say, sundown?"

He looked at his companions. They all nodded. "We'll be ready."

Shelby just sat there after they left. His mind was racing through all sorts of possibilities. They were really going to do this dangerous thing. And now others were involved. What if he and David messed it up, and good men were killed. Or worse yet, what if they started a war or something? The young Texan felt the heavy weight of responsibility and a little sick to his stomach.

It was just before supper that David and Vishti returned. They glowed with happiness and talked of the fun the day had brought. This was good for Shelby to see a different side of his companion that had been heretofore hidden in a cloud of insecurity. Vishti had changed him. He was something different, and regardless of what happened now, he would never be the same again.

Shelby hesitated to call David away, but he knew he must. He told him of the day's events and the conversation with the men from town.

David grabbed his arm and walked him a few steps seeking more privacy. "What does Sardisai say?"

"He proposed it."

David turned away as if in a daze. "Who would have ever thought it?" He faced back quickly and locked eyes with his comrade. "What happens next? You're for this, aren't you?"

"You know, I've pondered it all afternoon, and I am. I really am. But this has to be a Tekoan show. We can help, but they have to do it. Do you see what I mean?"

David walked over and leaned on the doorjamb. "Yeah, I do. But we're holdin' most of the cards. You see that, don't you? And imagine the odds. Oh man! I just thought of that! Look at the odds!"

"I'm not that worried about the odds, and I'll tell you why. I spent a lot of time with Sardisai today, and I have learned some things that are worth a whole army." Their conversation continued and became excited as they compared ideas and developed a plan.

They were still talking when Vishti called. "Do Texans eat or just talk all the time?" They broke off the conversation, but they had agreed on their strategy for later at the meeting. Shelby felt better knowing that David was in line with his thinking. Now they just had to convince the men from town.

Dinner was pleasant as usual with these folks. It was easy to enjoy their manner and respect for each other. Sardisai was patriarch and was treated as such, but his respect for the others' opinions and feelings was striking. Even when Bon told of some outrageous adventure, he was allowed his time, and no one teased or belittled him.

Vishti told of her exciting day with David. She carefully left out the part about Sorek not being around. They had walked to the river and taken a canoe upstream to one of the inlets. "The water is very low this year, Grandfather. We ran into mud up by Doe Springs and had to turn back."

Sardisai stabbed a potato from the serving bowl. "That is dangerous country, child, I'm surprised Sorek allowed it. Another twelve miles up that river is a Cartok garrison. I will have to speak to him." He looked around, puzzled. "I haven't seen him this evening. Where is he?"

David almost choked. "Uh...He went into town about something."

Vishti sighed, "Oh, Grandfather, I just wanted to show David the falls."

"Now Vishti, the falls are not running; the river is too low." Sardisai lifted an eyebrow, amused with himself for where he was taking this conversation. "What could you and David possibly do up there away from everything... and everybody?"

David was the color of the beets on his plate, but said nothing. He wouldn't step into this conversation with waders on.

Vishti flared. "Grandfather!"

Sardisai raised his hand for her to hush. "Easy, child. This old man is just having a little fun with his favorite girl. I trust you completely. And as for David, well, I rest easy when you are in his care."

Shelby looked over at David and could see sweat beads on his brow. He had seen that before when he ate peppers, but they had no peppers for supper. He grinned.

David and Shelby walked into town, watching the sky and quietly pondering the magnitude of what they had set out to do. The sun was setting and turning from white to gold. The rich colors streaked the sky with every color imaginable. They blended into each other with a radiance that defied description. The larger clouds were highlighted in gold. Crepuscular rays lifted and spread into the darker reaches of the oncoming night. Watching such a sight lifted their burdened thoughts and replaced them with awe.

They knocked on Kadian's door, and Lorina greeted them with a strong look of concern. She stepped back and gestured for them to enter. They removed their hats and wiped their boots, as was the custom among western men.

David spoke gently to her. "Evening, ma'am. You surely do look nice tonight."

The hard lines in her face relaxed. "Thank you, David. I'm sorry. I'm just so worried. I have nothing against you boys. I guess I should thank you, but somehow, I don't feel that yet."

"That's all right, ma'am." Shelby said. "We're pretty worried too."

The living room was warm and pleasant. A fire crackled on the hearth of a large, magnificent fireplace. Several men, locked in serious conversation, sat in groups around the room. That conversation stopped as they entered.

Kadian stood up and walked toward them. His head missed a ceiling beam by an inch. Shelby held his breath, and Kadian laughed. "Son, I put that there with my own hand." He waved his arm in a grand gesture. "I built this place, and no beam is low enough to strike me. There's only an inch clearance in some spots, but an inch is as good as a mile. Here, sit down."

Kadian made introductions and they all howdied. The boys only knew Kadian, Sorek, and an interesting little man they'd met in town named Deccan. Two of the others they had seen around, but didn't really know. The rest of the men were strangers. No matter, by the time this was over they would know these men well.

At length the warm room grew stuffy to Shelby, but he knew it was just him; he was nervous. His mouth felt dry, and his hands were clammy. He knew they waited, expecting them to speak, so awkwardly, he started. "We are flattered at your confidence in us, and we recognize what you have endured over the years. We've thought long and hard about this and what it means to you. We've thought about what you will write in your history books and what you will tell your kids. It's for these reasons that we've decided not to be your leaders."

The room erupted. They all spoke at once, almost yelling. Shelby paused, wishing he hadn't put it quite like that. Kadian bellowed, "Hold on now! Let the boy explain himself. I know they aren't backing out on us. You go on now, Shelby. Speak your mind."

"This needs to be a Tekoan effort. History needs to record it that way. How is it going to look for a couple of runny nosed youngsters, foreigners no less, to come in here and save a proud race such as yours?" He paused for reaction. They showed it in their faces and nodded to one another.

"We propose that we act as technical support. We'll help devise a plan, and we'll help carry it out. But you must lead your own people."

"Who can lead? We are not soldiers. We know nothing of this kind of thing." Shelby did not remember the name of the man speaking. He was short and balding, but powerfully built. He remembered him to be the one that cared for the ether electric plant. Before, he had been a jovial fellow, but now he was deadly serious.

"I have considered that." Shelby replied. "We need a leader who understands the Cartokian people. We need a man who knows Croseus and that evil sorcerer of his. We need a leader who knows the land and the territory occupied by the Cartoks. We need a man who knows the Cartok garrison. We need Sorek."

Sorek gasped in surprise. "Me! What makes you think that I'm any of those things?"

"Sardisai told me about you and why he chose you as Vishti's protector.

He told me great stories of your skill and bravery. He told me how you used to serve as captain of the guard in the Cartok army."

"What!" The men in the room spoke in shock as one voice.

"Wait! Let me finish." They stopped talking, but were as restless as a treed 'coon. "Sardisai also told me about your honor as a man and how you, and only you, stood against Croseus when he planned to march on this innocent town. It was you, Sorek, who convinced him to allow these people to live in service to them instead of not living at all."

Shelby turned his attention to the others. "He showed Croseus that you could be of benefit to the Cartoks by mining and building for them. So, because of this man, you live."

Kadian spoke with some doubt. "So why are you here now, Sorek, and not with them as a Captain?"

Sorek stood quietly and faced the men. "You are my friends. The best companions I have ever had, and I consider myself to be one of you. I am one of you! I'm Tekoan! I grew up in Valwon and was in the fields with my grandfather when the great mountain blew. We were covered with the gray dust, and he died there. I wandered away and grew very sick. I was only ten, you understand. A Cartokian woman found me and raised me. At sixteen, and searching for a place in life, I joined their army.

"Yes, there was a time that I held a position of honor as an officer in the Cartokian army. I was proud and enjoyed what I did. But that was before Croseus came. Once he was leader, things began to change. They continued to get worse until they were an army of animals, not men.

"I was a young officer in the garrison up the river. One day, eighteen years ago, we captured a Tekoan Chief. We were told that the Tekoans were threatening an attack and could no longer be trusted as friends. It was said that their chief had turned greedy for our land and had plotted war. He was, however, the most noble man I had ever seen. He was beaten almost to death for secrets he never divulged. He was tortured to submit to Cartokian gods, but never denounced his God or his people. I had never seen this in a man before. Such strength, such resolve. I thought 'This is a man...a real man.'

"Word spread quickly about this prisoner with no fear of Croseus. This of course, troubled our new leader. He did not know how to deal with such strength, so he arranged for a public sacrifice. It was nothing more than an execution by the high sorcerer.

"The story is complicated and long, my friends, but the short of it was, I could not allow such a man to die. Here was a man who had shown me what it was to be a man. I drew my sword, and in a brief battle during the ceremony, I killed three guards and cut the ear from the high sorcerer. We escaped together, and he promised me a home among his people."

"Sardisai?" Kadian spoke almost reverently. "You are the one who rescued Sardisai?"

"Is this not your leader?" Shelby said. "What more could you hope for?"

Regaining control of the meeting was difficult now, for these people had a hero. A quiet, unassuming man from among them had emerged as the secret character in a story that even their children knew. Here was the beast that had taken the ear of the sorcerer. Here was the unknown soldier who had rescued their beloved Chief.

As they began anew, there was an energy in the room that wasn't there before. An excitement, a courage, a will that had been the missing ingredient; an ingredient that no battle to be won can be without. This was a good thing, and it lifted much of the burden from the Texans' shoulders.

They spent several hours talking plans and ideas. None seemed to be the kind of solution they needed, and Shelby said as much. Sorek paused and sat back in his chair. "The boy is right. This is foolishness. We are vastly outnumbered, so we must plan with that in mind. A battle, no matter how well planned, would mean our end."

"I suggest, sir that we undermine Croseus as a god," Shelby offered. "Show his people that he is simply a man with no supernatural power. If we could somehow publicly strip his deity status from him, we would not have to fight the people. We would then fight only him and a few loyal followers."

He could see the thought sinking in, so he continued. "You know as well as I that their gods are simply objects made of stone. They reign under their supreme god who calls himself Croseus, and his only strength comes through the black magic of the hideous sorcerer. Think, my friends. How can we do this? How can we strip him of his high position in front of his people?"

There was silence in the room…only the crackle of embers in the fireplace and the tick of a wall clock. The truth of what he had said was searching their thoughts. These men did not believe in such gods and knew them to be only the vehicle of one man's greed for power. There is a supreme God, and He hates injustice. He was known well to these men, for He was their strength. The very idea that some arrogant man professed to be on such a level repulsed them.

Sorek had been leaning on the mantle, deep in thought. As he turned to speak, he attracted all eyes. "The Ceremony of equinox! It has been going on all week, and it ends in two days. All of the officials and priests are there as well as thousands of spectators. The Cartokian people hold this ceremony most sacred. They believe that their sacrifices provide abundance in the coming year.

"Once a day for a week they sacrifice some poor prisoner. Then, on the day of the equinox, they sacrifice three of their own. Most often they are teenage boys and girls who are chosen by the sorcerer. It is a time of grief to the people, but they believe it must be done.

"If there was a way to denounce Croseus, there would be no better time. It would be seen by all."

David walked over to Sorek. "Can we get in to see this ceremony tomorrow so we can plan?"

"Yes, that is easy. Remember, they have no reason to fear resistance. There has been none in..." He paused and said under his breath, " ...eighteen years. We can go tomorrow and plan for the final day."

The meeting broke up, and Sorek walked with them back to Sardisai's home. They walked in somber silence. Sorek pondered his new roll as leader. The Texans pondered the disgusting thought of attending such a ceremony. Shelby wondered if it was in his nature to be able to sit still and watch someone being killed so senselessly. He thought long of it as he lay in bed trying desperately to sleep. The persistent thought stalked him and found its way into his dreams. There it settled and haunted his restless night.

Chapter 7

Aryan sat quietly this morning. The sun beamed a golden bar through the narrow slit in the thick, stone wall. Dancing along the golden shaft were hundreds of glistening particles that jumped, looped, and pirouetted as he blew gently to give them life. Outside he heard a mockingbird trill. He had never seen the little bird, but he felt like he knew his feathered companion, for the little fellow sang to him a sweet song every morning. The scene out the narrow slit didn't offer much of a field of view, and the bird's perch was off to one side. Still, he imagined the sleek gray body with patches of white scattered along his tail and wings. He longed to see him.

He was especially somber this morning... a feeling of impending doom lulled over the room like a heavy cloud. He could feel it, but couldn't explain it. He glanced at the damp wall above his head where for one hundred and seventy-six days he had scratched his tally. A tally that he no longer kept and that was no longer important. His will was finally broken. He knew he should seek some thread of hope, but it wasn't in him to try. Not today... maybe not tomorrow.

Aryan had ceased scratching his time marks on the wall three days ago when the guards had cruelly teased him about his son. They had given him few details except that his young son had attempted to rescue him and had been captured. His attempt had incurred the wrath of Kadon, and he was killed by fire and taken away. No darker day could come. No heavier burden could find its way into his soul. And yet, despite the cheerful call from outside his window, he felt that this day would bring more sadness, more abhorrence.

"Aryan, my friend, you seem far off this morning."

"Ah, good morning, Kral. Yes, I find it difficult to want to live in this any longer." He looked around the small dungeon, dimly lit by what little light found its way through the slit. "I used to believe I could endure, that I could not be broken, but now..." His voice trailed off. Kral sat quietly for a moment, knowing the agony in his friend's heart.

"You give up at the sound of the lying guards? How can you believe them? They are cruel, and they will do anything to bring us pain."

"But how could they know so many details of Bon? They knew his age, and his appearance. This could not be a coincidence."

"Look, you have told me how cunning the boy is. You talked of all you taught him...all your father taught him. Don't give up so easily. You need that boy in your heart to survive this place, Aryan."

"Do you have a son, Kral?"

"Oh, I hope to someday. I will teach him as you have taught Bon. I look forward to that, Aryan, I really do. There can be no more noble role in this life than to be a father. But for now I am a Gedorian soldier, a prisoner..." then is voice turned bitter, "...of these horrid Cartoks."

"You are young, Kral. There is still time." Aryan stood and walked the length of his leg chain. "This war will not go on forever. It will end soon. It has to."

"Not as long as the shadow of Croseus darkens our land. Even though your people will fight no more, mine will, to the very end."

"It was too much, Kral. We fought until my people were almost wiped out. Do you know how few of us are left? We were no match for their huge numbers. To simply preserve what little we had left, my fath...." He caught himself, unable to place the blame on his father. "Our leaders surrendered. Now they leave us alone."

"They didn't leave you alone. You are here as a political prisoner, aren't you?"

"I refused to listen to our leaders, and I continued resistance. It wasn't a military resistance you understand, but it was indeed a rebellion. Our people have become far too important to the Cartokians. We provide products and services that they are too lazy to provide for themselves. I jeopardized that. I was simply in their way.

"Just look at what I have accomplished." Aryan waved his hand to take in the gray musty cell. "I sit here with my noble ideas, while my children go without a father and my poor wife without a husband. I may die here, and then what will I have accomplished? Nothing! That's what. Nothing, except the death of my dear son."

"You give up so easily, Aryan. Just what would that young son think? If he did die at the hand of those animals, it was for a cause, a noble cause. If that boy is dead it is because he tried to save his father. *You* were that noble cause. Do you want to take that away by giving up? What kind of man are you?"

Aryan turned away, festering with feelings he could not sort out. They talked no more. Each man was lost in his own personal agony brought on by this place. The day passed as all days had passed. The two men sat quietly, watching, waiting for the day that had just started, to end. From time to time their blank gazes were disturbed by the stir of a roach or a rat, but no other events occurred in these long, lonely days. By now they had learned to ignore the incessant flies, even when they crawled on their faces. Living, they were yet dead men in their hearts.

The long hours of silence broke as Kral questioned. "Aryan, do you think of our companion that died this morning at the hand of the sorcerer?"

"Indeed. This time yesterday we talked of the equinox ceremony and who would be chosen. With each day's end I wait in dread to hear the guards take another from among us and prepare him for his morning death."

"Soon they will return for another. Aryan, what will you do if they choose you? Will you fight or will you go quietly?"

"This morning I would have gone without resistance. Now, I am not sure. What about you, my friend?"

"I'm frightened. Somehow, I feel that they will choose me today. The feeling is within me, and I can't shake it." A long silence commanded the room and dared to be broken. At length he quietly continued. "Aryan, I have nobody to miss me. My family was lost in the war. I..." His voice trailed off.

"I would miss you, Kral. I would miss you greatly."

"Thanks, Aryan."

The afternoon stillness wore on with each man tortured by thoughts of being chosen when the guards returned. If they could just make it through this day, the last day for a prisoner to be chosen for tomorrow morning's sacrifice... tomorrow evening's choosing, for the day of equinox, would come from among their own people.

The hollow thud of a distant door reverberated through the dark, stone tunnels. As the footfalls of the guards neared, the men broke into a sweat of dread. Aryan's lips moved silently as he drew on courage from his Creator. Kral watched him. He had heard Aryan speak often of his God, and he wished now that he knew more of this... Jehovah... this powerful deity that had brought strength to his friend for so long. If he lived another day he would ask Aryan to teach him about his God.

The guards came to a halt outside their door and removed the bar. Time seemed to stand still for the men as every instant of their past played out in vivid clarity. Mere seconds passed, but the years marched on before them. The door swung wide and revealed four armed guards with a hideous cruelty in their eyes.

"I can't tell the men from the rats in this stinking hole!" one said, bringing a roaring laugh from the other guards. "Which one shall we take, boys?"

The agony of the moment brought on shameful thoughts in the mind of Aryan, thoughts he would carry with him to his grave. *Choose him, please,* he thought. When Aryan faced these hideous thoughts, he wondered what he had become in this morbid place. How could he wish for the death of his friend? But how could he wish for an end to his own life either, especially now that this friend had made him see its value.

Determination shaped Kral's face, and he stood up with the dignity of the soldier that he was. Stunned, Aryan looked up at this man, his friend, and saw there much more than he had ever seen before. Here was honor, loyalty and abiding friendship, adorned in their finest colors. A quote came to his mind and lingered. "No greater love than to lay down your life for another..."

The moment was shattered by the vile guard. "Maybe I don't want a Gedorian dog!" A sinister laugh worked its way through his broken, yellow teeth. Kral leaned forward and glared with eyes of steel and spit in the guard's face. Anger flared, and the guard drew back his scourge for a blow.

"Stop!" shouted Aryan, drawing the guard's wrath to him. Then, pausing for it to seethe just the right amount of time, he calmly continued. "Would you render a blemished lamb to your gods?"

The guard absorbed his anger and pushed Kral toward the door.

"Kral," whispered Aryan. They all paused and looked at Aryan. He stood, and with all the determination he could make visible, he scratched a mark on his counting wall.

Kral smiled, "Speak to your...Jehovah about me, my friend."

"I will. To my dying day the name of Kral will be on my lips."

Chapter 8

The ceremony was at dawn, so what restless sleep they got was brief.
They were up three hours before sunrise and began their journey to the great
fire mountain. Shelby remembered Tekoa, that magnificent volcano he had
first seen several days ago when they came through the gateway. It was
beautiful then, but in this early twilight of a new day, a day of death, it
appeared demon possessed, a ghost mountain. The wisps of smoke that lifted
from its mantle, together with the moan of the wind across the valley floor,
cried as spirits of the men it had consumed these past few days. It was there,
somewhere inside a huge cave within the mountain, that this day's horrid
events would unfold.

As they approached the mountain they met many people in route to the
ceremony. It was a simple matter to fall in step with them and become
completely anonymous. So they would blend in, David and Shelby had dressed
in some of Vishti's dad's old clothes.

They walked in silence, as did the entire group. The people were solemn,
moving with purpose, distracted by nothing.

Shelby, on the other hand, was distracted by it all. Approaching such a
mountain was ominous. He could feel life surging from it through the ground
they walked on. Warmth and trembling movement lifted through the grass
and ferns along the trail and found its way to his sandals. There was an ugly
smell of sulfur on the breeze. He sensed that this mountain wanted to explode,
to vomit the evil that had taken refuge within it.

He looked at Sorek and whispered his observations. Sorek held his finger
to his lips, and Shelby fell silent. A few moments later, as they rounded a
bend and were further from the others, he whispered, "It is always like this.
Do not be concerned."

Before them the earth opened in a giant crevasse; a wound in the mountain that they entered like germs into a sleeping giant. Shelby felt small and evil somehow, like an invader come to do harm. Answering a desperate need to vindicate his presence, he whispered to the mountain. "I did not come to participate in this atrocity. I came to stop it."

Once inside, he could see that the cavern was an erosion cave that had long since seen much volcanic activity. The passage through which they walked was a large lava tube with several branches extending from it. It was dimly lit by torches scattered along the route. He moved closer to one of the torches for examination and discovered it to be fired by piped in gas. He thought it strange and filed that as useful information before following the moving mass of worshippers into a large chamber.

The cavern room was immense and tiered like an amphitheater. The people scattered out and sat on the floor. The stage area was large with a fire pit at its center. Directly behind the pit stood a twenty-foot stone statue. It was proportioned like a thin, gangly man, but had the head of a strange beast. *Some ancient god*, Shelby supposed. Walkways surrounded the room on several levels but were roped off to the people. He imagined them to lead to secret chambers and be used only by a sacred few.

Heavy drums beat a slow ominous rhythm, one of impending doom. A chant began somewhere from the back of the room. It started slowly and quietly but quickly grew, and soon the entire assembly was caught in its trance. The mass of human bodies moved and swayed as one creature with a life of its own.

Several minutes passed, and Shelby began to squirm in discomfort. Part was due to being crouched on the floor, wedged among so many unbathed bodies. Part was the strange mood that had transformed this quiet group of harmless souls into something haunting, something…dangerous.

Suddenly the drums halted. The chant ceased. A hush fell over the room. Only the quiet, mysterious drone of wind through the chambers continued. Slowly, a deep rumble began and grew in intensity. As it increased in level and frequency he could ascertain its source. It came from the pit on stage. As it grew louder the pit began to belch fire and smoke. The room lit with sparkles and streaks of light. The torches flared, then subsided, as if announcing some event. That event quickly followed as the pit erupted with billowing white smoke and a loud rushing noise. As the white, churning cloud lifted, it left the form of a man standing as if he had appeared from nothing.

The people sat entranced. Shelby couldn't help but observe the ones closest to him. Tears glistened on the cheeks of their blank faces. *Did they even understand this?* he thought. Obviously, they were brainwashed, and with what little understanding they had of physical science, this was to them the doings of the gods. Here in this sacred place they had seen the power of their gods and didn't question it.

Shelby looked at David and saw him rolling his eyes. Everything they had seen was easily explained. No gods were at work here, and they knew it. It was, however, impressive as a whole, because this was something out of the past... something that had written history and given rise to legends. They were witnessing how down through time, a few men, using superstition and illusion, had controlled entire civilizations.

His thoughts were interrupted as the man moved around the stage, executing several illusions and blowing fire from his mouth. He wore a grand robe of dark blue laced with gold ropes. The robe's fabric was full and flowing, and Shelby was sure they knew nothing of fire retardant. This could easily become a real spectacle if he made a mistake, or if...Shelby dismissed the thought.

A plan began to form in his mind, and he searched the room for tools to use. He noticed a window in the rear of the cavern. Light entered, but the sun's rays were carefully blocked from striking the opposing cavern wall. They hit, instead, a curtain and he could clearly see the sun's glow on its surface.

He remembered then, the purpose and timing of this ceremony. It was an equinox ceremony, and tomorrow was the equinox. Tomorrow would be one of the two days each year when the sun was exactly in the east. Its precise position at sunrise was well documented by the magicians and holy men. Even Solomon's temple had had a hallway and special room aligned for the purpose of capturing the rising sun on the morning of this special day. Throughout history, the position of the sun at equinox has been used in sacred ceremonies. He thought of Stonehenge, Medicine Wheel, the Pyramids and Temples of the Maya. The list seemed endless.

And now, they would witness such a ceremony. In the morning at sunrise the sun's first rays would shine through the uncovered window and strike the spot where, he was sure, Croseus would be standing in a robe of reflecting jewels. The effect would be electrifying and confirm him as the highest god in the land. *Well, maybe not this time,* he thought. Yes, there were all the makings here for quite a show.

The drums started once more, this time with a quick, aggressive beat. A

man was led in and tied to a wooden structure near the pit. There was a
scream from the audience, followed by weeping. A murmur went through
the crowd and hushed with the raised hands of the sorcerer. He walked over
to the man and ripped off his outer garments with one quick, flowing move.
The prisoner stood firm and brave, refusing to flinch or cower. Such resolve
Shelby had never seen in a man.

Shelby wanted to be somewhere else, anywhere else. He found himself
holding his breath in dread. The sorcerer paraded around with his hands
open above his head, showing the audience that they were empty. He turned
and glared at the tied man from a crouched stance, much like a cat before a
kill. Slowly he approached the man. The drums kept pace as if they were
counting off the last few seconds of life for his helpless victim.

Shelby sat knowing he could do nothing. No power on this land could
stop the events that had been placed in motion. His hands were clammy and
beads of sweat covered his brow. *How can a human being treat another this
way?* he thought. It was beyond his thinking. *How can I just sit here? But
what can I do? Nothing! I am powerless. Maybe this time I'm powerless, but
never again.*

The sorcerer placed the back of his open hand in front of the man's face,
and horror struck the poor fellow cold. Slowly he moved his hand toward the
man's lower abdomen and waved it as if some magic were taking place.
Then instantly, in the blink of an eye, he raised his hand. The man's insides
fell to the floor, and the poor fellow looked down in disbelief. The drums
had halted, and the audience sat in deathly silence. Nothing moved except
the sorcerer. He reached into the man's chest and came out with his heart.

At some point the man died. Shelby did not know when…it had happened
so very fast. He gasped for breath and felt sick to his stomach. The sorcerer
stood facing the audience, holding the heart above his head. Then walking to
the pit, he dropped it in. Again the pit flared up as if some angry god had
accepted the heart as payment and was again content.

Shelby's anger flared and he started to stand, but Kadian's grip on his
shoulder held him down. "Be still, Shelby. If you lose control we lose all we
have gained. If you can't take this, what will you do tomorrow when he kills
three?"

Shelby glared at him through tears he couldn't control. "Never again!
That hideous butcher will never kill again. I take this as a solemn oath. Do
you hear me, Kadian? Never again."

"I hear you, Shelby. And I believe you."

They left the mountain at noon, but not before more scouting around and surveying the chamber. The Cartokians had long since gone, moving their events to the palace of Croseus. There they would feast and have a festival closing out the long season of winter snow. The little group had much to plan and do to be ready for morning, but there was plenty to work with, and their confidence was high.

Sorek led them to a little ravine a mile or so away where they made a cold camp and compared notes. Everyone talked excitedly about what they had found out or had located that might help. Slowly and methodically, their plan took shape.

By early evening they were resting, because they planned to be back in the cavern sometime after midnight. By then the magicians would have set up for the next ceremony and left. Deccan pulled the top off a bottle of whiskey and asked if he could pass it around. Sorek rebuked him and allowed only one swallow for each man. Then whatever was left would have to be poured out.

Deccan turned up the bottle and took his shot. "Wow! Now that stuff has authority!"

Noticing Deccan's reaction to the whiskey, Shelby asked, "Sorek, how much alcohol do you think is in that stuff?"

"I don't know. Let me see that." He took the bottle and smelled it. "Whew! A lot, I would say."

Turning his attention to Deccan, Shelby inquired. "Is there more of this to be had?" That drew a questioning stare from the others.

"Yeah. I found a room with barrels of the stuff."

"Fuel for the fire." Shelby whispered to himself, but Sorek heard his comment and tilted his head in question.

Shelby moved off into the brush and pulled some cedar boughs for a bed. Removing his sandals, he slipped into his soogan and lay watching the sky. Here again he was puzzled by another element to their riddle. This was apparently another world, yet the constellations were the same. Not only were their patterns the same, but they were correct for the seasons. He watched the Pleides, Orion, Gemini and the other winter constellations and groupings as they set in the west, making way for the stars of spring to dominate the night.

Around him the cedar, mesquite and magnificent purple sage were as much like home as the jackrabbits, the red-tail and the horned toad. He could easily be back home under the same sky or bedded down on similar ground and not know the difference. So how could it be that he was in another world? Where was this world? Was it in a different dimension or in a different place? These were questions beyond Sardisai, and for now, beyond Shelby. He drifted off to sleep pondering questions that he would probably never answer.

When Sorek shook him he was sure that he had just closed his eyes. "It is time."

"Right." he said, yawning, then felt around for his hat and boots. Then he remembered he was wearing neither on this trip. Grumbling, he slipped on the sandals and rolled his soogan. The others were just as slow to get moving. He glanced at the sky and found the reason. Only about four hours had passed. They ate some dried fruit and were off. It was a very humble beginning for a day that would surely change Tekoan history.

They entered the cavern cautiously. They didn't expect anyone to be there, but they took no chances. After a brief reconnaissance they knew they were alone. Sorek left a man at the entrance with David's radio, and they went to work. Everyone knew his task and went to it with a passion. These men needed no more motivation than the freedom this job promised.

David took Deccan and went to work on a "potato cannon." To the Texans, it had been a high school toy, but here it would be a decisive weapon. They wrapped rocks in cloth that would later be soaked in alcohol. Once lighted, they could be shot with accuracy and deadly force across the cavern. They planned to use the methane gas from the torch pipes to fuel the cannon, but that required some experimentation to get the mixture right.

Shelby put Kadian to work hauling whiskey barrels up to the walkways and positioning them so that, when opened, the whiskey would flood all the pathways that surrounded the room. Once the big man had the idea, Shelby left to work on a positioning device for a mirror. He used his flashlight to calculate where the sun's path would traverse the cavern wall, and his ingenuity to control that path.

The place was buzzing with activity and it wasn't long before David was blasting flaming rocks across the room. His first few had fizzled and gone only a few feet. He changed his fuel mixture by controlling the time he held the cannon over the methane pipe. When he finally got it right, he and Deccan had a frightening weapon…loud and nasty.

The lookout at the entrance called a warning over the radio. People were starting to arrive. No matter, they were ready. Shelby called for everyone to take their hiding places outside the cavern and wait. He moved to a darkened area in the rear of the cavern and hid.

There he patiently watched as Croseus' "stage crew" came in and made ready. One of them crawled down into the pit and after some clanking and vocal carrying on, it rumbled, and flames shot up. Once, twice, then the man climbed out and went about other tasks. Another adjusted the torches, and still another manned the sparklers. This was exactly like a production crew rehearsing cues before a play.

He held his breath once or twice as the men neared the Tekoan props, but they were well concealed and went unnoticed. Soon they finished their check and were sitting around laughing and joking when the High Sorcerer arrived. He barked commands at them, and they dispersed. The evil creature then walked the stage noting everything. It was as if he suspected something. How could he? He paused, looked out into the cavern, and stood listening.

Shelby turned away not wanting to look at him. There were men who could feel your eyes upon them… feel your presence. He himself had felt it. Was it a sixth sense? He often wondered. Purposefully, he diverted his attention to other things. He thought of the grand sunsets in this land, he thought of his family back home, his girl. He scattered his thoughts and diverted his eyes so the evil man could not perceive his presence.

Presently the Sorcerer's gaze fell in the young Texan's direction. Slowly, he walked toward Shelby's hiding place in the darkened area of the cave. Shelby slowed his breathing, fearing the man might hear it. Again he looked away and busied his mind, but the Sorcerer walked still closer. If he had carried a light source he would have been able to see Shelby, but it was dark. He leaned forward, squinting his eyes.

A man entered and called for him. He turned and replied, then walked back to the stage. Shelby's racing heart found reason to ease. Now that the man's attention was dominated with other tasks, he allowed himself a quiet sigh and settled down to wait.

The morning wore on, and the people arrived as before and filled the chamber. Today Shelby noticed a section near the front was being kept clear. *That must be for the high council.* He thought. Sorek had said that this day would bring the highest officials in the land.

As the cavern filled he could see his comrades move in and take their places. All was going as planned. Kadian was right up front. He had no trouble spotting a man of his size even though he hunched over to look shorter. After a few moments Shelby noticed him scratching his ear. That was his cue. He left his hiding spot and fell in behind some men trying to find a place to sit. He broke off and sat down beside Kadian. Their eyes locked, and he nodded. Nervously, Shelby again scanned the room for their other three men. They chose to leave the others outside just in case something went wrong. They were within an easy radio call.

Everyone was in place except Deccan. His last task was to open the whiskey kegs Kadian had placed along the pathways around the cavern. Shelby hoped he was allowing *all* the whiskey to spill out along the floor. If he got sidetracked... Then he saw him walking back into position and sighed in relief. All was ready then.

About that time David called over the radio. "It's a go."

"We're ready here too," Shelby whispered into the microphone.

The crowd hushed as twelve men in gray robes walked in from the back of the cavern and took their seats along the front near the stage. "Good." Shelby whispered to himself. "You guys are in for a great show." Kadian overheard and grinned but said nothing. He was loving this, as were the others. They had forgotten the rush that comes with virtuous battle, and this felt good in their veins. Finally they were men again. No matter what happened today, they would still be heroes. Their names would live on in the history books and on the tongues of the grandfathers and Chiefs.

The drums began, and the ceremony proceeded as the day before. The sorcerer came out and went through a ritual of placing several rhytons around the fire pit. These ceremonial pots had not been there the day before, and Shelby hoped they held no surprises. The torches flared, and the chants began. Soon, as before, the entire audience was in some kind of emotional trance, completely absorbed in the mystic event.

Shelby found himself in wonder of the moment, in awe of the control the sorcerer had over the group. *Are they really that stupid, or does he indeed have some kind of strange power over them?* He wondered. The sorcerer spoke with words Shelby couldn't understand and dared not ask Kadian to interpret. His words screamed with power and authority, and they worked up the crowd to a dangerous emotional level.

Their plan depended on stripping these "gods" of their power and having the crowd see them as mere men. That task was becoming more difficult as this continued, for the people seemed to worship this man. And Croseus hadn't even arrived yet. *Can we pull this off or have we been incredibly naive?*

A brief moment of panic went through him as he considered their possible failure. What was wrong with him? He had to get a grip. This kind of thinking was dangerous, and he must be positive. *I must grasp onto something,* he thought. *But what is there, a handful of men in a crowd of perhaps a thousand. This was...* But the drums started. They beat that distinctive rhythm. That rhythm would haunt him until he died. His mind snapped back, and his anger flared once more. This was the death beat.

From one side of the stage paraded Croseus, dressed in a robe of polished jewels that glistened even in the subdued firelight. He moved with precision to his marked spot on stage. The crowd bowed down, hands above their heads and facing the floor. So this was the great Croseus, the supreme god of these people. Shelby wanted to shout his disgust. What happens to a man to cause this kind of thinking? But he really knew. It was greed and power. From the beginning of time it has always been the same.

A gong sounded and reverberated in low resonant tones. The sacrifice victims were led on from the other side of the stage. Shelby gasped. These were not prisoners as before. These were youngsters, teenagers... two boys and a girl, all about seventeen. Then he remembered. Sorek had said it would be like this. He had forgotten, or perhaps he had just forced it from his mind. They were tied to the wooden frame and the drums halted.

From several places in the crowd he could hear crying and pleading, but no one moved. Croseus lifted his arms, and a chant began. The torches flared once more, then subsided. The energy in the cavern was laced with untrammeled emotion. Several in the crowd were chanting and ripping at their clothes. The state of the people was contagious, and soon it swept over the entire multitude.

At the height of excitement, the sun's image shot through the thick smoke in the chamber and struck the wall beside Croseus, missing him by ten feet. The audience gasped and fell silent. Croseus' face paled to a livid white, then glowed red with anger. The sorcerer stood motionless, stunned at the strange event. What had gone wrong?

He quickly regained his composure and shouted something as he moved toward the tied captives. His attempt to cover the incident seemed to fire his rage. He grabbed the girl's outer robe and ripped it from her body. She screamed, and he struck her in the face. That was Shelby's cue. It hadn't been planned, but it would do.

He stood up, allowing his outer garment to fall. He wore jeans and a red cotton shirt underneath, typical for him, but strange to all in this place. His interruption and appearance drew a stare and a murmur. He boldly walked forward and took his place on the stage. Kadian followed and stood like a giant beside him. "Stop, or I will kill you where you stand!" Kadian translated in a booming voice and drew a hush over the crowd.

"Who are you?" The sorcerer commanded in his tongue, but Kadian translated.

"I am a Texan."

"What is a Texan that I can not crush like a bug?"

Shelby raised his hand, and the image of the sun that had missed Croseus, that image of the sun that was to point him out as the greatest of all gods, slowly began to move across the stage and came to rest, on Shelby.

A susurration went through the room and hushed as Shelby spoke. "You will never crush another bug. You will never see another day."

Enraged, the sorcerer rushed Shelby and grabbed his shirt. So far their plan was flawless, for they had planned this very moment. But now, with him so close, his hatred so intense and his attempt to scare so real, Shelby hesitated. Time seemed to stand still, and all he could feel was the man's bitter wrath. He spit in Shelby's face, and that was his mistake. Shelby snapped out of it and regained control.

As the sorcerer glared into his eyes, expecting retort, Shelby emptied two vials of alcohol onto his robe. Unaware that he now wore a robe of death, he continued his aggression by making sure that Shelby saw the ring on his right hand. It had a razor sharp blade on its back side. That was how he appeared to disembowel his victims with empty hands.

Shelby knew the man's next move would be to use it on him, but everything was going according to plan. At least he hoped it was. Then Kadian reached over and grasped the sorcerer's left wrist. Shelby heard it crush like a bundle of dry twigs. He leaned over to the sorcerer and whispered in a harsh, nasty voice. "Sorek sends his greetings." The sorcerer's face paled, and he released Shelby.

He mouthed the name "Sorek," but no word passed his lips. He reached up and touched the side of his face where once, a long time ago, there had been an ear. He was in shock and surely in terrible pain. Then with a flourish, he backed up and attempted to gain command of the stage again, but he stumbled and looked unsure.

Shelby spoke with contempt. "You are not a god. Croseus is not a god. You have no more power than a child." Kadian made sure that his translation was well heard. It was, and it drew a reaction from the crowd.

Wheeling around, he screamed something about appeasing the gods. He rushed to the girl and placed the back of his hand near her stomach. There he crouched, coiled like a snake with hate and fire in his eyes.

70

Instantly, the image of yesterday's sacrifice flashed through Shelby's mind. He had vowed it would never happen again and yet, here he was, a blink of an eye away from seeing it once more.

"No!" Shelby screamed at the top of his lungs. The evil man didn't understand the word, but he understood the tone and meaning of what Shelby spoke. He hesitated. He had never been spoken to in such a manner and was taken aback for a moment. Shelby continued his dialog in a slow spell-casting drone. "Da...vid...hit...him ...with..the...flare...gun."

Instantly an explosion echoed through the cavern, and a red glowing ball of phosphorous thundered above the heads of the crowd and struck the sorcerer in the stomach. Upon contact he exploded in flame. The alcohol and that fancy robe made a fine combination.

As he flared up, the girl screamed in pain from the heat. "Kadian!" Shelby yelled, "The girl." The big man was immediately at her side shielding her from the burning, twisting mass that had almost been her executioner.

The crowd sat spellbound, quiet at first, but then they began to chant. "Kadon...Kadon." Shelby recognized it to be a familiar word, but at that moment he couldn't place it. They stood and continued the chant, almost jubilant.

Croseus had moved to a darkened corner of the stage lit only by his burning companion. He looked stunned by the actions of the past few seconds, but Shelby knew he was planning. He could see his power draining away, and he must save face now or never rule again. He moved to center stage and yelled to the crowd. "I command Kadon! The god of fire serves me; he does my will!"

"No! Your power is gone." Turning to face Croseus, Shelby remembered full well the name, Kadon now. The soldiers had screamed it the night they rescued Bon. Bon had used it in jest as he made fun of the soldiers. The people used it now believing that Kadon was responsible for this. When he had yelled for Kadian, they imagined he had said Kadon. He decided to use this small advantage. "I now control Kadon and I command him to destroy you."

Before Kadian's translation was complete, the next scene in their plan began. The potato gun was in full action, now, shooting fireballs into the walkways around the room. They flashed as they made contact with the spilled whiskey. In less than a minute the entire cavern was encircled with flame. The people were too stunned to panic. They sat dumbfounded by the events.

Croseus stood helpless to regain control, and they wanted to insure that he never did. The potato gun launched several balls of fire that smashed the stone idol and exploded all around Croseus, forcing him to dodge and run like a scared rabbit. But not before yelling at Shelby. "I'll kill you!" Despite David's best efforts to hit him, he disappeared into the darkness behind the stage.

Kadian spoke in a solemn voice. "We should have never let him get away. He will lose these people, but he will have the soldiers, and many of them will stand with him to the end."

As they turned to leave they found themselves standing face to face with the men of the high council. Shelby started to speak, but Sorek walked up and took command. "You remember me. I was a captain in your service. I left because of these evil men, the sorcerer and Croseus. I am back now, and I bring Tekoans and Texans. We have shown our strength here today, and we are only five men. We have become a powerful people, while you have grown fat and lazy. For more than a generation your life has been too easy. You have struggled for nothing. Your leadership has corrupted, and you have become pawns to these two men." He turned and gestured to the smoldering, stinking mass on the stage. "Now, one is no more, and the other runs like a scared dog.

"I know you men. What happened to your strength, your wisdom? You were just and honorable leaders before you fell under their control. Is it all gone, or does a spark remain that might be fanned back into the flame that made your people great?

"For us it is over, and you must know this. We will stand for no more of your oppression. If you disagree, speak now, and let this battle continue. We will start anew where we stand and before we move. But understand this, we hold the power at this very moment, to take your lives before you can draw another breath."

One of the men drew on enough courage to speak. "We have seen that power. It shamed our gods. What do you want, Sorek?"

"Only peace my old friend. You have nothing we want, except to be left alone. We are lovers of knowledge and freedom. We will tolerate no more of your dominance."

Shelby interrupted cautiously, "There is something we want... the son of Sardisai. He is captive in your prison." Kadian did his best to keep up with the translation.

"You want what we cannot give." The man that spoke was old and feeble, but he carried himself with dignity.

"Why, is he dead?" Shelby asked.

"We don't know. But if he lives, he is a prisoner of Croseus. He controls the garrison and the palace, and while after today he may lose many soldiers, he will surely have enough loyal to him to remain strong."

Sorek leaned closer to the men. "Now, where do you stand in this?"

"Sorek. Sorek." A very old man, robed in a darker garment than the others, spoke for the group. "We have grieved at what has happened to our people. We have seen the vicious and evil corruption Croseus has brought these past two decades, but we are old men and he is young and strong. Besides, he commands the gods, so what can we do?"

Sorek gestured with the wave of his hand at the still burning fires that circled the room, at the destroyed stone god that had fallen under the potato gun's attack, and finally at the smoldering mass of burnt debris that once was a man. "Do you think he still commands the gods? You may still think your gods are powerful, old man, but they are not the real God, and don't ever forget what we, mere men, have just done to them."

The small group of heroes left the stage to the men of the high council. They hoped the men would address the crowd and explain this to their benefit. They gathered in the rear of the cavern. Five of them stood together, drawing every eye in the room. Strangely, Shelby saw nothing in their faces but wonder and relief. The magnitude of what they had done this morning would slowly sink in, but for now they were simply confused by their feelings. So was Shelby. All was quiet. All was still. What were these people thinking?

As they turned to leave, a voice called…an uncertain, quiet voice. Shelby turned back to see a man and girl approach. This was the girl who would have been killed only moments ago. The man, Shelby imagined, was her father. He walked directly to Shelby. Tears filled his eyes, and he spoke something kind and gentle. The girl held out her hands and Shelby offered his. She kissed his hand and placed a small silver arrowhead within it. She then backed up a step and bowed graciously. Awkwardly, Shelby returned the bow and smiled. Later, he would ask Kadian to translate, and later he would find out that her name was Sinca, a beautiful name that seemed to match so lovely a girl. He wouldn't forget that girl, ever.

They left the fire mountain that morning feeling like they had made a difference. They had succeeded. But what was the next step? They needed to move forward quickly while the mood of the people was in their favor, but they hadn't planned that far. Somehow, they just hadn't thought they would be so successful, but superstition can be a strange force. Rarely does it work for good, yet this time it had, and in their favor. But how long would it last in the minds of such a precarious people? History is full of wars and tragedies that were the result of what happens when gods stoke the superstition of men.

Chapter 9

The rain fell for six days following the equinox ceremony. Its intensity gave purpose and life to crusted streambeds and caused havoc and local flooding around the low-lying areas of the village. Aside from providing for necessities, and shoring up against intruding water, the villagers chose the dry comfort of their homes to the daily tasks that could willingly be put off for a few days.

All was quiet and pleasant at Sardisai's ranch. The spring rain was a welcome wonder, and the pastures took it in with a great thirst. Sardisai sat on the front porch throughout the long days and rocked peacefully in his creaking, time worn chair.

The events of the ceremony had given him new hope, and he could readily see that hope expressed in the faces of his people. The millstone had been lifted from around their necks and the threat to their lives from the former enemy nation was gone. Only a renegade remained, and his power was dwindling with the passing days. Already, word had reached Sardisai that thousands of Cartokian soldiers had deserted Croseus. Only his most loyal and surely his most dangerous remained.

The old Chief pondered his options. He must move toward an alliance with the Cartokian Nation, but not too quickly, for the events surrounding Croseus would certainly shape the next few days. He thought of his son in the garrison dungeons, but those were still under the hand of the viscous wild man. "Patience. I must have patience." He muttered as he doubled his fist and struck the palm of his other hand.

Shelby walked around the house splashing through the soggy grass. Rain dripped freely from the brim of his cowboy hat and down the back of his slicker. The day was dark, but his wet coat glistened white as it reflected a nearby lightning flash. The young man looked up at the old chief and grinned. "You folks have the best storms." He paused for the thunder to punctuate his statement and roll off down the canyon to settle. "I sure love this stuff!"

The old man looked admiringly at the lean boy. He thought of how unassuming he was, how well mannered and respectful. Yet at the same time he thought of how well educated and quick he was. This boy had savvy and grit. He and his friend came to them as simple, easy-going Texans, but they had forever changed their lives, their history.

"Mornin', Shelby? What brings you out in this?"

"Just passin' time." He turned and pointed to a distant cliff at the edge of the front pasture. "There is a little cave up there. I've been sitting in it all morning watching this storm. I've always loved thunderstorms, even as a kid. Back home I made several devices to detect the lightning strikes. I put one in my car, but it cost me a few dates. Girls never seemed to go for lightning…never figured out why."

Sardisai listened with interest and nodded without understanding. These boys were forever talking of things he knew nothing about. What was a car and why would you need something to tell you that lightning is striking? He chuckled to himself, he may not understand Shelby's scientific interests, but he could sure explain the part about the girls. But then, maybe he shouldn't.

"Well son, sometimes girls are just hard to figure. I imagine someday you will find one that likes it, or at least pretends to. Girls can come to like all sorts of things for the right reasons."

"I reckon. Say, have you seen David this morning?"

Sardisai pointed with his chin. "He is in the house with Vishti. They are baking cookies."

"Get outta' here! David wouldn't do such a thing!" Shelby slung his hat off and slapped it across his leg.

"Boys do all sorts of things for the right reasons too, Shelby. Go easy on him."

Shelby caught Sardisai's contagious grin, then started for the door. "I'll go easy on him all right. This is going to be fun."

"Shelby! Why don't you leave them alone? My little girl is changing your friend, and it is a good change. I've heard you say it yourself. Sit out here and talk to this old man about the rain, the sky and the mountains.

"You're right, Sardisai. In fact, you're always right. Mind you, I was only going for the fun of the moment… I wouldn't hurt David for anything."

"You boys are close, aren't you? Where did you meet him?"

"We met when we were still in junior high. His family moved to the ranch country to get away from the city. David loved the outdoors as I did, but he never fancied ranch work. He shied from horses and didn't like cattle, sheep or goats. He took more to chickens, ducks and farming. That boy can make anything grow. Reckon he's got a green thumb. We went to high school together and took a lot of the same classes. After that, we went to A & M together. We're in our last year there now."

"What's A & M?"

"Oh that's a school, a university. The Best! Folks call us 'Aggies'. You probably heard some of the Aggie jokes."

"No. I don't believe I have."

"Well, I'm sure you folks have 'em. The names are changed, that's all."

They sat for several minutes, quietly watching the rain make little rivers in the yard. It fell heavy now and poured from the rain gutters. It rumbled and hammered on the roof so loudly at times they couldn't hear to talk. Shelby reached a hand out from under the porch and caught the big drops in his hand.

"I think this will end tonight." Remarked Sardisai. " I have been watching the clouds."

"It's sure been a real chip floater."

"A what?"

"A chip floater. You know, it floats cow chips. Get it?"

"You Texans speak so eloquently."

"It's a gift."

The rain ended during the night, just as Sardisai had predicted. It left the morning fresh and washed. The smell was wonderful, and the sky was clear. These were mornings to live for, and the two Texans were walking the road to the village enjoying every bit of it. As they approached the village a small boy stumbled into the street and fell to the ground. He caught their eye but not their attention. They imagined him to be playing until a man appeared. He looked down the street directly at them, then walked out and picked up the boy by the shirt. Suddenly, something was wrong here. No one manhandled a kid like that, not in their book.

They quickened their pace, moving with purpose toward the two. Once more the man looked at them, then drew back his fist and struck the boy across the face. He fell limp in the dirt, and the man began to run.

"Did you see that?" screamed David.

"DC, that's Fricher! Stay with him! I'll get the guy!"

David ran to the boy's side and carefully examined him. "Fricher! Fricher, can you hear me?" The boy mumbled something David could not make out. He noticed that several people were running up. "Go get his Dad!" He commanded, choosing a tall thin teenager with his eyes. As the boy ran off, David turned his attention back to Fricher. Blood trickled from his mouth and right ear. Gently, David turned the boy on his side so he wouldn't choke, then rested his head on a folded coat that came from someone in the crowd. He leaned over to listen to Fricher's breathing and determined it to be fine, so he proceeded to check the boy over for unnoticed wounds.

Concerned as the people were for the boy, the quick and competent aid that David rendered bred confidence. They kept their distance, leaving David plenty of room to work. Some of those closest to him began to talk to him and draw response. Fricher's eyes focused and slowly he regained awareness. As David asked him simple questions he alternately shaded and exposed Fricher's eyes to the bright morning light. Noting the reaction of the boy's pupils, David became more confident of the lad's condition, and relieved.

Kadian ran toward them, and the crowd opened. He knelt beside his son. "Who did this, Fricher?"

"I never saw him before, Pa. He walked up friendly like and asked about the Texans."

"What did he ask you about them, son?"

"He just asked if I knew them, and I said they were my friends. Then he started talking about the rains and the village and stuff. After a while he just threw me into the street. He didn't say why or anything. Then he hit me with something."

Kadian looked up, puzzled. "Make any sense, David?"

David looked up the street where Shelby had given chase. Sudden realization came to him. "Shelby," he whispered. "Kadian, I think it was a trap, and Shelby just took the bait."

Kadian instantly understood the situation. "David, I'll get the others, and we'll track 'em. Go, and be careful. We will be right behind you."

David nodded in agreement and ran off after his companion. When he got to the edge of the village he stopped and tried to sort out the many tracks. The damp earth held the tracks well, but a hundred people must have passed the spot. David walked further, then cut a wide arc, hoping to cross Shelby's boot tracks. After several minutes he found them and felt very inept. For an experienced tracker, this would have been child's play. The trail finally became easy to follow once it left the village activity and ran across the countryside.

David grew wary as he entered the more rugged terrain. The area was perfect for ambush, and Kadian didn't need two to find. He slowed to a cautious walk as he approached an upthrust of enormous boulders. Crouching low, David moved from one bush to another, pausing long enough to listen and look carefully, then proceed. As he eased around a turn and stood up, he came upon a tightly stretched length of barbed wire across the trail. He shivered as he touched the sharp, neck high barbs. Being from ranch country, he had tremendous respect for this stuff.

Off to his right, where the wire crossed the trail, blood sprinkled the ground and rocks. The ground was torn up from scuffle, and many tracks covered the area. Leading on from there, the tracks drug something. David's heart sank deep as his mind played out what must have happened. He sat down, deciding to wait here for the others.

Kadian, Deccan and Sorek were hot on the trail. Deccan was legendary as a tracker, and the others did well to keep up. At the spot where David had searched for almost a half hour for Shelby's trail, Deccan took a mere three minutes. Consequently, David had just sat down when the men overtook him.

Little had to be said…the evidence told a grim story. Sorek whispered a curse and drew the shock of the others. "I'm sorry," he said grimly, "but this is a cowardly deed."

"Look at this." Deccan invited.

The men clustered around the bloody wire and looked at the spot Deccan pointed out. David spoke first. "What are we looking at?"

"Hair. This may mean that things aren't that bad for Shelby. This is short hair, I would guess from his forearm. It would suggest to me that the wire didn't hit his neck."

"That's good to know, but it doesn't change my feelings about those guys." Kadian spoke with more anger than he could control, and David imagined the fate of the men when caught.

"From now on it's important that we follow some basic rules." Said Deccan. "My job is to track. Now, I can't be looking around the hills or worrying about getting shot while I'm looking down, so that's your job. You protect me while I follow sign. And another thing… you guys always stay off to one side, and never, ever cross the tracks. You never know when I might have to double back a ways."

With that said the band of rescuers were off following a trail left by apparent idiots. For some time the others wondered why they couldn't just rush on… after all, the trail was painfully obvious. After an impatient hour of walking when they felt they should be running, Deccan paused, looked around for a moment then continued with an even more vigilant pace.

In another ten minutes he stopped. "This trail is a decoy." He stated matter-of- factly. Then without further word or hesitation Deccan began to backtrack, and within minutes he was off again in a new direction.

Sorek mused. "They sure had me fooled."

The new trail led across large flat boulders that had been wind swept and polished by time. Onward he led to the utter amazement of the others. He seemed to follow an invisible trail. But whatever he followed, he did so with great determination. Kadian chanced a doubting question. He had tried to hold it, but couldn't. Finally, he simply said, "Deccan?"

"Shelby walks a little now. They don't drag him anymore." The response only drew more wonderment.

Presently, they left the rocks and were back on dirt where once more the tracks were plain. The men exchanged glances and followed with confidence. The trail plainly showed Shelby's boots with no attempt to cover them from view. They moved quickly now, almost at a run, until they hit the river. It was evident to all that a large number of men had camped at the spot. Markings on the shore showed several canoes had been pulled up on the grass. The canoes were now gone, taking with them all clues and leaving an empty feeling in the hearts of the rescuers.

Deccan remained busy scouring the camp for details that he pieced together like a puzzle. The others watched with a sick feeling of failure. Presently he walked to the rest of the men. "More than twenty soldiers. They camped here for several days while a party of five went to our village. They left here in seven canoes a few hours ago and went downstream." David stared in disbelief at the tracker, with his head cocked a little and his mouth twisted in doubt. Seeing the look on David's face, Deccan added quickly. "The canoes had red seats and green gunwales." He paused, then laughed. "You must trust me David. I am a very good tracker."

"I know, Deccan. I have read about men like you, but I always thought the stories were exaggerated."

Deccan grinned. "I don't know what you have read in your books my young friend, but what I read in the sign left in this place is as clear as if it were in a book. Except the part about the seats and gunwales."

David accepted that with a trusting smile and followed the others to the riverbank. The heavy rains had caused the river to swell beyond its boundaries.

It raged and frothed past, carrying with it uprooted trees and broken branches.

Sorek looked puzzled. "The Cartokian soldiers are not good in fast water. They have no training for such an angry river, and their canoes are made for smooth water."

"Isn't that a good thing?" David asked. "They'll have to stop if they have trouble."

"They may not recognize the danger." Sorek continued. "And if Shelby is bound…" It wasn't necessary to continue. They all understood.

After a moment's pause to ponder the situation, Deccan said with confidence, "This is what we will do. The village of Moorok is a half day's walk downstream. We will go there as quickly as possible, looking all the time for signs of their coming out of the water. If they passed the village, the people will know of it. If they did not, we will cross and backtrack on the other side. What do you think, Sorek?"

"It's a good plan, Deccan. Let's go."

Shelby stuck to the fleeing man's trail as he darted around trees and brush. His anger was so fired by the vicious attack on a helpless boy that it had not yet occurred to him what he would do if he actually caught the evil bully. Neither had he noticed the baiting tactics of the fleeing man.

Shelby was fast and gave a good chase. He loved to run and had been a high school track star. His best trainers had been the jackrabbits that he chased through the pastures on his West Texas ranch. He had lost few races in his young life, both with the rabbits and with human opponents. Yet, he had run those races in bare feet… today he ran in big, clunky cowboy boots that ruined his naturally smooth stride and rhythm. His speed was only half what he was capable of, and while he found that discouraging, yet he could not know that within the next few seconds, it would save his life.

It infuriated him to be losing the race, but he pushed on, driven by the grisly image of Fricher's bloody face. He ran through stands of sage and jumped ditches and prickly pear. Thorns tore at his arms and legs, but he did not tire or waver. Rounding a turn, he again saw the man not twenty yards distant. He also saw and ran into a cloud of gnats hovering above the trail. Instinctively he closed his eyes and raised his hand to brush them from his face. In that instant he covered ten feet of unseen ground. When his eyes opened they caught the shiny glint of sharp barbs on the stretched wire. With no time to react, Shelby buckled at the knees, but too late. The wire never made it to his neck, but instead he caught the full force of it with his already raised arm and stretched the already taut wire to its limit. As it sprang back, the tight wire threw him to the ground. He lay dazed and bleeding badly from an open gash in his forearm.

As the blur cleared from his vision he looked up to see a man standing over him with a broken limb drawn back in his hand. Then several other men appeared, laughing and slapping each other on the back. They were soldiers. The man he had chased walked up breathing heavily, and between gasps for breath, said something hoarsely and kicked him in the side. A moment later that broken limb turned club, struck him in the side of the head, and Shelby saw no more.

The soldiers made no attempt at concealing the evidence of their deed. They picked Shelby up and roughly dragged him along for the next few miles. They cared nothing for his condition except that he be delivered to Croseus alive. That was the order. They had seen how their leader had dealt with those opposing his will, and they now joked at the fate of this young man.

None of them had been at the ceremony, but they had certainly heard of it. The details were now well known. Individually, each man actually had a fear and respect for their captive and wondered about the extent of his powers. Collectively, they were driven by mob mentality and showed no fear. Those that dared, kicked and spat on the unconscious lad, attempting to cloak their insecurities with bravado.

With a few miles behind them they paused and dropped Shelby in the dirt. The jolt stirred his consciousness. Through clouded vision he watched two of the men continue the journey, dragging one of their companions. It made no sense, and Shelby was not interested. The soldier who remained walked over to the shade. Also seeking shade, Shelby rolled over under a small bush. An hour later, all three returned by a different route. Shelby then realized their amateur attempt to plant a decoy trail and chuckled to himself.

Now that he was awake the men were more wary. They pulled him to his feet but were no longer as rough as before. They picked him up and walked to a huge outcropping of rock that extended across the meadow beyond the range of sight. There he was allowed to stand while one of the men returned and sifted dirt over their tracks. With this complete they walked on across the large bouldered expanse, confident that they could not be tracked on such rock.

Shelby walked awkwardly between two soldiers. His head was splitting with pain and he felt a bit nauseated, but he was thinking and lightly marking his trail across the rock with a drag of his boot now and then. The rubber heel left a nice black mark. He didn't have to look back to know it was there… his mother had warned him enough about boot marks in her kitchen. His efforts went unnoticed by the soldiers and they walked for another hour across the rock.

Shelby began to hear the roar of water and soon they came to a white-water river well swollen out of its banks. There were seven canoes resting on the grass, and nearby several Cartok soldiers lounged in a sloppy campsite. Some were sleeping; some appeared drunk and others just sat in the shade whittling. Shelby's second look at a Cartokian bivouac site confirmed his earlier opinion that these were not real soldiers. They were a disgrace to the word military.

Shelby pulled himself together and stood tall. These men who knew no dignity or honor were going to see it in him. Despite his pain and obvious wounds, he carried himself with ease and confidence drawing bewildered looks from the men. As they watched this young man stand proud among them and remembered what he had done to Croseus, they felt uneasy. What if he could unleash that power against them? But there was strength in numbers, and that is why they were all here.

The soldiers began to break camp and put their equipment into the canoes. Shelby walked to a large sycamore, sat in its shade and watched the disorganized activity. His hands were bound behind his back, but they had not checked his pockets or taken his possibles kit. His shirt had come untucked and covered the small belt kit, so it had gone unnoticed. If Shelby could keep it that way he would have what he needed to escape.

Two soldiers came after Shelby and took him to the canoes. At first glance he was shocked. These were not fast water canoes. At the first sign of stress they would disintegrate. They were birch-bark with little sheathing along the bottom, and the ribs were a good two feet apart. They had been built well, but were made for smooth water and no heavy cargo. It was clear the Cartokians had stolen and not made these canoes, or they would know better. It was also clear that they came here before the rains, when the river was still down and calm.

He was directed to follow one of the soldiers into the canoe and lie down. The other covered him with a tarp, shoved off and got in. As he peeked out from under the tarp he could see the others cast off and frantically fight for control of their canoes. The water was bad, here but Shelby knew it would get worse and that his life lay in the hands of these inexperienced men. The water beat against the canoe and stressed the splints that had been lashed into place to form the sheath along the bottom. Shelby cringed and thought, *one well placed rock and this thing is going under, broken apart like an egg.*

Further thought brought Shelby to the realization that he must quickly be rid of the ropes binding his hands. He worked unnoticed under the tarp in an attempt to get his hands in front of him where he could reach his pocketknife. In less than a minute his hands were free.

The soldiers were fighting the water with all their attention and might. They realized their danger, but it was too late. They were committed to the river and what it held in store. After almost a half a mile of white knuckles and cold sweat, the river widened and the water smoothed. The soldiers regained some of their confidence and yelled jokingly to each other.

Another few miles and Shelby noticed a small group of people walking along the bank. He pushed his head from under the tarp for a better look. That drew a sharp vocal attack from the stern paddler who quickly recovered Shelby. Now he understood. They didn't want him seen. Apparently they were afraid of how well known he was and who might be willing to help him. That brought hope and the beginnings of an escape plan.

Shelby knew that if he was to escape, it needed to be soon, while they were not well organized. And if he could do it while they were distracted by the river, his chances would improve. He considered jumping overboard but rejected it. There were too many canoes following theirs, and the soldier who had yelled at him was too wary. His mind moved quickly over several options but none seemed viable.

Again he heard the distant roar of fast water, and men began to yell warnings and instructions. Immediately the canoe leaped and plunged. Like a cork, it bobbed and bounced. He chanced another peek and witnessed total chaos among the soldiers. Their own canoe was now sideways, and where they were headed looked wicked. A nearby canoe broached on a large rock, then broke free before it wrapped.

The idea came to Shelby, and he seized it immediately. The timing was perfect, and their position on the river was superb. He noticed several large boulders downstream and knew there would be eddies behind them… calm water, if he could get to it. He went to work cutting the lashings holding the sheathing splints in place. As he cleared away some of the floor strips exposing the vulnerable birch-bark, he discovered a thick leather bag. It held an assortment of dried fruits and nuts. He would need these, so he shoved the bag inside his shirt.

A few seconds of work exposed about two square feet of the birch-bark. *That would do nicely,* he thought, and peeked out for a final survey of the river and position of those large rocks. *Now! I have to go now!* With speed and determination, Shelby put his knife to the birch-bark, and it easily yielded under his sharp blade. In the span of three seconds the water rushed in and Shelby rushed out through the hole and into the cold, raging river.

Instantly, he went into shock. The water was so cold that he couldn't move; his arms and legs seemed useless. His mind fought for control, battling the onslaught of panic that was surging through him and threatening to take command. The water churned wildly, and Shelby was caught in its turbulence, helpless to determine his orientation or depth. After moments that seemed like minutes, he gained enough mental control to extend his body to full length and attempt to relax. His body desperately wanted air, and he was certain if he didn't get it in the next second, he would surely die. But no, he told himself, he had held his breath for much longer at other times… he was not going to die. This was a mind game, and he knew it. Momentarily he floated to the surface and gasped for air.

He could see debris and pieces of his abandoned canoe, along with its occupants, bobbing along in the violent, white froth. They had no interest in him, at least not now. The other canoes had passed, and he had escaped undetected. At the speed they were going, his absence wouldn't be noticed for some time. They might even think him dead. After all, they had tied him and would consider it impossible for him to swim with his hands behind him.

The water had him in its clutches and wasn't about to let go. Shelby knew he must work with it and not against it, so he turned, pointing his feet downstream. They would offer protection from rocks as he backstroked toward the boulders. He missed the first one and aimed for the next without hesitation. He hit it hard and grabbed on like a leech. There he rested for mere seconds as he was pinned against the rock. This was a dangerous spot, and he knew it. He could be crushed by a large floating tree or stabbed by some smaller branch. Carefully the young adventurer worked around the rock to the downstream side. There he found the calm water he expected, and rested. For the next twenty minutes Shelby moved from eddy to eddy behind the big rocks until he reached the shore.

His strength was gone, but not his faculties, so pulled his tired body out of the water with care, knowing he could not leave tracks. He stepped from rock to rock until he was well away from the river and into the tall grass, then on to the woods beyond, where his chances of detection were slim. Only then did he rest and contemplate his next move.

Chapter 10

There were no tracks along the river except for those of a few hunters. The canoes had not docked, at least not on this side of the river, so David, Deccan, Kadian and Sorek raced on toward the village. The villagers had indeed watched the soldiers pass less than an hour ago. Six canoes and two dozen or so soldiers; that seemed right so they moved on, now with a new problem. There were no more villages downstream, so they must somehow cover both sides of the river. That task was complicated by the fact that they had no means to cross and search the other side.

"What do you want to do, Sorek?" asked Deccan.

"Let's keep moving downstream, Deccan. There is a garrison several miles down river. That's probably where they're headed, but I'm hoping they won't make it that far in those canoes. If they rip them up in that river and decide to walk, we've got a chance."

"Good." replied Deccan. "David, your job is to watch the river and that other shore for any place the canoes might have come out. Kadian, you watch out for David and me. Don't let anybody slip up on me while I'm looking down. Sorek, you scout up front so we won't get surprised by anybody. Stay away from the bank so you won't mess up any tracks."

Without a word Sorek disappeared into the woods ahead. The others fell in behind Deccan and let him set the pace. The afternoon was hot and muggy with swarms of insects adding to the discomfort of the trek. Their lazy hum, along with the sounds of the woods, were masked by the roar of the water. The men didn't like their inability to hear approaching danger, but then they knew they couldn't be heard either.

Another two hours they walked before David pointed to debris from a broken canoe hung up on the rocks. "Somebody bought it," David observed.

Deccan paused and surveyed the wreckage for a moment before moving on. He was puzzled by something but unsure about its importance, so it went unmentioned. The river looked deadly at this point with large boulders holding strong, refusing to yield to the powerful water. The roar was deafening, and the spray settled on their faces. David pointed to smaller bits and pieces along the shore, and these they checked for clues.

A small distance further they discovered another canoe, this one wrapped around a tree. Its occupants were gone. Deccan searched for tracks but found none. The next mile of white-water devoured three more canoes and left evidence of its deeds scattered along the bank. Tracks of a dozen men now marked the mud, but none were Shelby's.

Sorek came back to the group. "Two canoes are pulled up on shore just ahead."

"Any sign of soldiers?" asked Deccan.

"None, but I stayed back in the brush. Let's spread out and check the area. If it's clear, Deccan can move in and check it out." With his hand he directed the others where to go, and they slipped into the brush and trees.

Twenty minutes later they reassembled under a large cottonwood as they had been directed. The last two canoes had indeed been abandoned, so Deccan began his search for clues. He walked around the area several times, then back to the canoes before motioning the others to join him. "Shelby isn't with this bunch. I don't see sign of him anywhere."

"Maybe he got out on the other side," said Kadian.

"Maybe. I'm thinking he escaped, and I think these guys know where he is."

"How?" David asked. "It looks like they just took off down river and gave it up."

"No." Deccan said as he pointed to several tracks. "Look at these. They double back the way we came. I figure we just walked right past two of them back there someplace. The others are heading for the garrison, dragging and carrying several hurt men. These two went back to locate Shelby. I'm sure of it. And I've got a hunch they are back by that first canoe."

Sorek knelt down and touched the marks in the dirt, a move that seemed to aid his concentration. "They will bring help, and probably lots of it." He stood and looked down river. "The garrison is about another six miles, I figure. By tomorrow this area will be crawling with soldiers, and they won't give up without that boy."

Sorek knew that the only way Croseus could save face and regain power was to destroy the Texans in front of his people. Only then would they know that he was greater than the Texans. The thought weighed heavy on Sorek, for he knew personally the workings of Croseus' mind. He turned and commanded through clinched teeth. "Deccan. Let's follow those men back up river."

The tracks were well inland from where they had previously walked, and it wasn't surprising that they had missed seeing them. After a few short minutes Deccan knelt down near some thick brush. "Sorek, look at this." He pointed to a spot of crushed grass under the brush. "They lay here in hiding, not more than a few minutes ago, I would say. The grass hasn't had time to recover."

"That means they are very close." Sorek whispered.

"Not as close as they were, Sorek." With that comment left to sink in, Deccan pointed to a fresh footprint less than three feet from the depressed grass. "Yours, I believe."

Sorek looked stricken, not from fear, but from the realization that he had been so careless. He quickly regained his bearing and said, "A lesson for us all, I hope. Move on, Deccan, and mind you all, when we passed them before, we were distracted by our search for Shelby. This time they are apt to be more dangerous knowing we've discovered them."

They followed the tracks back up river about a mile to where the first canoe wreckage had been found. The tracks veered off into the woods, but Deccan's interest was in the canoe. Earlier in the day something had seemed strange about it, but it didn't seem important at the time. Now it did. The largest piece of it clung to a rock about twenty feet from shore.

Deccan stood studying it, then said, "I need a better look at that birchbark." With that, Kadian went into the woods and returned with a long sapling he had uprooted. After whittling off the branches, he contrived a hook on its end and waded into the river as far as he dared without being swept away. With little effort the big man dragged the canoe wreckage ashore.

Deccan leaned down and examined the bark. "Just what I thought…this was cut with a knife."

"Shelby did it… he must have. That means he escaped," remarked David.

"Well, Shelby did it, but we don't know that he escaped. All we know is that he apparently had a plan, and this was the beginning of it," replied Sorek.

Deccan stood and pointed across the river at the huge boulders. "If I had planned this, I would have headed for those rocks over there. There would be calm water behind them, and he could work from one to the other, all the way to shore. That would mean he is on the other side. Sorek, I think we…"

Deccan's body jerked, and he stood motionless, frozen in mid-stride. His words trailed off, and he collapsed, falling into the water. The others looked on, bewildered, then quickly went in after their companion. Kadian eased him from the water, already turning red with his blood, and rolled him over. A knife was embedded in his back near the left shoulder.

Before words could be formed, the explanation was clear. From behind, the brush moved, and receding, running footfalls were heard. Kadian took chase and crashed through the brush like an angry bull elephant. David knelt beside Deccan and pulled open his shirt. "Clear a spot on the grass so we can lay him out," he ordered. Sorek rushed into action, kicking away the stones and brushing aside the twigs with his hands.

David eased Deccan down to the prepared spot and began careful examination. The knife had to come out. They were too far from home to let it stay, for it would do further damage. Deccan's eyes were wide and wild. He hadn't yet figured out what had happened. He weakly attempted to form words, but only blood came from his mouth. It trickled down his cheek and spotted the ground. David noticed the blood was bright red and bubbled. "Looks like it got his lung, but judging from the knife's position, I think it may have only clipped it."

"I will start a fire and gather some herbs for a poultice." Sorek said as he raced into action.

David eased Deccan's belt and prepared him for treatment. He dared not remove the knife without clean water and a dressing to seal his chest. As he worked he looked around at Sorek blowing gently on a little curl of flame. It quickly caught, so Sorek turned his attention to the canoe and began to rip birch-bark from its hull. He fashioned a small bowl from the bark, filled it with water, and placed it over the fire. *Now there is a real woodsman,* David thought. He had read of mountain men and Indians; he had heard of their skill with these things, but to actually watch such a man in action was truly amazing.

As he carefully observed, he wondered how these men knew about such things. David had learned from a book that the water in the bowl would draw off enough of the heat from the fire to keep the bark below the water line from burning. But who had first stumbled across such information, and when? The same could be said for the poultice that was being prepared. And he was sure that the treatment wouldn't even be in one of his books.

With the boiled water, David cleaned the wound, and Sorek mixed his herb poultice. They placed a cool cloth over a lump on the tracker's head where he must have hit a rock in his fall. Deccan came around and began to talk. "What happened? Did they get away?"

"I don't know," David said. "Kadian went after them, but that was several minutes ago."

Sorek poked David and pointed to the river, saying, "No, Deccan, they didn't get away." Deccan followed their eyes to the river and saw two bodies floating in the thrashing current. Like lifeless rag dolls, they rolled and bobbed along in the white water and disappeared swiftly out of sight.

Kadian came back and knelt down beside Deccan. "I'm sorry, my friend. I only looked away for a second. This is my fault."

"Quiet, you big ox. This wasn't your fault, and I don't want to hear any more of that kind of talk. Now, boy, you gonna' pull this thing out or look at it all day?"

"I'm going to pull it out, Deccan." David said firmly. "You just hold real still so I won't do any more damage."

The knife came out hard, and David cringed and felt faint but showed none of it. He knew the pain would have made anyone else pass out. "Give me that poultice of yours, Sorek." With that, he dressed the wound quickly, preventing air from entering the chest and collapsing a lung. "Well, Deccan, the rest is up to you and the good Lord." With that David stood up and wiped his hands on his pants. "Let's get him home."

"What? You finished? I was still waiting for you to start!" Deccan whispered hoarsely.

David grinned at the old tracker and thought, *these men have grit*.

Sorek stood looking across the river. "Well, we've kept them off of Shelby's back. Maybe he can get a good head start before the rest of that bunch gets back." Then turning to David he continued. "You know we have to go back, don't you? Knowing Shelby, he is going to be mighty hard to track, and without Deccan we don't have much of a chance. And if it's any comfort to you, those Cartoks don't stand a chance either. The best they can do is swarm that country like ants 'cause they'll never find his sign."

David knew it was true, but hated to hear it said. He would have willingly gone on by himself if it could do any good, but he knew better, and said as much. Saddened and heavy with failure, they made a travois for Deccan and started home.

Chapter 11

Shelby lay under the low limbs of a graceful sycamore. Its leaves, spring fresh and green, whispered in the gentle breeze. There in the soft, cool sand, completely hidden by the thick foliage, he slept, regaining strength to a body exhausted by the elements and bruised by man. Even in sleep, his mind worked, and his keen senses stood guard.

His friends assembled across the river, searching the rocks that only moments before had been his refuge. Now he slept, unaware of their close presence, except for a brief moment when, for some strange reason, he felt a sense of alarm. His body jerked tense, then relaxed. What had startled him? What had given him that glimpse of tragedy? Through a foggy mind his eyes tried to focus on the hypnotic movement of the leaves above, but groggy with exhaustion, he gave it up and drifted back into slumber. Whatever had stirred him eluded his consciousness. Whatever had attempted communication with him went unexplained and misunderstood, yet at the same moment, his friend and rescuer fell limply into the raging water.

Shelby slept through the afternoon and night without stirring, and the morning found him rested and alert. The cheerful song of a mockingbird announced the day and lifted his spirits. He looked up through the gold-flecked leaves and watched his little companion singing without worry. The little fellow sensed no danger or concern for what the day might bring. He simply made the best of the moment. Shelby thought there must be a lesson in that somewhere.

He lay quietly, planning his day, thinking of what he must do, where he must go. Suddenly, his companion hushed in mid-song and took wing. Shelby sat up cautiously and looked around. Nothing. He waited for several minutes, but failed to see or hear anything out of the ordinary. He finally determined that he was too jumpy. The little bird probably just didn't like his company.

Shelby sat back and ate some of the dried fruit, although it was now quite soggy. As he spread the contents of the leather bag on a rock to dry, an idea came to him. He must get rid of his boots; they were clumsy in this terrain and slowed his speed. They also left footprints that were difficult to hide. He turned the leather bag in his hand, examining it carefully. "This will do nicely," he said aloud.

For the next hour Shelby cut strips of leather into cord and carefully shaped pieces. He then laced the pieces together and fashioned a pair of moccasins. Slipping into them he stood up. They felt good on his restless feet, and he was eager to move on. But he had one more task. He needed a weapon, and the remaining leather was enough for a sling. He had made them many times before and required only fifteen minutes to complete the effort. He could do considerable damage with one of these and could accurately heft a rock a hundred yards. He chuckled to himself, remembering when he had first learned to use one of these. Before any accuracy set in, he had put a couple of rocks through the wall of the barn and lodged one in the siding of the house. He rolled up the completed sling and put it in his pocket.

Suddenly, he wanted to run. Like a young horse too long in the corral, Shelby wanted to stretch his legs and feel the wind rush past. Running was wonderful to this young Texan. It was almost like flying.

Shelby stashed his boots in a tree fork and covered them to look like a nest. Maybe someday he could come back for them. After all, a good pair of broken-in boots were worth more than most of life's little pleasures. He stuffed the remaining nuts and dried fruit into his pockets and crawled out from under the tree branches. All seemed normal. Even his singing companion had returned to a nearby tree and was calling his mate.

The spring morning was fresh in these mountains, and the air was crystal clear. He took a deep breath and felt its coolness deep within him... then he turned toward Tekoa and broke into a lazy jog. Slowly, he warmed and stretched his muscles, then quickened his pace and lengthened his stride. It was naturally smooth, and it came easy... almost too easy... for he was lost in it, absorbed by the exhilaration of what was much like a controlled fall. He hurdled sage and flushed birds and rabbits. He darted around prickly pear and Spanish dagger, seeking out dim animal trails that mapped endlessly across the rugged land. To run was to live, for it brought him such joy.

Most cowboys wouldn't walk across the yard if they could ride. It was not from laziness but rather a pride in what they were. Consequently, their boots were made for riding, not walking, and certainly not running. They had pointed toes, a rigid, narrow shank and high heels for getting in and out of the stirrups without getting their feet hung up. The heels were angled for leaning back on a rope and digging into the dirt. Yep, cowboy boots were made for a purpose, and most top hands were quick to remind you, "If you can't do it on horseback, it ain't worth doin'." But from as early as he could remember, Shelby would rather run than ride, and that drew a lot of ribbing from the other ranch hands. But it was a ribbing that never changed him or dimmed his urge.

This morning his youthful excitement suppressed his good judgment, and he ran for the pure joy of it. Foolishly, he topped a small hill in mid-air and landed inches from a lounging soldier. He had run headlong into a Cartok patrol on break. Fortunately, they were drinking and lazing around—a condition that, when coupled with their poor military training, caused a slow response and call to action.

Adrenaline surged through Shelby and his mind snapped into reality. He bolted behind a small berm and was quickly out of sight but could still hear them yell the alarm and begin pursuit. Looking back would accomplish nothing, so he focused on places of concealment before him, and it was there he ran with all his might. He heard several shots, but they were far to his left and well behind. He had eluded them then, at least for the moment, but he knew they would be well on his trail in a matter of minutes.

After making some distance he came to a small, jagged heap of upthrust volcanic rock that was scarcely fifty feet high. He worked around it and up as high as he could easily climb. From his vantage point he could survey the terrain and the proximity of his danger. The patrol, almost a half mile behind him, was as easy to spot as a herd of cattle. Their movement raised a dust cloud and their undisciplined manner of travel filled his ears with the clatter of equipment and the chatter of excited voices in pursuit.

Northward, Shelby saw the great sheer walls of Mount Pequepe, a mountain mesa lifting a thousand feet into the air and flattened like a great table. Sardisai had told him of this mountain. It was laced with legend and was completely unscalable. Earlier generations of his people had supposedly come from the mountain. But that was long ago when they were a very different and superstitious people. It was during the time they had turned away from their God and served many deities made with their own hands. They had learned much over the years, but their roots were still important, and the tabletop mountain retained its hold on their culture. The mystery path to its summit, however, had been lost, and it had stood untouched for a thousand years.

From the hollow that lay beneath his viewpoint, mounted a gradual slow-swelling slope that rolled gracefully to the base of the great mountain. The expanse of ten miles distanced him from it and gave rise to tall, volcanic spires, leaning, cracked and ruined as powerful evidence of a violent past on this serene landscape. Birthed from the mountain, the sparkle of water peeked through trees and brush as it snaked around the jagged crags and followed the path of least resistance to the river framing the southern border of this immense picture.

There to the west, where the stream passed closest to him, it became lost in a thicket... five square miles of dense briar and willow, vines and shrub so thick a man could disappear for days. That would be his immediate goal, his refuge from the soldiers. But he must get there, and to do that he must cover at least two miles of relatively open country. Quickly, with a sharp eye and careful photographing mind, he took in the country and lay plan and route through the thicket and on toward the tabletop mountain, Pequepe.

The soldiers had closed the gap but had not yet seen him. He slid down the slope and ran northward to gain distance. Only then would he turn west toward the thicket. A bullet screamed overhead as it tumbled through the air. A moment later Shelby heard the dull boom of a black powder musket. He had been seen then, but he puzzled over the sound of the bullet. Then came several more. None even came close. Instead, they whined overhead harmlessly into the distance.

Distracted, he looked back and ran into a Spanish Dagger. The narrow spear of the vicious plant dug deep into Shelby's leg. He fell to the ground and examined the puncture. It was painful, but the dagger had pulled out without breaking off. He lay back for a moment, catching his breath and rubbing his leg.

From his hidden position, he could hear soldiers yelling from the north. Startled at their presence he whispered aloud, "Where did they come from?" Their words were lost to him, but he could certainly detect anger in the voices. Then came more yelling from the south. Then it was clear. The soldiers following him had shot at another patrol coming from the north. He was between two groups, now screaming at each in anger. *Typical for such an undisciplined mob*, he thought. *They shoot at anything that moves.*

He ran in the direction of the thicket. He could not see it, but he knew where it was. From behind, came a volley of gunfire, then bullets cut the air all around him and ripped at the brush. He didn't have to look back...the sequence of sounds told him they were close. He ran with all the speed he could muster, darting back and forth around mesquite and sage, as much to avoid it as to make a difficult target.

There was no place to hide on this flat plain. The tallest vegetation within view was beneath his shoulders. He ran and the shots continued, but he could sense the distance widening. From the corner of his eye he detected movement. Another patrol, and it was moving fast to cut him off from the thicket. The men were almost a mile distant, but so was the thicket. The shooting ceased for the moment as the soldiers ran to follow. Shelby chanced a quick look. They had spread out and formed a wide line behind him and were coming fast. Again he took careful measurement of the patrol to his front left. At their pace they would cut him off unless he aimed more to his right. That would mean more distance to run for them both, but the advantage would be his.

Another round of bullets whizzed past, some striking dangerously close, then the volley of distant booms. Without exception, every bullet tumbled and whirred through the air as though it had been a ricochet. That puzzled him on a subconscious level but never surfaced to demand any thinking time. They were simply too close, and that was all that mattered.

His breath was coming in great gasps now. His chest heaved in an attempt to take in more air. His legs began to feel heavy, and sweat soaked his shirt and stung his scratched arms and face. Twice he fell and tumbled in the dirt. Each time he rolled to his feet like a cat and ran on without loosing his stride.

Shelby was far enough ahead of his pursuers that they had ceased to shoot, but the ones ahead of him drew closer with each step. He veered more to the right, trying to gain distance on them, but he was wearing down fast. There was little to work with now. Exhaustion had set in, and he ran like a rag doll. If he ran any more to the right he would parallel the thicket and they would have him cut off. They could simply wait for him to stop running.

His side was in wretched pain from the killing run. His mouth felt dry like dirt. He could hear a gasping, wheezing sound like from some wounded animal. The realization that the sound was his struck a fear that he was almost cashed in. A flash of surrender came to him… anything would be better than this moment… but he fought it down. His vision was clouded by tears in his eyes and sweat from his brow. The pain dulled, and the sounds around him fused into one thunderous roar. The mesquite blurred gray as it passed behind him. And still he ran.

Years of hard ranch work and tough country boy play had prepared him for this moment. His physical and mental condition were superb, and while he thought he had taxed his body to the limit, he had a reserve. No city boy could call upon what it took now to complete this race. He was less than a hundred yards from the wall of the thicket and perhaps two hundred from the approaching patrol.

The soldiers realized his lead and opened fire, but they ran as they shot, and their aim was nonexistent. The bullets splattered the surrounding brush but didn't slow Shelby. He saw only the dark thicket and heard only the rush of wind. He had one focus and with a strength unknown to him he surged forward and into the thicket.

Immediately he fell, tripping over the tangle of vines. But where he fell began a small game trail, a tunnel of sorts, routed out beneath the brush by wild hogs and used by a host of creatures. Shelby crawled furiously and the sunlight faded. Like some wild animal in a flight of terror, he clawed and scrambled his way through the tiny wooded passage. The branches grabbed at him, some to hold, some to tear, all to resist and thwart his escape. Finally he broke free and halted in a small break. He stood up to survey a new route. He stood in a small, six foot opening but could not see through the twenty feet to the edge of the thicket. He heard the soldiers as they attempted to enter the thick brush. He doubted they would be able to follow very fast or come very far, but he knew they would at least try. So he walked briskly on, still heaving for breath and stinging from sweat-soaked cuts and scratches.

In a last ditch effort, the soldiers fired blindly into the thicket. The bullets cut through the foliage and snapped saplings. They were striking dangerously close. Shelby instinctively ducked and caught a ricocheted bullet that would have hit his chest but instead it struck his head with a dull thud. He wheeled and fell. His fall seemed endless and in slow motion. But it did end, and he lay still on the dirt beneath a false floor of twigs and small, dead branches. Blood trickled from his head, but he felt nothing. Men crashed through the brush, but he heard nothing. Motionless and unaware he lay as soldiers walked almost on top of him. They ventured in only a few yards and searched the outer edges of the dense brush but quickly gave up, beaten back by the strength and torture of the unyielding thicket.

The soldiers' clamoring assault on this strange and mystic sanctuary drove its creatures to darker, safer regions within. Their retreat brought an unnatural silence and stillness rarely known to this zone of teeming life. The copse held its breath and nothing moved. Nothing disturbed the silence that was left alone to guard the fallen Texan.

Chapter 12

The night came and passed into morning…still Shelby did not move. The afternoon sun beat down on the thicket, but only dark shadows danced within, and they found a stir of movement in the once stone-still body. A fly buzzed and landed on an open wound, then buzzed again and rested on the forehead and rubbed his legs together. Shelby opened his eyes and looked up through the heap of twigs and debris through which he had fallen and that now served to completely cover him. He lay still, listening, and trying to piece the puzzle together. The past events were a blur, but he worked to sort it out. His hand fumbled for the wound on his forehead and found it caked with dried blood. He had been shot, but as far as he could determine, it was not very serious. His body ached with pain, and he felt nauseous. His tongue was thick and dry…signs, he knew, of serious dehydration.

His desperate need for water outweighed the demands of his wracked body to remain still. To move was to invite pain, but to ignore his body's warning was to embrace death. Grabbing a young sapling for support, he got to his knees and managed to crawl from beneath the debris. He stood and took a quick survey to determine his direction of travel. Shelby knew the stream was west of where he had entered the thicket, and the sun now hung low in the afternoon sky so that it was in the southwest. Quietly, he walked westward, yet even the deft touch of his moccasins on the copse floor seemed harsh to his ears.

Travel was difficult, but in it he found comfort and believed no soldier would dare follow into this briar patch. Much of his travel consisted of climbing on top of the brush and at times not seeing the ground at all. Other areas demanded crawling on his belly beneath a canopy of dense vines and sharp bramble. The leafy covert was hot and windless this time of day, and nothing stirred but the relentless insects. Their ceaseless drone and insistence to swarm in his eyes and nose dominated his attention and aggravated his thought. It was very difficult to be careful and watchful with such distraction. Still, he carefully moved through the saplings and underbrush, threading his way like an Indian.

Fatigue had always been unknown to him. Even after his death run, which would have been just that for most men, he had recovered quickly and now felt no residual from it. Except for his dehydrated condition and its accompanying symptoms, his endurance was still intact, and his mind-set was firm. He would get water and plan his escape.

He heard the stream before he saw it, and caution touched his senses. The soldiers might very well be there waiting. After all this was a logical destination. Carefully, Shelby moved closer and took up a position where he could watch a section of the stream. The birds seemed content and so did the cicadas, so after a few minutes of careful scrutiny he moved in and drank. His training had taught him never to drink from a stream without first purifying the water, but that was in his world of pollution and millions of people. He doubted if five humans had been within ten miles of this place in a hundred years.

After drinking, he sat back to rest and let his body use the water. Then he drank again. As he sat there he pondered where the soldiers might be, if they were around at all. This rugged place on the stream was completely closed off with thicket, and he realized that if the rest of the stream was the same, he would have concealed access to water as he traveled. It would be slow, but it would be relatively safe.

His line of travel brought him to a large cottonwood, which he quickly climbed for reconnaissance. It was late, and the afternoon sun waned into a red-gold sky. He was well within the middle of this thicket. The tabletop mountain stood dark and foreboding to the north, drawing not only his attention, but his presence, to it. Why did he feel drawn to the mountain? It could not be climbed and would therefore offer no sanctuary. Perhaps it was simply its mystery that called him. Whatever it was, he would go.

A flicker of light caught his eye, and he studied the spot until he saw it again. It was a fire...a campfire. As he watched he noticed others lit around the perimeter of the thicket. By dusk he counted twenty-five fires scattered around him. In the time he had slept, more soldiers must have come and joined the search. Of course there may have only been two soldiers at each fire, but the number of fires made it appear that he was surrounded by a massive, overwhelming army. He must lay hold of his imagination lest it defeat him. Shelby thought of the old story of Gideon and the Midianites and chuckled. He would not let so many fires frighten him. He climbed down but was met by a horde of vicious, hungry mosquitoes and decided to go back up where there was a breeze and the possibility of a little sleep.

He climbed around in the fading light looking for a branch that would offer a good place for the night. Finding one, he wedged down in its fork and tied in with his belt. He had slept in worse places but never one so laden with danger. Leaning back, he wiggled and squirmed in search of a position that offered at least a little comfort, but there didn't seem to be any.

Finally, despite his discomfort, he was asleep, but his subconscious mind worked on the problem of escape. He had learned long ago that he could solve problems in his sleep, just as he had learned to control the outcome of his dreams. At home he kept a notebook beside his bed for those ideas that came to him in the night, ideas that would surely be gone in the morning. He was well conditioned to wake and write down things of consequence. To him it seemed normal, but many of his friends thought it extremely strange.

After about four hours he had all the rest he could tolerate in that tree. Noticing the surrounding fires had died down, he decided to see how alert the soldiers were. Climbing down he began to move through the brush, leaving the stream and pushing north toward the mountain, on to what he did not know. But he felt its mysterious call and a need to answer.

The scant moonlight was little help in the dense thicket, dark with shadow. Scattered here and there were silvery pools of light, but they were scarce and positioned to be of little value. Several times something moved past him in the brush, something large and deft in this snarled and tangled place. Whatever it was it had no interest in him, and that suited Shelby just fine. The chorus of insects and night birds brought a melancholy mood to this dark, mysterious woodland. Was that what they intended, or was it simply his grim mood that read it that way?

Shelby pushed on, sometimes guided by the dim slivers of silver moonlight that penetrated the thick canopy above him, and other times by feeling his way, groping along in the utter blackness and trusting his senses. Instinctively, he employed his night vision where he was able and picked his trail through the tangle of brush and trees. Shelby's dad had taught him well. He had night skills that would be envied by an Indian. He had grown up using his night vision while hunting and playing night games, but never had he relied on it as he did now. Subconsciously, he thought of his dad, and the night he had first taught him the skill. Shelby was told to focus his attention on the object he wished to see and actually look a little off to the left or right instead of looking directly at it. That would cast the image of it off of the retina and onto the surrounding rods inside the eye. While it seemed strange, it was not a hard technique to learn and allowed him to see quite well.

Three hours of threading through the thick brush brought him near the northeastern perimeter of the thicket. He could see the dim glow of the campfire and a sleeping soldier nearby. Carefully he moved closer. He must know the possibility of getting past this guard post. Suddenly, a glistening line appeared before him. At first glance he thought it to be a spider web reflecting the light of the moon and started to wipe it away but caution arrested his move. Gently he touched it…a trip wire. He had certainly underestimated these men. He wouldn't have thought it possible of them but here it was, carefully placed across the most logical escape route.

Shelby doubted any serious danger here, this was most likely a simple noisemaker and not a detonating device. Still, he needed to know the extent of their threat. From his possibles kit, he removed a pack of dental floss and carefully tied one end around the trip wire. Then as he unwound the floss he eased back into the thicket a safe distance and gave it a yank. As expected, the clang of tin cans and glass clinks were followed by an explosion of wild gunfire and yelling men. Perhaps he should try another spot, maybe further west where the stream entered the thicket.

Shelby glanced at the eastern horizon. He still had another two hours before daylight, so he moved off to the west where the stream entered the thicket. He kept on, wondering what his next attempt would bring. His body was stinging from the numerous scrapes and scratches to his face and arms. Thorns had torn at his legs and sides and his shirt was shredded. Despite this he felt strong, undaunted, and his will to escape was fervent.

Something snorted in the black shadows near him, and an icy chill ran down his spine. He jerked back instinctively and cowered behind a tree. The brush crackled and gave way to something monstrous. He sat motionless, and his heart pounded at the sudden scare. Slowly, his mind took control, and he attempted to identify the noise and its potential danger. Vaguely he began to make out a shape as the giant moved around in the brush and slowly settled down. It came to Shelby that he had disturbed the beast, and his presence was a continuing source of irritation to it. Whatever it was, the silhouette outlined against the dark, star flecked sky, was well over six feet high and he could not ascertain how long or wide.

Deciding not to move closer for identification, he trudged on, working through the growth with a greater skill, now that he had acquired some experience. Soon he heard the rhythmic chorus of insects and night birds add to their wonderful symphony the rich, melodious voices of the frogs, and he knew the stream was near.

His first action was to wade in and sit down in the cold, dark water. It chuckled gaily over the rocks and tumbled off of large flat boulders in small falls as it swiftly threaded through the thicket. Shelby leaned back in the fast water and let it massage his tired muscles and soothe his scratched body. He drank a little and relaxed, pondering his next move. He was perhaps a hundred yards from the perimeter and soldiers. It was still dark but a faint glow in the sky announced the coming twilight and told the trained eye an hour of darkness remained. It had been a long, wretched night, and he welcomed the coming day, even though he did not know what dangers it would bring.

Refreshed, he stood and waded upstream letting the sound of the rushing water mask his approach toward the soldiers. He moved on until he could see a parting in the black trees and dark blue twilight sky beyond. The soft glow of fading campfire embers marked the edge, and there guards would surely be waiting, huddled around their fires. Some were sleeping, some in a dazed, half awareness brought on by exhaustion and a lack of commitment to this miserable chase, but all were waiting.

Shelby lay prone, half out of the water, with searching eyes locked on the campsite. There was no movement, no sign of life at all. Was it a trick, or had the careless guards left their post? He lay motionless as dawn's gray light disclosed the darkest shadows of the night and laid bare the open landscape toward the huge mountain. The sage and mesquite looked so inviting and free; yet they offered little in the way of concealment. Once on that open plain he would be exposed for a good six miles before he could reach the base of the mountain. He could only hope that its base might offer a small cave or a crevasse, a place to hole up until the soldiers grew weary of this as he knew they would. Their hearts were not in this chase or some would have ventured into the thicket after him. It was the bidding of that evil Croseus, and they were here out of fear of him.

For a brief moment his thoughts turned to Croseus. *What turned an innocent child into a man like that? What turn of events, what experiences led a man to think so highly of himself while seeing all others as mere dogs? What was it he had said? Yes, he said he was going to kill me.* Shelby remembered that well. *Well, he was certainly doing his best to try.* Then the thought struck him strange, and he whispered aloud. "He spoke in perfect English! Where did he learn that? From the Tekoans?"

With his judgment clouded by the nearness of freedom, Shelby allowed carelessness to push aside discretion. He left the protection of the thicket and edged ever closer to the open plain. His stomach knotted as he realized what this dangerous move meant. Behind was safety and beyond lay freedom, but if he moved out and the soldiers cut him off... He would have a six mile run with no place to hide.

He took a few more steps, and caution gripped him hard. He knew then it was a foolish mistake, and he turned back and ran for the thicket. A dozen soldiers jumped from behind clumps of brush and rushed him. He darted around them and zigzagged through the sparse brush as they yelled and shot wildly. The bullets whizzed and zinged harmlessly off into the brush. There was no attempt to shoot at him, only to frighten him. Apparently, this group of soldiers had been reminded to capture him alive, something the earlier patrol had obviously forgotten. In the wild chase, the soldiers grabbed and ripped at his clothes as he dodged and fought them off. Some tumbled into the dirt and gave up, but others remained determined to bring this ordeal to an end.

There were several close calls, but he managed to break free only to face two soldiers moving in to cut him off. One quickly got into position between two large mesquite and crouched waiting. Confidence was on his face, for he had closed the gap...the last route to the thicket. Shelby was cut off. He stopped and wheeled. He ran and darted in short bursts, then turned again like a desperate, trapped animal. The soldiers moved in and tightened their circle. All were yelling with excitement except the man who had originally cut him off. He looked demon possessed as he crouched, seeming to know that he would make the capture. Shelby thought of the many scared, trapped animals he had seen in his life. He thought of the wild look in their eyes, their will to attempt the impossible in the face of certain death. Shelby was one of them now, and his actions reflected the terror of capture and the tremendous will to survive. In one last, magnificent effort, he ran toward the man with all the speed he could manage in that short distance. He yelled and crossed his raised arms as if to knock his opponent down. The soldier crouched and braced for impact, but Shelby leaped high into the air and was over the man before he could react. In seconds he was back in the thicket and ripping through the brush in an attempt to gain distance and safety. Behind, the shouts receded, faded, and finally blended with the voices of the cicadas and the sinister drone of winged squadrons of gnats and mosquitoes.

Shelby stirred for a better position. The sun was hot on his back and several antagonizing flies buzzed in his ears and tickled his nose. They woke him from a sleep he did not remember entering. He lay near the stream in dense brush not too far from the edge of the thicket. He knew this because he could hear soldiers in the distance. He rolled over and looked up into the sky, trying to remember what had happened. Brushing the sand from his face, he discovered a good sized knot on his forehead. It was evident that he had run into a low branch and had been here for some time. Fortunately the soldiers had not pursued, or he would now be their captive.

The pangs of hunger gnawed within his stomach. He felt for the dried fruit in his pocket, but it was long since gone. He knew he could survive. He had water, and could do without food for many days. But he wasn't just trying to survive, he was trying to escape; and that took energy, lots of energy. He had been so preoccupied with escape, he had not even thought of food until now. And now he needed it... desperately. He thought of the mountain and what might very well be a six mile adrenaline run to the security he hoped to find in its shadows.

The thicket offered a variety of edible plants, now that he attempted to find them. Most plentiful and easiest to prepare were the young, tender bamboo shoots near the water. There were berries, but it was too early in the season and they weren't yet ripe. He also constructed small animal snares along the runways beneath the thick brush. By evening Shelby was no longer hungry.

As he sat back relaxing near his small, smokeless fire he heard a crushing, powerful movement through the brush. It was slow, easy and methodical. It would pause for a moment, then proceed again. Shelby's first thought was of Cartok soldiers, but upon scrutiny, he decided it was an animal. He sat still, listening. Whatever this creature might be it was big. Perhaps it was the beast he had almost met the previous night. Curiosity was a weakness of his, and he got up to investigate. Dowsing his fire, he moved toward the sound on cat feet and from the downwind side. The closer he got, the bigger it sounded and more distinct were its noises. He heard snorts, grunting and chewing. When he determined he was within thirty feet, he settled down to wait for it to emerge.

Waiting was always hard for his inquisitive mind, but his good sense told him it was wise. The sound moved closer, and he remained undetected. If the breeze shifted or if he made a move or sound, he might be considered a threat, and that could be dangerous. Why hadn't he thought of that earlier? The nearest climbing tree was a large cottonwood a good thirty feet to his left, too far to do him any good if the situation got sticky.

Faintly now, Shelby could make out scant features of this massive beast, still hidden in the thick brush. It paused and he heard it sniff the air. It eased forward like a tank in tender saplings, unstoppable and going precisely where it wanted to go. Suddenly, it broke through and stood in plain view not twelve feet away. Shelby held his breath in astonishment. Before him stood a creature of legend, a hulk of unprecedented stature…a magnificent white buffalo.

The large bull seemed to look at Shelby with contempt, then he lazily turned to feed once more. Perhaps he didn't see him at all. Buffalo tend to rely on their keen sense of smell and hearing. To be seen as something of consequence, he would have to move, and that, he did not plan to do. Shelby was mesmerized. He had only read of such animals. Many Plains Indian tribes considered the rare white buffalo to be supernatural, and held elaborate ceremonies in their honor. No animal was more esteemed than the great white mutant, considered to be the leader of all buffalo herds.

The splendid animal moved off toward the stream and waded in, seeming to enjoy the cool water and lush foliage. Shelby watched, but his mind turned back to the soldiers not two hundred yards distant. They sat patiently waiting for him to emerge, and their only duty was to deliver him to Croseus. They had plenty of time and good reason to carry out that duty. Shelby did not have time. He could survive here for several weeks if necessary, but his friends probably imagined the worst had happened, and he cared too much for them to allow that to continue. And besides, this was no game. He wanted to be free of these savage, undisciplined soldiers.

Shelby leaned back against a tree and twitched a blade of grass in his teeth. While he unconsciously watched the old bull his mind searched all possibilities of escape. He needed a diversion, something that would distract them long enough for him to get through their lines. But they would probably expect something like that. His prospects looked pretty dismal.

The breeze stirred, and a small branch from above dropped on the back of the white bull, now shoulder high in the stream. Absent-mindedly, Shelby looked up to where the branch had come from. A pair of squirrels darted about, playing on a thick limb. His eyes followed the limb back to the large cottonwood he had earlier noted.

As quickly as the idea came to him, he tried to dismiss it as stupidly dangerous. But remaining here was dangerous. What if they sent in dogs or set fire to this place? No. His idea was far-fetched, but not stupid. He would ride that great white buffalo out of here. Perhaps the superstitious Cartoks would be awestruck at the sight of the beast and not shoot it down. Perhaps they would be taken by surprise and not be able to react in time. In any event, if he could manage to hang on long enough, this buffalo could take him miles from here in a matter of minutes.

Shelby considered what must be done and laid a plan. He waited for the buffalo to turn away from him then he carefully crept toward the tree. Quietly, he climbed it and worked his way over the top of the buffalo. Twice he stopped as the questioning animal looked up and sniffed the air. At length, he was directly above him. The drop would be about eight feet and he would have to land perfect, solid, and straddling the huge bull. If he missed or the bull moved, he would be trampled by two thousand pounds of sheer terror.

Shelby whispered words of confidence to himself. After all, he had ridden lots of bulls in the rodeos and around the ranch. This couldn't be that different, although he hoped to stay on longer than the regulation eight seconds. He held his breath and leaped from the limb.

Shelby hit square and solid. His fingers dug into the long, coarse, stinking hair, and his toes searched for the bull's flanks. Fortunately, his initial grip held, because there was no chance for a better one. The huge animal grunted. His tail came almost straight up, and he lunged through the water toward the shore. He moved like a runaway barge pushing a wall of water that churned white and rushed over the narrow banks. Grunting and panting, the great animal left the stream, bounding like a gazelle along the bank, and in the direction of least resistance, out the thicket. There was no graceful or manly way to ride this creature, so Shelby simply clung like a baby possum to its mamma.

The initial bounding jolts rattled his teeth and shook his insides, but he held on for life. Finally, the buffalo settled into a less painful running gait but added a few short bucks and swipes into the trees. He gathered speed and crashed through brush that almost ripped Shelby from his back, but the knowledge that he would never get a better chance than this gave him the will to endure the torture. He buried his head in the thick hair for any protection possible. The branches grabbed at him, tore his clothes, and lashed at his skin. The buffalo didn't flinch. His hide was like armor coating. With the wanton drive of a linebacker, he would charge a wall of brush that looked impassable, and it would shatter like chaff.

This miserable battering brought second thoughts to Shelby's plan of escape. He could have been beaten with barbed wire and faired better. The seconds passed as endless, agonizing minutes until suddenly they broke free of the thicket. The white bull crashed through the last of the brush and scattered the wide-eyed, screaming soldiers. They had heard him coming and were alarmed and dumfounded. Now they were wild and frantic, seeking any possible escape.

Several soldiers instinctively raised their muskets to shoot but quickly lowered them upon recognizing the venerable creature. In mere seconds Shelby and his steed were through the line of soldiers and galloping across the open plain. The feral beast gathered speed, and with nostrils flared, thundered out of sight over the horizon toward the great tabletop mountain. On his back, a young Texan clung in the ride of his life.

Chapter 13

Once clear of the thicket Shelby raised his head to gain his bearings. He had no hope of directing this unstoppable hulk, but he wanted to know where he was going. The buffalo raced still faster, and the mesquite blurred to a streaking, gray-green wall. Tears streamed from Shelby's eyes, and small branches slapped his legs with a sharp sting. He thought of jumping, but not at this speed. How long had it been, and how far behind were the soldiers? When would this white marvel slow down? His mind raced for control and his every nerve was strung tight.

The white bull made a good four miles before slowing and jolted almost to a halt. Shelby quickly seized the opportunity and leaped for the dirt. He rolled on impact and came up on his feet ready to run if Big Medicine turned. "Big Medicine. That's what I'll call you, old boy. I name you after another of your kind that put a mark on history. And thanks! You sure saved my neck." Shelby spoke aloud to the puzzled, lumbering buffalo as if the animal had the ability to understand. Big Medicine turned and simply grunted before trotting off out of sight.

Shelby spent a panting moment taking in the country and gathering his wits. He removed his hat, beat the dust from his jeans, and took tally of the damage to his clothes and body. Looking skyward, he wiped a sleeve against a sweaty brow and let a long, dry whistle pass between his teeth. A missed trickle of sweat born on his hairline began a journey along his cheek, leaving behind little tracks of mud. The cuts and scratches began to sting with salty sweat, and he wished he could bathe his wounds. He knew the cool stream ran from the mountain toward the south, and he thought it passed him to his left, but he had lost track of exactly where.

The tabletop mountain stood before him and several silent minutes passed before he seemed to grasp the wonder of it. Then, as if possessed, it called to him, bade him come forth and seek refuge in its mysterious canyons and dark caves. The feeling was strange, but the draw was strong…too strong to ignore…so Shelby walked north to the mountain and just enough west to bring him to water.

In mere moments his trek crossed the stream, and he entered the cold, swift water, drinking first, then washing his wounds. He sat down in the water and looked back to where he expected to see the advancing soldiers, but there were none. He had a good head start and figured he should keep it, so he moved on, keeping his travel restricted to the stream bed where he could leave no trace of his passing. The Cartoks were poor trackers, but why give them any advantage?

A half mile further, the stream entered the mountain through a scorched, jagged ravine. The walls were stained red cliffs of cracks and caves covered with broken shale and ancient scrub oak. He climbed steadily up a rugged, natural staircase of rocks and crags that evolved into a strange otherworldly place. The mountain stream through which he walked fell from ledge to ledge in delicate, dwarfed waterfalls that chuckled pleasantly beneath his feet, seeking the fastest passage out of this strange place.

The elevation changed quickly, and soon he had a good view over the rise to the south and could see the distant thicket where he had taken refuge. A faint cloud of dust told of an advancing patrol. They had not given up, but then he had not expected them to. How could they face their cruel leader with such an incredible story of defeat?

He turned back to the distorted gulch, open like a diseased mouth and daring him to crawl over its decayed and twisted teeth. Its denuded walls lifted like a deformed precipice, ruined and deprived of everything good. Except for the stream seeking a rapid escape, the place had the look and feel of the devil, and he wondered if he could indeed find safety here, or would he become trapped in this God-forsaken hollow? He gave it serious thought, then went on. The sheer walls of the canyon might very well close and become a dead-end trap. But if they did, it was rugged enough to easily hide from a tired, unskilled army that had no stamina for this.

As he climbed, so did the sun. The heat rose and the breeze stilled. His forehead dripped with sweat and his scratches and wounds stung. Several times he paused to bathe his arms in the stream and soak his torn shirt and bandanna. He filled his hat and put it on, letting the cool water fall where it may.

The afternoon sun finally moved from the narrow strip of bronze sky above his head returning it to blue, and dark shadows began their trek up the east cliff. With that came relief, and Shelby sat down on a flat rock in the stream to rest. He was tired but not done in. It had been a day to write about. David would love, this story and he would enjoy telling it.

He lay back on the cool rock, looking up at the strip of blue framed by the sharp notches of the rim wall. A buzzard crossed the narrow strip and disappeared only to return and trace out lazy, narrowing circles above him. Undoubtedly, the grim creature had eyed him for some time, hoping for an opportunity to visit. Shelby chuckled to himself and spoke aloud. "If you're waiting for me, you'll starve to death."

Then, deciding to have some fun, he lay very still, appearing to be dead, while watching the buzzard's actions. Within ten minutes there were others. Still, Shelby didn't twitch a muscle. After all, he was quite comfortable and could wait and see if they would approach. The coolness of the rock against his back penetrated deep within him and he relaxed. The sound of the stream dulled his senses, and his eyelids grew heavy. Soon his body lay limp, not from any game he played, but from sleep.

An hour passed and the sky above was empty. The buzzards were gone. So were the other birds in the small ravine. The cicadas hushed, and all was quiet except the chuckle of water and the wake of a clatter approaching from down stream. One lone Red-tail watched from the cliffs above. He had been closely watching Shelby, but now his keen eye ranged on the clamoring soldiers coming up the gulch. Their undisciplined racket and threatening appearance advanced, bringing an unknown spectacle and obvious threat to his small, remote canyon. He took wing. His piercing call was clear, penetrating and untamed. It belonged here, as much a part of this wild land as the scarred crags and tortured, strange rock walls.

Shelby's eyes opened and his heart raced. Something was deadly wrong, but what? Instinctively, he rolled to the nearest boulder offering concealment and tried to sort out the danger. Then he heard the soldiers, still distant but still deadly. He broke into a run and rounded the bend out of sight. His eyes searched the scrawled walls, but the places he chose would be too obvious. He ran on, following the stream, leaping from rock to rock with the precision of a mountain goat. Each bend brought new surroundings and possibilities, but each he rejected and drove on, careful to leave no trace of his passing.

At length, the ravine ended just as he had dreaded it would. The walls were impossible to climb without rope and lots of time. The stream ended here at its source, a pool not thirty feet across and deep enough to be dark. A splendid waterfall emptied into it from a ledge eighty feet above. The water sprayed and dampened everything while ferns covered the walls and bank. The cliff around the fall appeared to be mostly calcium deposit. It was very ornate with strange, delicate formations.

Shelby weighed all possibilities then waded into the cold pool. He swam for the falls and planned to go behind them. As he approached, the water thundered, displaying its immense power. He held his breath and entered. The falling water beat like a hammer on his head. His felt hat took the shock, but he was driven under, amazed at the power and force of what appeared to be a delicate waterfall.

He emerged in a hollow behind the falls where it was cold and shaded. The mist swirled like steam and settled on the smooth, time worn rocks. He climbed out of the water and stood on a small ledge, shivering from the icy spring water. It was exhilarating, and he felt refreshed as he bent down to look through the falls. He moved around a bit seeking a spot that he could see through and found it.

The soldiers were just coming into view and he nervously looked around for a better spot to hide. His eyes were adjusting to the darker area now and he could make out several small caves. Their openings were scarcely large enough to crawl into, and they appeared to connect like tunnels within a honeycomb, but they would have to do. He began his climb over the slippery rock and noticed water emerging from several of the small openings. Working deftly, he maneuvered to the largest of those found and entered. Water rushed out and over him as he squeezed through the opening on his stomach. He found himself in a round room large enough to sit up in, a chamber that had been the work of thousands of years of eddying water. The walls were smooth as glass and captured the scant outside light with a ghostly but pleasant glow.

He felt safer here. The soldiers had not seen him, and he had left no tracks, he was sure of that. They were merely checking all possibilities, but for them to follow him in here was extremely unlikely. The place had looked like a box canyon with no possible way out, and Shelby hoped they would accept it as just that. Still there was a need to do everything possible to distance himself from them.

He unzipped his possibles bag and took out a small flashlight. If there was more to this place he planned to find it. Being careful to keep his light from the opening, he scanned the area and noticed first that the opening he had crawled through was actually much larger. It had been plugged with rocks. About a dozen fifty to sixty pound rocks looked to be *stacked* in the opening. The method left little doubt. Someone had done it on purpose! Close examination of the water erosion indicated that the work was ancient and very clever. The rocks had been placed to not only block the entrance, but to divert the water. Then another realization occurred. The work had been done from the inside! There was another way out!

Shelby turned and beamed his light toward the back of the small cave. There was a tall narrow passage half full of running water that seemed to disappear just beyond a large speleothem, a spectacular, glasslike stalagmite. He moved into it and realized that it did not. Had his need for escape not driven him on, his curiosity would have. Carefully he eased into the waist deep water and followed the narrow chamber as it wound past beautiful formations and shimmering pools of eddying water. These small eddies were as certain to carve this rock as a pick and hammer. Their meager effort would take a few thousand years, but here in this timeless place that didn't matter. Perseverance mattered, and given enough time, these small currents would take down this entire mountain. Gently though, with delicate, artistic fingers they would carve and polish, shape and reshape until nothing remained. And over the course of eons, their work would always be seen as beautiful and beyond the skill of man. How many such places existed where such breathtaking beauty would be so carved, and yet go unseen except by some small passing animal that would not even notice?

He climbed from the pool and ascended a steep, slippery path of polished walls and imposing dripstone. The water crisscrossed the path and disappeared into the walls, only to reappear at some other unlikely spot. In some areas it poured, in others it dripped from a thousand places in the ceiling. Still others remained relatively dry. But in all, the ever-present sound of water, dripping, running, rushing and always echoing through the maze of chambers, prevailed.

At length, Shelby found himself at the top of the waterfall beside the wide stream that poured over the ledge. He dare not look over the edge for fear of being sky-lighted and seen by the soldiers below. As impossible as it seemed, he needed to know if they followed, but he would resist the urge to look from this spot. There was plenty of vegetation beside the stream. He would postpone looking over until he got to it.

Once there, he crawled to the edge, and well under the cover of brush, he peeked over. The soldiers were resting near the water. None seemed to be looking around or showing any signs of suspicion. Shelby's confidence grew. Perhaps they would rest and simply leave, so he settled in to wait it out. He had to know.

It wasn't long before several of the soldiers began to splash around in the water. That changed as they got wetter, and finally three of them were swimming in the small pool. Shelby grew concerned as they got closer to the falls. What if they went under as he did and found his cave? He watched intently, keeping track of each one of them. There were the three swimming, five sleeping, two more sitting under a large manzanita bush, and one was fifty yards down the gorge throwing rocks at something on the cliff wall. Two others had gone beyond him another fifty yards and were engaged in conversation. They were apparently in charge of this shiftless bunch.

Suddenly, one of the swimmers went under the falls and Shelby held his breath. Long, anxious minutes passed before he emerged, yelling and motioning for the others to follow. Shelby wished he knew what the man was saying. It didn't sound urgent, but it did sound like he had found something and wanted the others to join him. Shelby had to find a way to call them off. If they went in there, it could mean he was in serious trouble.

His eye again caught the movement of the man throwing rocks. What if he hit one of his leaders or came real close with one of those rocks? Now that would be a diversion. The idea came to him and he grinned with pleasure. He backed away from the edge and found a smooth, round rock, one that would fly silently and not cut the air. He placed it in his sling and observed the man below. He watched him and attempted to match his timing. Then, as the man pitched, Shelby whirled his sling and released his rock. It arched high and sailed true. It seemed to take forever to traverse the distance and finally it disappeared from sight. Then it hit. He saw the two men duck and run before he heard the sound.

No sooner had Shelby's rock come to rest than the two were running toward the others yelling. All eyes were on them as they came up the ravine like two angry pit bulls. One attacked the man throwing rocks and knocked him to the ground. Then he began screaming at the others, barking commands and waving his arms.

The swimmers got out quickly and dressed. In a matter of minutes the soldiers were headed down the little canyon at a brisk trot, and behind them their angry leaders raged and ruthlessly barked their commands.

Shelby rolled up his sling, kissed it, and placed it back in his pocket. He turned then, confident of not being followed, and strolled up the stream at a leisurely pace.

The upper crevasse through which he now walked took on a grandeur that the lower gorge lacked. These walls were sheer cliffs of polished granite separated by a creek bed only twelve to fifteen feet wide. The narrow pass had seen seasons of deep rushing water that had deposited dry brush high on the walls. Now the stream flowed gently over rounded rocks worn smooth by eons of wind and water.

Along the cliffs rose a faint murmur of the wind sighing in mournful contrast to the happy chuckle of the stream. Shelby's keen ear marked them as the only sounds to be heard on this late, sultry afternoon. For two hours he continued his climb through the narrow pass and noticed the change in vegetation and the dwindling of the stream. At length the water ceased all together, disappearing into the sand, reappearing perhaps in some silent dark cavern deep beneath his feet. It had been born of scores of small springs along the way and added to by the continuous flow of water hidden beneath the rocks and sand in the bed. Now he walked atop that bed, dry but well worn, and routed by the fierce mountain storms and the flash floods they birthed.

Nearer, still nearer he came to the rimrock spires that he hoped marked the top of the butte. Could it be that he had actually found the long lost trail to its top? Excitedly his pace quickened at the thought of reaching the sacred plateau of which Sardisai had so reverently spoken. He wondered what might still remain of a site the Tekoan people had called their "Beginning Place."

Shelby stopped to rest at a point that seemed impassable. The slope before him was one of loose shale and extended for a hundred yards before the solid shelf resumed. Beyond, lay the top of the mesa. He was a half mile from the crest of the tabletop mountain, but it may as well have been ten. His eyes searched for a path around the shale but were unsuccessful. Yet he was not prepared to give up so easily. Shelby was absolutely convinced that he had found the lost trail, and if that was the case, then this could not be the end.

Again he looked at the slide of shale. It could be relatively recent, but that he doubted. The slide had probably been here when the Tekoans were, so how did they circumvent it? Absent-mindedly he picked up a small piece and hit it with his knife handle. It sounded dull, so it was indeed shale. The earlier slate he had encountered had a nice strong ring to it when struck and sounded crisp when walked on. It was of no consequence to Shelby, a slide of either was too dangerous and too impossible to climb.

He chunked the piece of shale against the cliff and it splattered. Enjoying that, he did it several more times, then the boy in him looked for targets to hit. He wanted hard targets that would splatter the shale missiles he threw. At first he chose other rocks scattered about, then his aim moved up the cliff to small holes along its edge. Suddenly, Shelby paused in mid-throw. Those holes caught his attention and drew him closer for examination.

"Footholds!" He exclaimed as he ran his fingers along the rough surface. He backed up and surveyed the carved out steps... steps so weathered by time they had gone unnoticed to his casual eye. Instantly, he scrambled up the side of the cliff and around the slide, using the chiseled out steps and hand holds. No doubt this young Texan was the first to use these steps in over a thousand years, a thought of which he was well aware.

In a matter of minutes he had reached the solid shelf above the slide of shale. It was a large expanse of rock that lifted toward the mesa above. Winds had swept it clean of weathered shale, and rains had washed it free of dust. It lay polished in the late afternoon sun, enticing, calling, and the last trek before the plateau.

As Shelby walked across the shelf he noticed several large battlements of rock along the rim above him. The distance between them, along with their strategic placement, indicated the hand of man against an enemy. He could see smaller rocks wedged at their base... rocks that could be easily knocked free, allowing the huge boulders to crash down and begin a rockslide of immense proportion. An invading enemy would be buried in the loose shale and have no hope of survival.

Shelby reached the top and walked to one of the large rocks poised on the edge of the cliff. He felt a little chill and a strange feeling in his knees as he looked over the edge. He thought of the men who had placed this weapon here, this last line of defense against an army of invaders. He looked at the other rocks. So much effort had gone into this. There must have been much to defend. Shelby looked back over his shoulder toward the mesa. What would he find?

Chapter 14

This young explorer had seen things in the past two weeks that transcended the limits of conventional thinking. He stood in another world, perhaps another dimension of his own. He had been exposed to possible answers to questions his people had asked for centuries. Yet he did not recognize those answers, for they were cloaked in a fog of mystery and intrigue.

He walked across the mesa toward the setting sun, already appearing to grow larger as it changed from white to gold. There it would rest, and for a breathtaking moment it would set fire to the sky as if announcing some grand event, then gently slip from view.

In the last gold light Shelby could see that the tabletop mountain wasn't really flat as he had imagined. It was rimmed with rock that fell away to a shallow valley. Before him he could make out large areas bordered with stacked stones. They appeared to be fields, but they were now chaparral, spotted with scrub cedar, cactus, and yucca plant. The rimrock was a broken escarpment of toppled boulders, and there Shelby could see several caves, even in the waning light.

He saw no need for shelter on such a night, so he gathered dried wood and built a small fire on the open field. As it grew darker he prepared a bed and stretched out. With his knife he peeled the spines from several prickly pear tuna and roasted them over the fire. They were a bit tasteless and not quite ripe, but they were food.

There were no night sounds, no crickets, no birds, no coyotes or owls. It was strangely quiet. He thought his presence was the more logical reason for it…after all, any creature in this high place would have never seen a man, or a fire.

Restless, Shelby got up in the moonlit darkness and decided to walk to the rim and look over. He wanted to know how committed his pursuers were. Climbing over the boulders that marked the boundary of the butte, he stood on the edge and caught the cool updraft blowing along the cliff wall. Below him, the silver light of the moon illuminated the floor of the plain. It was dotted with Cartokian campfires. Most were back near the thicket, but a few were scattered toward his mountain.

Still, perhaps two hundred soldiers waited, searching for this Texan who had so easily made fools of them. In those camps, soldiers secretly talked of abandoning the search. They were disturbed by his ability to summon their gods to do his will. They had seen him ride the sacred white buffalo, a feat beyond imagination. Some had even seen what he had done to the High Sorcerer and Croseus. Those who hadn't, had certainly heard of it. Before dawn, scores of these men would abandon their posts and their nefarious leader.

Shelby sat there with his legs dangling over the edge admiring the grand view and pondering how long they might hold out. The floor of the plain lay peaceful a thousand feet below. The Cartok campfires flickered far beneath him, and the bright stars sparkled just above his reach while he hung suspended between them in this amazing place. In the distance he could see the volcano, Tekoa, silhouetted against the dark velvet sky. Above, the Milky Way stretched across the heavens toward the north. *The Chief's road,* he thought. He had read that somewhere.

After several breath-taking minutes Shelby walked back to his small camp and slept. Sometime during the night he awoke with a start. He lay quietly trying to figure out what had disturbed him. The wind was softly whispering along the rimrock, but that wasn't it, he was sure. Yet, he felt watched. But what would be up here where no man could be? The ancient Indians said that witches prowled these mesa tops. He certainly knew better than that. Perhaps his dreams were a little out of control in such a place as this. Whatever, it brought him little concern, and before the next meteor streaked across the sky he had again drifted off to sleep, never discovering the reason for his awakening.

A warbler announced the twilight, and Shelby was up, eager for every moment of daylight. It was good to hear a bird in this place of almost absolute quiet. It also made him wonder what other wildlife might live on this flat-topped mountain. There was little to his camp, so after spreading the ashes from his fire and the boughs from his bed, he was off to explore the mesa.

He walked for an hour and saw nothing but the flat, chaparral-covered plateau. Disappointment began to mount within him. True, it had been over a thousand years since any civilization lived here, but he had hoped to see some sign of it. Perhaps they had never been here at all. It might all be legend. Disgusted, he walked toward the edge, now almost a mile distant, hopeful for a small cave, a shelter in the rimrock against the mounting mid-day heat.

He puzzled over a shimmering mirage before him and felt the sun's warmth on his back. Within the mirage he noticed geometric shapes... man-made shapes. They were straight lines and right angles. At first he ignored them as mirage tricks, but as he walked, they became more defined, more architectural. In the next moment he was running excitedly toward the ruins of a long departed people.

There had been a depression in the plateau, and there, within that depression, the remains of a city. He had found it, the *Beginning Place* of the Tekoans. Carefully he walked, now fully aware of his find, knowing that a clumsy step might destroy a clue to the past or a priceless artifact.

The city ruins appeared to cover slightly less than a square mile, and from his vantage point he could see its border structures. Erosion over millennia had worn the walls, and much of it was mere rubble. There were, however, many rooms with all walls intact, and it was these that caught Shelby's attention. He saw T-shaped doors like those of the Anasazi buildings he had studied in school. There were many other haunting similarities with the Anasazi, and what he did know of that ancient people could be seen here. He was no scholar at this, but archeology had been his minor at A & M and he definitely knew what he was looking at.

The afternoon sped on and Shelby was lost in fascination. He had filled thirty pages of his notebook and had barely started to explore. There was more to discover here than one of his learning could glean, but he was well disciplined, so he handled very little. Perhaps the day would come when the people of this world would become scientists and historians. This mystery was theirs to unravel, and he had no right to disturb it.

By mid-afternoon he noticed the adobe structures connected with the rimrock, and upon closer examination he discovered a large, sheltering cave where they met. Immediately, the structures took on a different appearance. The large cave protected them from the elements, and they were completely intact, preserved beyond belief. A little dust had blown in over the years and sifted over the floor, but the floors had ceilings. He entered and walked through the rooms of what looked to be a type of clan house or Pueblo. These had many rooms in a line, sharing common walls. Some were two story...all were amazingly solid.

He knelt down near a cooking pit. Stone scrapers and wooden tools were there as if placed only moments ago. He looked up, almost expecting their owners to walk in and resume work. Gray pottery, typical of the Anasazi, was abundant, but he dared not touch it. With his knife he gently poked in the burned pit. Seeing a large bone of some kind among the debris, he reached in and carefully picked it up. He rolled it in his hand and suddenly, it disintegrated into white powder.

Across the room he observed a mano and metate for grinding cornmeal. Walking over, he picked up the smaller mano stone and held it like they must have done so long ago. Thoughtfully, he dragged it across the larger, bowl-like stone. The sound was hollow and reverberant in this silent place. Quickly he halted, feeling guilty for causing such an intrusion. An amused smile cracked his lips as he thought of the women chewing up the cornmeal before cooking it. They had no sugar, so they used their saliva to turn the starch in the cornmeal to sugar, thus flavoring the family meal.

Standing, he walked to another room, and there, scattered on the floor, were the remains of several woven mats. Nearby were three ollas. The water jugs were unbroken and maintained the distinctive gray color that he had seen on all the pottery. He knew that to be characteristic of the period when pottery was fired in very hot open fires that sucked away the oxygen.

Strangely, he understood more of this world by standing among its ruins than he had discovered from its living, breathing people. The Tekoans had been kind and friendly to him, but what were they? Indians? Not exactly. They were a cross between the Indians and the early American settlers. Their clothing, their homes and even their villages didn't fit any known archeological pattern. Rather they were a mix, a smearing of time and place.

Where he now stood was right out of a textbook, far better preserved than anything he had ever seen or read about, but it was here...the pattern was right. He had held in his hand what his books could only describe. Here in this silent, immense ruined castle with its dismantled towers and time worn walls, the story was real. He had seen now with his own eyes and touched with his hands the evidence of that reality.

The ancient civilization didn't seem so distant anymore. In school he had examined and coldly studied the artifacts of those who had vanished. Now, as he stood in this wondrous dwelling and held a delicate necklace of shells and turquoise, he felt like an intruder in someone else's home. Gently, he lay the necklace back in the dust where it had rested for over a thousand years and whispered. "Just lookin'."

He turned, seeking something less personal, but it was *all* so personal. Everything was as if it had been placed by a returning owner. This wasn't like taking a specimen from a labeled drawer back to your desk for study. Here it was easy to attach the people to their things. Here it was easy to see their pride, their intelligence. Here it was easy to see the love and care they had for their families.

Looking down, he noticed a Kachina doll carved to look like some ancient spirit and nearby, a cradleboard with worn cords still attached. He remembered studying these and thinking, *What stupid parent would tie their child's head against such a board and cause it to grow wide and flat.* But, now seeing it all in context, he knew they could not be an ignorant people…they were, in fact, very intelligent and gentle.

With the last light of evening Shelby came to the place where he resolved to spend the night. He had walked into a great kiva. It was at least seventy feet across with a roof still held in place by four massive timbers. The wear on the stone bench that encircled the main floor offered little clue to the number of decades that had passed since it had seen its last ceremony. It had been worn smooth by use and not by the simple passing of time.

He sat for several minutes taking in the grandeur of it. It was the kiva, more than anything else that had originally stirred his interest in archeology. These ceremonial centers were like the great temples and cathedrals of his world, and it was here that the true mystery of these people lay silent. And somewhere out on that darkened floor should be a deep hole; a sipapu. To the ancient people the hole symbolized how the first people came onto the earth. He would find it in the morning light. For now all he could see to do was stretch out on the bench and try to find sleep for a weary body and an excited mind that wanted no part of rest.

The night in the kiva was dark and still until the hours after midnight when the rising moon found its way into the cave through the few weathered holes in the roof. With silver rods it probed the darkness and caught the stirred dust of an intruder entering from the opposite stairway. A pebble moved and sand trickled. Shelby's eyes snapped open in alarm. In a place where silence is master, one tends to hear his own heart beat, his own breathing, and certainly anything that might stir where nothing had moved in a thousand years.

Something was here in the kiva with him. He could feel its presence as it crept in the dark shadows across the kiva. As Shelby looked up into the scattered moonbeams he saw movement in them; it was dust, sifting and settling after eons of stillness. Directly above him, the moonlight struck the face of a stone mountain lion. Its fierce features were stark and hard as it cast its eerie shadow on the nearby wall. The mountain lion was said to bring hunters success in tracking game, so it was common to have a creature such as this carved cat here in the kiva. But still, in the moonlight, in such a place as this, it seemed so imposing, so real. He unzipped his possibles bag and reached for his flashlight. His action brought movement across the way and his light caught a blur of something large as it scurried back up the steps. There would be no more sleep this night. He had been thoroughly scared and he wasn't ashamed to admit it.

He lay restless, jockeying for some small comfort on the cold stone bench and counting the minutes as hours while he awaited the morning light. He wondered what he would find in that light. Would the evidence mark a man or a beast? Suddenly, a chilling thought struck him. *What if it left no evidence?* Now Shelby had an open mind, and he knew there was an awful lot humans didn't understand, but to entertain the thought of a ghost... Well, he would wait and see.

He lay in the waxing light as the dark shadows revealed their secrets. He watched the stone lion face turn from a sinister creature of mystery to simply a carving of volcanic rock covered with dust. Encircling it were several rows of elk antlers. As soon as there was enough light, he was up and seeking clues. He walked the distance across the kiva floor to where he knew he would find the sipapu. It was there, and it was girdled with boot tracks! They led out the stairway. He knelt down and studied them. It appeared that the tracks had been made over a span of time and they had gone back and forth several times. They were, however, made by one man.

Shelby yielded one moment to apprehension, then gave another to curiosity. Finally without further hesitation, but with definite care, he followed the tracks as they led out of the kiva and across the ruins to the outskirts of the city. There had been no attempt to conceal them or make his job more difficult, so he spent little effort in his pursuit. After half an hour of easy tracking he came to a small camp by a large stone cistern.

There was a welcome abundance of water, and he had gone a day without, so he drank long and savored the moment. Looking around, he noticed jerked meat drying on a rack of lashed branches. He had forgotten his hunger in all the excitement. He thought back to when he had last really eaten. It had been in the thicket. Since then he had grabbed a few roots and sprouts and eaten maybe a dozen prickly pear tuna. So without hesitation, he took a small strip of meat and tore it with his teeth.

It was plain enough now... he was not alone. The camp showed evidence of one man, but where was that man, and was he friend or foe? Shelby gnawed on the dried meat and pondered the situation. The camp had been here for several months, but was clean, well kept and showed great ingenuity. Whoever he was, he was well disciplined in the ways of outdoor living and Shelby admired that.

Then it hit him like a brick. They were *cowboy boot* tracks he had been following. He had seen no man in this world wear cowboy boots. These people had boots that were crude and flat-heeled. This man wore cowboy boots. Could it possibly be Robby? Up here? It was a far-fetched idea, but the evidence was there. He must make contact. He had to find out for sure who this man was. That might not be so easy after last night. The man would have no idea who he was and might be afraid of him. If it was Robby, he needed to know he was a friend, and if it wasn't... he had to remain careful. Methodically, Shelby devised a plan, and with a stick he began to scratch something in the dirt.

Refreshed now with the food and water, Shelby walked to the rim to again check on the Cartokian pursuers. He pulled out a small monocular and scanned the plain below. All the camps near the mountain had been abandoned. They seemed to have pulled back to the thicket, and even that group looked very small, perhaps around fifty. They were dwindling then. They had no endurance or desire for this game. Even as he watched he noted a small patrol pull out to the west. It occurred to him that he, too, might leave and make it back to Tekoa around dark. But he must let his plan play out...he had to know about this other man.

Shelby leaned back in the shade and continued to observe the dwindling army. Their telltale wisp of rising dust told of their movement away from him. He noticed, too, the mile long shadow of his great flat-topped mountain stretch across the chaparral landscape. Above, a vagrant, white puffed cumulous cloud drifted and added its racing shadow to the plain.

An hour passed, then two. All remained still and lifeless. Shelby looked back toward the city and noted a broken, stone tower he had missed before. It stood there, diligently watching over a city of stillness; a city that time could not destroy; a city where silence was master. It stood like a lone, wounded soldier refusing to leave his post. What could have been its purpose, and how long had it been since it had heard the laughter of children or the sounds of labor and commerce? It stood strong and proud, as if it guarded, and waited for their return. It stood worn and tattered, this sentinel of silence.

Chapter 15

A boot crunched on sand and Shelby turned to see a big, deeply tanned, shaggy man standing in the shadows of a gnarled juniper. He started to speak but out of caution, decided against being the first. After a long gaze, the stranger broke the silence.

"What do you know 'bout Polly?" the man gently asked.

"Depends."

The stranger took a step into the light and Shelby could see he was not much older then he was. But he was a big man with a black beard and long stringy hair. He looked to be a few inches taller than Shelby and powerfully built. He was clearly a man that had spent his life outdoors under the hard, punishing sun of summer and the biting cold wind of winter. That he was a working man, a cowboy, was plain enough. He carried himself like a gentle bear and reminded Shelby of the TV character, Hoss Cartwright. It could be Robby, but he needed more. Polly's description was somewhat exaggerated perhaps, but then women often describe their man in a way the world could never see.

"You left a name back there scratched in the dirt. You wrote my Polly's name. Who are you? What are you? And how do you know Polly?"

"Shelby Ferris, hombre. I'm a friend of your family. They sorta' sent me after you."

"What? How could they? Nobody knows where I went."

"It took some Texas size detective work, and they gave us a lot of clues."

"What do you mean us? I ain't seen nobody else."

"I've got a pardner, name's David. We came down from Odessa to see your Pa."

"So then, you're a real, honest-to-goodness Texan!" He rushed forward with his hands extended and excitement on his face. "Bob Remes, friend.

How is Polly? She all right?"

"Well, when I saw her last she was about as sad a girl as I ever laid eyes on. I hope you have a good reason for being here or I'm gonna' take it pretty bad."

"You don't think I'm here on purpose, do ya?"

"I don't know what to think, Robby. Maybe you should just sit down on that rock and tell me."

"She always called me that, bless her heart. Didn't like it none. Told her I'd outgrown it, but she liked it. My dear Mamma did too. How is she? And Dad! How they doin'?"

"They're all fine, but they are also pretty low about this. I think that deep down they think you're dead. They won't admit it, but it's there. Well, on second thought, maybe not your dad. He is a pretty strong old codger, and he seems to have a lot of confidence in your ability to take care of yourself."

"Look, Ferris, I don't know what you think, but I been lost and alone for a mighty long time now. I never planned to go off fortune hunting or whatever it is you think I did. I stumbled onto a cave one day and discovered this place." He gestured with a wave of his hand. "Well, not this exact place. It was 'nother place with right fine people. I couldn't figure out where it was or what it was. I bought some pretty things for Polly there. I shoulda' been content with that, but I wasn't. I went back. I guess I thought I might find something..." he dropped his head in shame. "Something that might make me and Polly some quick money."

Shelby quietly listened. The cowboy was carrying a guilty load. He had been the cause of his family's hurt and wanted to talk it out. "I went back." he said quietly and with a dazed look in his eyes. "I went to that same cave but somethin' happened, somethin' was different. I couldn't go the way I'd gone before, it was closed up tight, so I took a side tunnel and came out in a big room over yonder in those ruins. It was powerful strange, but everything was strange so I gave it little thought, 'til I tried to go back into that hole I'd come out of. It was closed off too! And it's been closed off every day since. I know 'cause I keep checkin' it.

"I've walked every inch of this mountain top looking for a way down. There ain't none. Even if there was, where would I go? There's nothin' down there, I've looked! And I don't have any idea where I am!"

"Did you just give up hope?"

"I reckon I did, 'til the other night when I seen your fire. I walked over there, but I was afraid of what you might be. I seen some strange things up here so I decided to leave you be. Then I watched you prowl around some yesterday, saw you was a man, but I still wasn't sure 'bout who you was or why you was here."

Shelby decided to change the subject. "So, how did you get food? Meat?"

"There's a meadow yonder." He pointed to the east end of the mesa with his chin. Shelby had not been there yet. "Lots of rabbits and field birds. I've even kilt a mountain goat now an' agin. The cistern yonder stays full of rain water so I never had no problem there."

He sat for a long, quiet moment with his head hung. "You know, Ferris, I even prayed about it some, but I don't think God knows where I am. I got myself plumb lost in the strangest place there is."

"Well, don't worry about God not knowing where you are. The fact that we got together in a place where nobody has been in a thousand years… a place so remote that no one even knows how to get here is pretty strong evidence against that."

Shelby's statement finally struck home with him and he turned facing Ferris with a stern, questioning look. "How'd *you* get here? How'd you know where to look?"

"I wasn't exactly looking, Bob. I was escaping."

The afternoon wore on as Shelby told his tale. He started at the beginning and left nothing out, for Shelby loved to tell a story, and this was a great story. Bob sat as if glued to the rock where he sat. From time to time he would ask a question, then quickly hush to let Shelby continue.

At length, Bob stood up and rolled his dirty, sweat-stained hat in his hands. "That's a powerful lot to swaller, Ferris. If I hadn't been *here* I wouldn't believe it 'tall. You best think on that before you tell it to anybody on the other side."

The other side, Shelby hadn't really thought of it like that before. It *was* like the other side… but other side of what? And he knew his story would be tough to swallow. Now that needed a lot more thinking.

"So, Ferris, when do we start home?"

"Morning, I reckon. We've got a good eight or ten hours travel if we don't meet any soldiers. You got anything to carry water in?"

"Yup. I made me some goat skin bags."

"Good. Rustle up all the grub you've got and all the water we can carry. We will leave as soon as we can see in the morning." With that, Shelby got up to leave.

"Where you goin', Ferris?" There was a definite alarm in his voice.

"I want to go back to the kiva, Bob. I love this stuff. And don't worry, I won't leave without you. I wouldn't miss the look on your pretty little wife's face when she sees your ugly mug. In fact, it would go a lot easier on her, and the rest of us, if you'd clean up a mite."

Shelby pulled his hat down firm and walked back toward the kiva. Bob watched him go and reached up, fingering his unkempt, shaggy beard. Then, lifting one arm he sniffed under it. "Reckon I could take a bath."

The morning found them both ready and eager for their journey. Bob walked with a spring of zest in his step, but Shelby was quiet. He had purposely avoided mentioning anything about Bon's dad yet, or how they still had to try to get him free before they left this world. The big guy thought he was heading home and Shelby labored over how he would tell him otherwise.

When they reached the spot where Shelby had spent his first night on the mesa, he led Bob toward the edge. Shelby wanted a last look before starting down. Even before he took out his glass to look, he noticed smoke in the distance. "What could that be?"

"Saw a big fire there last night, Ferris. Prairie fire I figure."

"Why didn't you wake me?"

"Now what good would thata' done?"

"That's Tekoa! Or mighty close to it!" He said, fear mounting within him. "That's where we're headed. It looks like something is terribly wrong down there. Hurry! Let's get going!"

Shelby took off at a good clip leaving Bob panting and falling behind. It wasn't until they reached the canyon above the shale slide that he noticed Bob's condition.

"You can't do that all the way to that smoke, boy. You'll kill me!" Bob said heaving for breath.

"Sorry, Bob. I just have a feeling of doom ridin' with me. I have to get back as soon as I can."

"Well, I won't hold you up no more'n necessary. But you better figure on them soldiers. I promise, Ferris, if you will hold a sensible pace, I'll stay with you."

"You're right. If I go barreling down there I'm liable to stir up a passle of Cartoks."

The trip took on a sensible pace then, and Shelby regained his keen and careful eye. The big man kept his promise and proved to be strong and agile. They negotiated the foot holds in the cliff easily, and Bob marveled that he had not seen them. The cave gave Bob a bit of trouble with its narrow, slick passages and small crawl spaces. Shelby was patient and helpful through the tight parts and avoided ribbing his new friend about the difficulty he had. The waterfall was cool and pleasant. Here the big fella had no trouble and took to the water like a fish. They left there refreshed after the short swim to the edge of the pool.

As the day wore on Shelby grew to enjoy Bob's high spirits and easy laughter. He didn't know it, but there was a charted effort on the part of Polly's man to repay a debt and ease Shelby's worry.

Bob was hungry for conversation, yet keen enough to realize his new companion wasn't in the mood to talk. He was, instead, a careful thinker and planner. At first Bob simply lumbered along following Shelby like a trusting dog might follow its master, but it wasn't long before he followed out of respect. It was plain to see that Ferris was a true outdoorsman. He hung to the low ground and moved like a poised cat on a hunt. From time to time and for reasons Bob couldn't see, he would abruptly change direction that might take them a mile out of the way before resuming course.

"Hey Ferris, I thought we were in a hurry."

"We are, but we have to be careful."

"Fine, but why do you keep going where we don't need to go? It would be a site easier to cut across there heading for that jagged peak."

"It would. But if we're being watched we would be perfect for ambush. This way nobody can set a trap for us 'cause they don't know where we're goin'."

With that Bob fell back into silence and was content to learn from Shelby's actions. He thought of how he had lived on the land all his life. He too was a good outdoorsman, at home in the wilderness, but this was different. Now the wilderness wasn't the challenge or the danger, the Cartokian soldiers were, and with that kind of threat he had no experience. But then, neither had Shelby until very recently.

By mid-day they had made only about eight miles, but the rough terrain was behind them now and traveling should go easier and faster. Shelby stopped under a large Juniper and lay back kicking up his feet on a branch. "How 'bout some grub?"

"Man, that suits me fine. I thought you would never stop."

"What! You tired, you big ole bull?"

"No! 'Course I'm not tired! But my stomach shore thinks my throat's been cut."

They ate and rested for a half hour in the sparse shade of the Juniper before Shelby got up. "Stay put and enjoy your lunch. I'll be back directly." With that he walked to a small hill and crawled up the last few feet to its top.

Bob watched admiringly as Shelby lay among the rocks studying the terrain. *This is a man to ride the river with,* he thought.

A few minutes later the young Texan returned. "There is a dry ravine over there a bit." He pointed with a head nod as he reached down to pickup his load. "And there's something mighty strange out there we ought to check out."

Bob's body wanted a little more rest, but Shelby's comment stirred his mind. He sluggishly pulled himself up with the help of a Juniper limb that would never be the same again. They circled the small hill, found the gully and slid down its steep bank. The bottom was a streambed, crusted and dry, taking on the look of a large puzzle... each piece separated by a wide crack about an inch deep. This had been soft, oozing mud teeming with life, but it was now baked hard like brick by the sun. What life remained, had long since burrowed deep and encased itself in a dry mucus, waiting for the coming rains that would release it to come to the surface and again sing its songs to the night. Shelby kicked at the hardened surface and wondered how many frogs and other adaptable creatures lay dormant beneath this hard, dry floor.

The sun beat down on their shoulders and cast small pools of black around their feet. Shelby walked and watched the little patch of black that mimicked his every move. He had always liked to watch his shadow... it was a good shadow and he liked the way it looked. He cocked his hat back to give it a change. *There,* he thought, *now that has style.* The breeze that had whispered in that juniper couldn't reach down below the rim of the arroyo, so the heat was stifling and the air was heavy.

Neither Texan complained. Heat was no curse to them. They had worked in it all their lives, and they knew how to deal with it. The animals here also understood the mid-day sun. They found shade and remained still, something these two would have done, but they had someplace they had to be.

When Shelby had gone his calculated distance he pointed up the bank, and the two scrambled out of the gully and immediately found concealment under the chaparral. All was quiet. Nothing stirred, and they seemed to be alone on the vast valley floor.

Shelby pointed with his chin. "Yonder."

"I don't see nothin'."

Shelby reached up and pulled the brush back out of Bob's way. "You're a real cut up, you know that? Over there, three fingers to the right of that ocotillo, about two hundred yards out."

Bob stretched out his arm and extended three fingers. Then, sighting along them he said. "Looks like a pile of junk to me."

"Surely does. That's exactly what has me puzzled. Let's have a look-see."

The two walked toward the spot, each step revealing more to their eyes and stirring more disbelief in their minds.

"Bob?"

"I see it, but I don't believe it. I nev—"

A covey of quail flew up and frightened them both, but each managed to hide his startled reaction from the other.

They stood breathless for a moment. Shelby whispered, "It's an airplane."

"A Curtiss P-40 Warhawk to be exact. 1941."

"You sound sure."

"War planes are my hobby. I had one of these babies hanging in my room when I was a boy, 'cept it had shark's teeth painted on it like the Flying Tigers. I collected all kinds of models, but this one is my favorite. The Warhawk was probably the most underestimated war plane of World War II."

"Why was that?"

"It just got some bad press about dog fights with zeros or something. I've read that with the right pilot this plane was awesome. It had power, speed and above all, you could get shot to pieces in it and it would still get you back home."

They walked closer for examination. The plane had crashed here and was pretty banged up, but it hadn't burned. Birds and rats had made nests in it, and the blowing sand had given it a good beating, but it was a plane! And it was here!

Bob was ecstatic. He climbed up on the wing and used his sleeve to wipe off the canopy glass. Cupping his hands around his eyes he peered inside. "Hey Ferris! There's an old binder in here. Maybe it's a log book."

Together they worked at the latch and slid back the cockpit canopy. The seat was cracked and dried, and a light dust covered everything. A black widow had stretched her web under the instrument panel and set up shop. Rats had left their calling cards on the seat and floorboard.

Shelby watched as Bob ran caressing fingers along the controls and uttered soft sounds of wonder. "Why don't you hand me that book while you do your gawking, Bob?"

"Sure," he said, as he gently picked up the old book and handed it to his companion. Shelby blew the dust from the old book and sat down on the wing, carefully paging though the old binder that was in fact a logbook. Bob took a small stick, spooled up the widow web and gave it a toss to the ground. After a careful look for the old lady, he proceeded to climb into the seat.

"Hey, Bob." Shelby yelled, "Where is Luke Field?"

"Over Arizona way I think. Why?"

"Listen to this entry:

"'November 21, 1941. 1500 hrs. Navigation training mission out of Luke Field. I lost my instruments. My compass was spinning. Could not recognize any familiar terrain features. I circled near my last known point until I ran out of fuel. I hit pretty hard and I think I broke my leg.

"'1530 hrs. After further examination, I did break my leg. I got a splint on it but that doesn't help the pain. Looks like I've got about two hours of daylight left. I will stay right here tonight. No sign of life but the sky is sure strange. I am puzzled though. I have flown all over and around this base. I know its terrain features but I don't recognize anything I see here. Maybe I'm just dazed from the shock of the crash."

"'Cpt. Chris Crawford'"

"Wow! Imagine that." Bob replied. "What do you think happened, Ferris? How do you reckon he got here?"

"I figure he got here about the same way we did."

"Well, he sure didn't fly this thing through no tunnel in the ground. What you gettin' at?"

"I think there is a dimension warp, a ripple or shift in our dimension barriers. They seem to be caused by some massive change in gravitational or cosmic forces. I don't understand that part yet, but it causes openings between dimensions that aren't normally there. Gateways. Some open predictably, and others are completely random.

"That's pretty wild, Ferris. You expect people to believe that?"

"Oh, I don't know. I have been thinking about that since I came to your mesa city, and I'm not really sure I want the modern world to believe it."

"They'd ruin it, wouldn't they?"

"Yeah. The money trail would bust the gateway plumb down. I gave it a lot of thought the other night in the kiva. You know, the Anasazi called it the *underworld*, and access was gained through the Sipapu in their kivas."

"That's how I came through, right?"

"I think that's exactly how you came through, Bob. The Tekoans and other ancient cultures have known about places on the ground or in caves, where a rift occurs and bridges the space between dimensions. For thousands of years they have tried to keep track of the 'Sacred Gateways' where entire civilizations have passed from one world to another."

"I could understand why a few explorers might do that, but whole civilizations?"

"You got it. Entire civilizations. Sardisai told me about it. They would pass through to escape famine or war. Some, like the Tekoans, returned after the threat disappeared. Others never chose to go back or they lost the gateways and were trapped."

"Like me," Bob said gravely. "I would have been a goner if you hadn't come along. But that don't explain the Warhawk."

"I believe the same ripples or warps could exist at certain places in the sky. They can't be seen so a plane flying along when one occurred would simply fly in and disappear from his own world. If he had been on a radar screen he would simply vanish. He shows up here, and as we just read, he can't recognize anything. I bet the same thing happens on the ocean. And I'll bet a new saddle that this is the explanation for the hundreds of strange disappearances of ships and planes around the world."

"Wow! What an idea!"

"How else can you explain a P-whatever, Warhawk in a world that has never even seen a car?"

"Man, you got me convinced. Here, let me see that log."

"We better get moving," Shelby said as he handed the book to Bob. "We'll take the log with us. Somebody's gonna want to see this."

Together they walked away to the southeast toward a drifting wisp of smoke that was their destination. Shelby, deep in thought, pondering the idea he had just posed, and Bob, with his attention glued to the pages of the old leather logbook…pages that continued to reveal an incredible series of events, and written by a pilot that crashed here twenty-some-odd years ago.

From time to time, because of the big cowboy's absolute attention to the leather-bound document, he would stumble over some bush or rock. Then, undaunted, he would plod on, his lips quietly moving, forming the words he found on the dog-eared, yellowed pages.

Suddenly, a notion commanded Bob's thoughts and he whispered audibly. "What if he's still alive?"

Shelby Ferris stopped and turn back, "What'd you say?"

"Oh, nothin', I was just thinking out loud."

Chapter 16

Silently, the two walked into the afternoon following their short mid-day shadows. Little puffs of alkali dust swirled at their feet and rose to sting their eyes. The sun's heat beat down, and their shirts grew damp with sweat and stuck to their backs. They found themselves savoring the cloud shadows as they passed and raced over the chaparral toward the horizon. The drop in temperature certainly wasn't significant, but the brief respite from its searing glare was good for the mind and pleasant on the skin.

Shelby raised a goatskin to his lips and squirted water into his dry mouth. Bob noticed and expressed his censure with a short expressive grunt. "Better save that stuff, Ferris."

"If you know something I don't, then maybe you better share it."

"It's just that you shouldn't be wasteful with that water."

"Wasteful, I'm not! Being careful, however, I am! The water in your canteen never saved anybody. It's the water you drink that does that. We're packin' enough water to last us into tomorrow, easy. And unless you fall down and break your stupid leg, we're going to be in Tekoa in about two hours." Shelby took another long drink and grinned at Bob. "Maybe you should try it... just might help your disposition."

"I don't need much water. I can go most of the day without it. 'Sides, I got me a pebble in my mouth...an old Injun trick."

Now, Shelby liked his new companion, coarse as he was, and they had both began to get a certain satisfaction out of needling each other. Herein was opportunity to eat on him a bit.

"Where'd that bone-head idea ever take hold?" grumbled Shelby.

"What you gettin' at?"

"Just that havin' a pebble in your mouth only keeps your saliva moving. It might make you feel better but it has nothing at all to do with your need for water!"

"Well then, college boy, if you're so smart, why is it I can go so long without it?"

"'Cause you're an idiot. That's why. Do you have any idea what happens to your body when you play tough guy like that?"

"No. But I'm sure you're gonna' tell me."

"Yes. I'm obliged to do just that. First off, your senses dull and your reflexes slow. Say now, I think maybe I've got you figured out."

"Come on, professor, get to it."

"Look Bob, you exhale about a glass of water an hour, more out here. You've gotta' replace that or your body will start a rationing process to prevent damage to your brain and kidneys. It tries real hard to save you from yourself, and that messes up everything from your judgment to your energy. Now, this is no place for that to be happening. We've got trouble enough."

"Well, I didn't know that. It always prided me some to see how long I could go without. And besides, I'm not even that thirsty."

"Thirst is not a good indicator of needin' water… judgment is, and paying attention to your body. By the time your mouth is dry you're already dehydrated. You gotta read your body's signs."

"Body's signs, humph!"

"You need to keep track of how much you drink. Your old carcass is gonna use a good half gallon a day whether you drink or not. Soon, you'll just dehydrate. Notice the color of your urine. It oughta' be clear. If it's dark yellow and has an odor, then you can bet you're good and dehydrated. Pinch the skin on the back of your hand. When you let go, it oughta' snap back down. If it goes down slow …you're dehydrated."

"Naw! You're pullin' my leg."

"Scout's honor!" Shelby said as he held up three fingers. "Didn't you learn that in Scouts?"

"No. Wasn't in no Scouts. We lived too far out. I suppose you were a Hawk or a Buzzard or somethin'."

"I was…I am an Eagle, cowboy, and don't go makin' fun of that."

"Shucks, I wouldn't. And if I did, it would be only to rile you some, wouldn't mean nothin' by it."

Two hours passed before they topped the rise overlooking Tekoa valley. Shelby went limp and whispered a soft sigh under his breath. Before them was a smoldering sea of devastation. Blackened fields, surrounded by tangled wire fences, lay in waste. They were dotted here and there with dead and bloated livestock. The burned remains of what had been farms and heaped rubble of charred boards stood silent now, leaning and pointing upward like the ribcages of some long-dead beast on a battlefield. A few small fires remained, feeding themselves on whatever had managed to survive the initial attack. Smoke drifted across the grim scene carrying with it a sting to the eyes and the smell of death.

Shelby began to run down the long slope toward the small, scarred village, still a mile distant. It had been the most peaceful landscape he had ever seen. Now, about half of the village remained. The flowers were trampled, the trees and buildings were burned and the once lush fields destroyed.

He passed people standing silent and stunned. Others picked through the remains of what little they had. Children, marked forever by the night of terror and events they didn't understand, whimpered and clung to their parents. There were faces he recognized; some were sad, and some were bitter. He wondered what was behind those faces. Would this snuff out the dim light of courage that was just beginning to take hold, or would this light a fire that could never be stopped?

They had been passive, gentle people, but they had been slowly pushed to their limit. They had lived in peace, but peace without freedom is short-lived and breeds discontent in the hearts of just men. Shelby knew that, and maybe now the Tekoans knew that. And now they must know that freedom has a price tag. But would they pay it?

Shelby's heart ached for his friends here, but still he ran, searching for Deccan or Sorek or David. He had completely forgotten Bob who ran and panted and stumbled a quarter mile behind him.

Suddenly there was a yell from a side street. "Shelby!" It was Sorek, and Shelby halted skidding in the dust. "Shelby! Where have you been?" He rushed forward and grabbed the Texan by his shoulders. "We looked for you, old friend. We looked long and hard. What happened?"

"Long story, pardner, mighty long story. I did find that guy we were looking for though. Sorek, meet…" Shelby turned and gestured behind him but nobody was there. Looking up the street he saw Bob stumbling into town. He was trying to run but his legs were flopping like rags.

They watched as Bob slowly jogged to them. His face glistened with sweat, and he panted and heaved for breath.

"Man…you run like a coyote, Ferris…You liked to…killed me." He gasped for air between words and leaned down placing his hands on his knees.

"Sorek, meet Bob Remes. This is the hombre we were looking for." Bob raised a hand and waved loosely before returning it to his knee to steady himself.

"I have seen you before. You worked here for a while."

"Right," Bob gasped as he leaned against a hitching rail and fanned himself with his hat.

"You're outta' shape, ole man," Shelby teased. Bob just groaned.

Shelby turned his attention back to Sorek. "How bad is it? The people, I mean. Where do they stand with this?" Shelby's voice carried an urgency and concern that the clever old soldier read like a book.

"Ever stir a hornet's nest?"

Shelby grinned. "Good! Now, where's David? I need to see him!"

Sorek rubbed his jaw and broke a sideways smile. "He's down at the doc's. Seems like he took a pretty hard blow to the head. Don't worry though, he'll be fine."

"What happened?"

"Maybe you better ask him yourself." Sorek led off down the street. "Come on, I'll show you." Bob waved them on and said he would catch up.

As they walked toward the doctor's office several people turned to greet Shelby and shake his hand. In spite of their distress, they showed genuine happiness in seeing him. Suddenly he realized from their concerned looks and comments that he looked a mess. His clothes were torn and filthy. His face and arms were scratched and caked with dried blood. Embarrassed, he pulled his hat down over his eyes and followed Sorek closely.

"I need to get cleaned up. I must look a sight."

"That you do, my friend. Looks like you've been sorting wildcats." They stepped up on the porch. "I'll take you to clean up after you see David."

They entered a darkened room, and it took Shelby a few minutes to adjust his eyes. A cocky, over-enthusiastic, young man approached and immediately began to examine the Texan. As he poked and squeezed, Shelby pulled back. "No offense, but I'm okay. I just came to see David Carson."

"Here, here, I'm the doctor's new assistant. You really should let me clean those cuts. Sit down over here while I get a lantern."

"Thanks. But later, all right? I really just want to see David."

The little man acted put out but finally consented and stepped back pointing to a door at the end of the hall. "He is in there," he snapped. "And may I say he was just as stubborn as you." He turned to leave with an impudent grin on his face. "But I got the best of him."

"What's that suppose to mean?" Shelby yelled after him.

"Oh, nothing." The little guy pranced off smugly. "I think he should sleep for about two… days." He closed the door behind him firmly, punctuating his remark.

Shelby looked at Sorek and walked toward the door. "What was that?" Sorek responded with a shrug so Shelby continued, "Well, let's go in and see him."

"I'll just wait out here and get word to Sardisai that you're back. You go on."

Gently, Shelby pushed the door open and stepped in. It was a small room, cluttered with equipment and lit only with a shaft of sunlight peeking through a thick set of curtains and falling across the foot of the bed where David lay. It was still, with only the sounds of the street stealing in and the drip, drip of something across the room.

A movement caught his eye and he focused on someone sitting quietly and silhouetted against the gray wall of the claustrophobic room. Almost immediately, the dark figure noticed him as well and stood up. Even in the dim light Shelby recognized the graceful move and gestures of the elegant Vishti.

"Vishti?"

"Shelby?" Her voice quivered then warmed with recognition and she rushed toward him. "Oh, Shelby I've been so worried. The men searched for you until Deccan was almost killed." She threw her arms around him and held on tight. Shelby drew back, his first impulse was to hug her, but he was so filthy he couldn't stand the thought. She was so… so refined and all. Sensing his tenseness she pulled back and looked up at him.

"Shelby!" she exclaimed. "You're hurt! You're all cut up!"

"It's not as bad as it looks. It's mostly dirt. But tell me, Vishti, how is David and how is Deccan? I didn't know anything about him!"

"Deccan was tracking you and leading the other men. I guess he got too close, because he took a knife in the back. It was bad. The doctor said it clipped the top of his lung. We all thought we had lost him for a while."

"And?"

"Oh, he's fine now. It's been all the doctor could do to keep him here. All he wants to do is get out of here and go back after you."

"And David?"

She moved closer and gently placed her hand on Shelby's arm. Tears welled up in her eyes and rolled down her cheeks. Shelby felt one fall on his hand and a torrent of emotion rocked his soul. Fear surged through his veins.

"What's wrong? Tell me, please!"

"Oh, Shelby, I'm so sorry, it's all my fault."

"What? The guy in the other room said he was just sleeping! What's going on here?"

She started to cry and Shelby felt helpless. "Vishti, please. Start at the beginning; nothing is making any sense."

She turned away, wiping her eyes and regaining her composure. "When the Cartoks came yesterday, before they burned the village, they sent a messenger saying they wanted the Texans. If you were delivered they would leave. Well, you can imagine the reply they got.

"A skirmish started when they burned the store down the street, and it quickly turned very bad. There were about a hundred of them, and they were well armed. We only had crude weapons, and it looked hopeless. David started out to give himself up. I begged him not to go but he wouldn't listen to reason. He said if he didn't go they would destroy the whole village. Now do you see?"

"No. I don't see. What does that have to do with him lying there unconscious? Did they get to him?"

"No... I did it." She almost whispered the words and dropped limply back into the chair and buried her head in her hands. "I hit him with a broken table leg." Again she stood and her temper flared. "It was the only way I could stop him! Now there! I told you! You can hate me for it, but it's done!"

Shelby stood stunned for a moment trying to sort out the strange emotions that were running wild in this girl. When it all finally made sense, his face broke into a small grin and he chuckled.

"What's so funny?" she flared.

"Nothing. But I'd like to have seen that. I know how stubborn he is, and there's no changing his mind." He laughed again. "I'll have to remember your technique."

"You mean you're not mad? You're not upset with me?"

He reached forward and gently placed his hand to lift her chin. "No, not in the least. You did the right thing, and thank you. You probably saved his hide."

"Do you think he will see it that way?"

"Probably not. But I can't see him being mad at you either."

"Shelby, you're insane. He'll never speak to me again. I just know it."

"Now, Vishti, I know you're not blind. Anybody can see that he's crazy about you."

She blushed and turned away just as the door opened and the doctor walked in. "Well, you must be Shelby. David asks about you constantly, and your disappearance has certainly been the talk of the town."

"Yes, sir. I'm Shelby." He held out his hand and shook the doctor's.

"You need cleaning up young man. I'll have Ovon heat you some water while I look at some of those cuts. Will that be all right?"

"Yes sir, I reckon it will. And while you're at it, would you tell me about David and Deccan?"

"I imagined that would be on your mind." He walked over to David's bed and opened one of his eyelids with his thumb. He looked studiously into his eye. "Strange. I expected him to be alert by now. I guess he was simply too exhausted." He continued his examination then turned back to the two companions. "Vishti, if you will excuse us I'd like to take our young hero into the other room."

The next room was as small and cluttered as David's. The curtains were pulled back, and it was very bright. "Take your shirt off while I call Ovon. I'll be right back."

Shelby labored with his shirt. It would have been easier to cut it off, but he needed it. He looked into a mirror, and for the first time saw the reason for the other's concern. He really did look bad, but upon closer examination he determined that what he had told Vishti was probably right. It was mostly dirt.

The doc returned and they talked while he cleaned up some of the bad places on Shelby's face and head. He learned of Deccan's condition and how bad it had been and how quickly it had improved. And the doc assured him that David would soon be his old self as well.

"Doc, that frenzied assistant of yours, Ovon?"

"Yes. Quite a character, don't you think?"

"Yeah, quite a character. He said he gave David something to make him sleep for two days. Is that wise?"

"So, that's the explanation. I'll look into it. I think I know what he gave him. Those two sure locked horns. Ovon's quite incessant when it comes to nursing. And that young friend of yours couldn't stand it. Just two stubborn young bucks if you ask me."

In an hour Shelby had bathed and cleaned up. Vishti went home and brought back one of her dad's shirts. He felt like a new man and was just tucking in that shirt when there was a loud commotion outside. He rushed out and joined Sorek and Vishti on the porch.

A boy ran past and Sorek called to him. "Hold on there! What's going on?"

"A Cartok officer came to town with a message. They are talking to him down by Kadian's place. Shelby stepped down and followed the boy. The others joined him. Part way down the street he passed Bob, sitting back in the shade of a wagon.

"Get up you lazy sidewinder! You're gonna' give these nice folks a tarnished view of Texans." With that, Bob grabbed hold of the wagon wheel and stood up. He took his hat and beat the dirt from his clothes. A cloud of dust plumed around him and caused him to cough. Shelby locked his thumbs behind his belt and rocked back on his heels. "You know, I just left a tub of hot water back at the doc's. Why don't you go use it? Tell the little guy you're David's friend and you'll get special treatment."

A crowd had gathered, and some men were talking to the officer who had ridden in on a beautiful black mare with three white stockings. Shelby moved closer for a better look at the horse. *I never forget a horse,* he thought. The words of the officer needed interpreting, so they were of little interest to him at the moment, but that horse now… *And I've seen that beauty in Sardisai's corral!*

Vishti eased up beside him, and he sensed her tension. "What is it? What's he say?"

She held her finger to her lips and continued listening to the officer. Shelby studied the reactions on her face and tried to read their meaning. Suddenly she went pale.

"Vishti?"

"They are offering one last chance for the village to give you up. If we don't…he says they will not only wipe out every living thing here, but they will dig up our graves and cleanse this valley of any Tekoan presence. It will be as if we never were." Her words were quiet and came slowly. She turned toward Shelby and sought his comfort. Her head relaxed against his shoulder and he held her.

By now the men were violent and about to attack the officer. Obviously their answer was "no." The Cartok stepped back but remained composed and sure. Kadian raised his hands and calmed the angry mob. "Stop! He is only a messenger, and we are honor-bound to let him return with our answer."

Shelby whispered to Vishti. "Is that Sardisai's horse?"

She stood on tip toes and looked over a man's shoulder. "Sable!" she gasped. "Shelby, that's my horse! They took her yesterday! The nerve of that awful man to ride her back here and parade her in front of us."

"It is kinda' nervy, isn't it? And stupid." Shelby looked around slowly and let go of her. "Excuse me gal, I'll be right back."

He pushed through the crowd, motioning to Sorek as he went. "I need a little translatin' help."

"What do you have in mind, Shelby? Nothing crazy, I hope!"

"I'm not sure yet. I'm kinda' lettin' this one come together as I go, but I need you." As he left the crowd, he passed a man he had seen many times but didn't know well. He remembered him because he had seen him with a bullwhip hanging from his belt. "Do you have your whip with you?"

"Uh yeah. Why?"

"I really need it for a minute, Okay?" The man stood puzzled, but he knew these Texans and he trusted them. He reached down and untied the whip and handed it over. "Thanks. Ten minutes tops. I'll bring it right back here." Shelby ran around the buildings. Sorek shrugged his shoulders at the man and quickly followed.

It took him a few minutes to catch up with Shelby, and when he did he saw him crouched behind some barrels beside the street. He started to speak but heard a horse trotting up the street and saw it come into view. As it passed, Shelby stepped out and unfurled the twelve foot, rawhide bullwhip. He whirled it above his head, and it made a wicked scream as it sliced the air. Instantly, he snapped his arm and the whip cracked like a rifle shot above the Cartokian officer's head, knocking his hat into the street.

Shelby loved the feel of a good whip. He loved the sound it made as the thin, braided popper at its end reversed directions with such incredible speed that it broke the sound barrier. The sound thundered against the buildings and echoed down the street. It brought the soldier to a dead stop and drained the color from his face.

Before he could turn, the whip was again cutting air, and its awful shriek was spelling doom for its victim. Deftly, Shelby steered the whip, and it coiled tightly around the soldier's neck. A sudden jerk and the man was flat on his back, under the horse, eating dust and wheezing for air. He looked up with sheer terror in his eyes and clawed at the leather braid around his neck. He was in a death grip, and he knew it. After a brief struggle, he realized that while the coils around his neck could squeeze his life away, the man at the other end of the whip held the decision. He calmed down and simply stared.

"You got something that belongs to a friend of mine, hombre." Shelby spoke calmly, yet almost cockily. Sorek, startled by the turn of events, attempted to translate.

The man looked around wildly. His eyes fell on the black. "The horse? Take him! Take him!" He gasped. His voice was strained, and the words wheezed.

"Thanks, I plan to," Shelby said as he flicked a little slack into the whip, allowing the coils to ease a bit.

The man's breathing returned to normal, and with it came his anger, then recognition. "You are a Texan!"

"Yes, but I'm just a little one and not very dangerous. You better hope you never meet a big one, like my dad."

The man realized he was being toyed with, and he started to stand up. "This is demeaning. I am an officer of the Cartokian army and a servant of Croseus." He attempted to release the whip from his throat. "I shall leave at once and report this atrocity."

Shelby gave the bullwhip a little tug to remind the man who was in charge. "Take off your boots." He said calmly. Sorek gave Shelby a strange, 'what are you doing' look, then proceeded to translate.

"What? Are you crazy? I demand…" Shelby gave another tug and the man scrambled to remove his boots.

When it was done, Shelby gave the whip a couple of flicks, throwing slack, and it fell free. "Now. Get out of here, and deliver your message."

"Oh, I'll deliver my message all right, and we will return here and erase this place from the valley." He turned to Sorek. "All your grand ideas and inventions will be for nothing. We will laugh at your great knowledge and forget you ever existed."

Sorek listened solemnly, and Shelby saw that he was disturbed. "What's he saying, Sorek?" Shelby listened to the interpretation. His mind took the officer's words, and the shadow of a plan moved across his face revealing a sinister smile, which he quickly quenched. "Cartok." He said solemnly and acting a bit, as if beaten by the man's words. "You come back tomorrow night, and you can take us. But you must then leave these people alone."

Sorek interrupted, but Shelby held up his hand and winked at him. His opinions fell silent, and again he began to interpret.

Shelby looked across the scorched fields and twisted barbed wire to the huge copper dome of Wardenclyffe looming above the trees. He pointed to it. "Tomorrow night, two hours after sunset, I will wait there. My companion, the other Texan, will be with me, and we will have torches so you can see us."

"You finally make sense. I will be there, and it will be a great pleasure for me to take you to Croseus," he snapped as he turned to walk away.

"Cartok. You had better bring many soldiers to keep us, because once we have been delivered to you, all bets are off. These people will have kept their bargain."

The soldier scowled and tried to walk off with dignity, but he could not. Each step was a stabbing pain as he negotiated the rocky road. Sorek watched him limp away and grinned. "You've got grit son, I'll give you that, but I hope you also have a good plan. That man is going to come back mighty mad and swinging a very big stick."

"That's just what I'm counting on, Sorek. When a man plans in anger he leaves his judgment behind. By the time he gets back to camp he should be so mad and humiliated that he would chase me clean back to Texas in his underwear."

"Strange plan, Shelby; certainly not a military tactic I would use or trust."

"You may be right, Sorek, but it worked for John Wayne."

Chapter 17

There was much to do, and the word of the exchange spread like a wild fire. But there was a plan, too, and everyone wanted to be part of it. Vishti was tasked with getting David up and around, for he was desperately needed. Everyone ran to their duties as Shelby had laid them out.

The plan sounded simple really: lure the Cartoks to the great copper dome and defeat them. The Tekoans were eager for action and although they didn't understand all the details, they were ready for the fight. Little did they know Shelby was planning an event that not only would enter their history books, but be the subject of tavern talk for a long while indeed.

Shelby was in hog heaven. He stood inside the small building beneath the great copper dome in complete awe of the workings around him. Here was the reality of something he had only read about. Here were the great machines, coils and condensers that Nikola Tesla had used to baffle the most learned scientists of his day. In fact the scientists of Shelby's day would do well to understand how the man did the things he had done. Here were the devices to create millions of volts of electricity. Here were the kinds of apparatus that Tesla had used to shoot bolts of lightning from his hands the night he stunned the world. And here, in this room, Shelby's incredible plan took shape.

He pulled the two giant knife switches at the heart of the complex, and the hum and crackle ceased. He closed the geothermal vent valves, and the room fell deathly quiet. The blue-violet corona atop the immense insulators vanished and only the smell of ozone remained. Before, it had looked imposing, almost wicked in nature, but now it all looked old and tired. One would expect cobwebs stretched around such a room as this, but of course nothing could or would live in this place.

Outside, the people were busy digging trenches and laying the heavy insulated wire that had been coiled in the back room. Others were bringing loads of obsidian chips and piling them into a great mound just beyond the door. All was according to plan. The question was: would the plan work? The young Texan had dabbled in this high voltage stuff as a hobby; he had studied Nikola Tesla and his work in depth. But now, to try to duplicate a part of an experiment that had caused many to think of Tesla as some kind of supernatural being, seemed ridiculous. Yet all the stuff was here. He didn't have to make anything. He had only to....re-wire it. He chuckled to himself, *you are one crazy Texan, Shelby Ferris.*

David showed up with Vishti, and they both glowed like two twitterpated, love-struck kids. It was a warm welcome, and David had a million questions. They talked, but they worked also, and David quickly fell into the routine, understanding Shelby's intent. "Well, there seems to be enough power here to fry that whole army. You too, if you make a mistake."

They went over the plan, and Shelby explained how he planned to disconnect the copper dome and run that high voltage electrode wire outside through an insulated tunnel of obsidian. From there it would pass up through the mound of glass rock, and connect to two metal wands. The obsidian was the best insulator he could think of, and enough of it should not break down. Then, they would expose a web of ground wires farther out where the soldiers would stand and drive metal posts into the ground all around that position. With the area wet down, the path of least resistance would be between the mound and the web of wire connected to those metal posts.

"Whew! I sure wouldn't want to be standing on that web of wire when you pull the switch. That whole area is going to be nothing but blue lightning!"

"I'm not pullin' the switch, DC. You are! I'll be standing on that pile of glass holding those metal wands in my hands."

"Are you crazy? Wait let me rephrase that. You, my friend, are absolutely insane!"

"Look, I've thought this through. This must have been, at least sorta, how Tesla did it."

"Sort of how he did it! Shel, if that stuff doesn't insulate you, and you're holding several million volts in your hand... well, there won't be anything left to pickup."

"It will work. I know it will!"

David turned shaking his head. "I know better than to try to talk you outta' this, but I sure wish I could." He walked a few steps and turned back. "Okay, what do I do?"

"Good! I knew you'd come through! Now, come in here and let me show you what *you* have to look out for."

"Me? I thought you were doin' the dangerous stuff?"

"Oh, I am." Shelby grinned at David as they went back to work on the details of the operation, and by late afternoon everything was ready to test.

"I'm not sure we should risk a test." Shelby said seriously. "We might only get one shot at this before we destroy our stuff."

"Now look, Shel, I draw the line right here." David was waving his arms and getting intense. "You're stubborn when you think you're right, but so am I. You know that better than anybody. We have to test this, if only for a second. If this fails to work we're in pretty deep. Remember, you've gambled, using us as chips, and we're not getting away from those mad Cartoks again. Croseus will have us right in his evil hand. And if it works wrong, you're crispy and dead. We're testing this thing. You got that?"

"I got that, pardner... loud and clear. And I appreciate it; you seem to balance me out pretty good." Shelby and David had been together too long for him not to listen and take heed. They were both men that "pushed the envelope" and they knew it. They also respected the other's judgment in matters where one might be too close to something to show good sense. This was certainly one of those times.

"Okay, David. We can test it with the wands mounted on sticks at about the height I would hold them. We can tie a rabbit or somethin' on the mound of glass. And hope that at the first sign of melt down we can shut this thing off before it self-destructs."

With the plan of action clear to everyone, they prepared for the test. The Tekoans left the area and took up a safe distance. The Texans took refuge inside the building, David, at his post near the huge knife switches and Shelby at the door behind a protective screen of drain wires, where he had a good field of view.

"I guess we're ready, DC. Open the vent valves and listen for everything to wind up to speed. Then close those switches for no more than two seconds; sooner if something fails."

The valves released the immense power trapped in the steam deep below the earth and the room came alive. It whirred and whined up to speed, then settled down to a powerful, steady drone. They made eye contact for a moment, then Shelby looked out the door and dropped his hand in signal. The place roared and crackled with frightening power. The prepared open area out front lit up as long arcs danced and searched out every ground wire exposed. As quickly as it happened, it stopped. They looked at each other with a pale, 'did we do that?' look. The event had been awesome; the rabbit on the pile of obsidian was still tugging at his rope, and nothing had blown up or melted. David doubled a fist and stuck up a proud thumb. They grinned. They were ready.

In moments, the Tekoan workers appeared showing anxious looks, then broke into jubilant yells.

The evening came, and everyone was ready and confident. The two Texans stood alone at Wardenclyffe. The Tekoans were concealed in the distant brush, ready for Sorek's signal and action they hoped would put an end to the threat of Croseus. It grew dark, and all were restless and quiet. The moments before battle are always sober and thoughtful and weigh heavy on a man's heart. Each man knew he might not go home tonight but he had to believe he would. They all knew they were out numbered by an army that was equipped with muskets and sabers. They knew, too, that they were no real army; they were farmers and storekeepers, craftsmen and ranchers. And they hid in the brush with pitchforks and shovels. Yet each man had confidence. They might be out-weaponed but they had a cause worth this fight, and they definitely were not out-generaled. It was that confidence that gave them comfort in these long, dark, waiting moments.

The torches stood like beacons in the night, marking the way for the approaching army. They encircled the deadly web of wire and opened only at the point where the army would enter. The plan depended on the fact that the Cartokians believed no threat could be mounted against them. The Tekoans had lost the battle only nights before and offered no real resistance. Besides, they had no true weapons to speak of. It was this foolish confidence, and Shelby's "John Wayne" tactics that would make the soldiers walk into this trap.

A runner came through the darkness announcing the approach of the army. The word spread, and tension strung tight in every nerve. Shelby took his position atop the pile of obsidian and picked up the two wands. He heard the soldiers before they could be seen. Nothing but overconfidence and arrogance would make an army so undisciplined and noisy. They sounded as they always had, like a gypsy caravan of tinkers' wagons. They laughed and joked, rattled and clanged.

Shelby took a last look around. Nothing stirred. Only the oil torches flickered around the perimeter and cast dancing shadows on the dark trees.

The stillness of the evening allowed their black smoke to hang low like ground fog. It gave the place a haunting presence. He took a deep breath and spoke quietly over his shoulder. "Here they come, David."

The glistening metal they carried caught the first torchlight, and they began to appear first as ghosts before materializing into men. As if by some rehearsed choreography, they filed in and took their places within the circle of torches. The officer to whom Shelby had given his special treatment swaggered to the front and announced his presence.

The fact that these soldiers were surrounded by men hiding in the brush was not a part of this equation. Even if they had detected their presence, they would not be concerned. And the men alone could do nothing but get themselves killed. Shelby's plan had to work. It was their only chance. And now it had a chance of working, for every soldier stood atop the wire web within the circle where he would benefit most by the upcoming show.

"I see you got a new pair of boots," Shelby said to break the silence and give this thing a jump-start. He had no sooner spoken than he realized his first oversight. There was nobody here to translate. No matter, this wasn't about conversation. There were no deals to be made or treaties to discuss. This was a last ditch effort. Shelby pointed to the man's feet and grinned. The message was understood and brought about the officer's wrath. He yelled something and ordered several men to advance.

Shelby called to David, and the night's darkness shattered. The fiery bolts of lightning belched from Shelby's hands and knocked down the first several rows of men. Their weapons were their demise as each piece of metal attracted an arcing blue-white bolt of death. The streamers danced and crackled, splitting the night with thunderous claps of deafening power. Men screamed and ran, trampling each other, clawing for escape. There was no escape. The fiery fingers sought out each man; some they merely frightened and shocked; some they scorched; but to most, they snuffed out life.

The deadly dance of fire stopped and left a stench of burned flesh and ozone hanging in the air. On command, the Tekoans came from their hideouts wielding farm tools and sticks. They yelled like Banshees, and the remaining Cartoks screamed and ran as if being chased by demons.

The Tekoans took chase, and battle began with an enemy that wanted to be elsewhere. Sorek called them back. "Wait! Let them escape and tell of this night. Their stories will do more than the deaths of a thousand men." He was right of course. The tale would be told and retold. No one would ever mount another attack against them. The terror of this night would even be on the lips of children not yet born.

Shelby dropped the wands, and David shut down the turbines and walked out beside him. It got very quiet as the Tekoans turned and stood facing them in awe of what had just happened. They had won, and not a single Tekoan was even scratched! No one spoke. No one moved. Only the oil torches flickered and the shadows danced on the dark trees. The gray-black smoke hung low, and its delicate fingers touched the still bodies of those that only moments before had thought themselves invincible.

Here in the dim, yellow torch light, lay the last of the powerful army. Those that left here screaming and scattering into the darkness would never again reassemble. Only their tale was left to be told of this dreadful night when a surrounded Texan shot bolts of lightning from his hands and destroyed their army. Such a tale would be told, over and over, and it would find the ears of frightened comrades. Croseus would then be left with a mere handful of followers; followers wary of those gods they called Texans.

Chapter 18

Only a few torches remained. Those still lit merely flickered in a slow death. Their smoke had cleared and the dust of battle had settled. The Tekoans were gone, eager to tell their families of this fateful night. The lifeless bodies of Cartokian soldiers littered the charred circle. The stench of their death lifted on the night breeze. Not a night creature moved or made a sound. Stillness took command over the grim scene, and Shelby Ferris sat alone on a pile of obsidian at Wardenclyffe.

Before it had happened, it had all seemed like some glorious game... the planning, the strategy, the outwitting and defeat of an evil force. It had been easy to get caught up in the excitement of it. The righteousness of it seemed so evident and noble. He had not thought past his careful plans. The reality of the price tag simply hadn't entered his mind. He knew men would die, but that was so distant then. He almost expected to be able to say, 'Okay, guys, we won, so you can get up and go home.'

But now, the cost had been counted, and its victims lay motionless... clasped in the eternal grip of death. He looked at their faces, some still twisted in the terror that had taken their lives. Most were old and hard... probably men who had no one to care. Perhaps for them, their passing would go unnoticed. But some were young, not innocent by any man's standards... but they were now as old as they would ever be. And surely they would be missed. They would be mourned. Shelby knew his name would be a curse on the lips of children, as the slayer of these men. This alone was a heavy weight, and he was not sure he could bear it. What had happened to that contest of wits where good would merely conquer evil? But then, he knew. As in all war, it had gotten so very real, and it was never a game.

A moving torchlight beyond the circle caught his eye, and he looked up.

A big man approached on the path from town. He knew by his size that it was Kadian and he was probably coming to check on him. The battle's decision was an hour old but Shelby had remained behind, needing the time to sort it out, alone.

Kadian walked over and stuck his torch in the end of a pipe. "Folks are askin' about you, son."

"Yeah, I know. I just needed to sit here a bit. I had to know this was the only way."

"I figured that. You know of course, if it hadn't a' been this way, there'd be a lot of weepin' women and kids back in town. They'd be cryin' because somebody they loved didn't come back home tonight. And don't forget, they'd also be cryin' because this thing wouldn't have been over, but now it is."

"There are still a lot of women and kids crying tonight, Kadian. And that's what's haunting me."

"Yes, but they belong to men that chose this action, this aggression. These men…" He gestured with his hand over the area. "These men chose to do this. They could have quit like all the others, but they wanted the glory of capturing you and destroying us. These weren't loyal, honorable soldiers, Shelby. Those kind of soldiers are long since gone. These were the bloodthirsty dogs that remained. And this was the price they paid!"

Kadian took up his torch and walked inside the building. Shelby heard him rummage around for something but gave it little thought. He got up and started across the dark path toward town, figuring Kadian would catch up. A faint sound caught his attention. A moan, a quiet cough. Startled, he paused and listened, then heard it again; one of the soldiers was recovering. Instinctively, Shelby rushed to the man thought to have made the noise. He reached down and felt his neck. It was warm and the pulse was strong.

The young Texan had cut his teeth on the experience given to him by the land and the dangers of the wilderness. He possessed a wealth of knowledge from his books and his schooling. His wisdom, however, was still callow, and he approached this moment as one naïve to the dangers of real battle.

Vulnerably, he bent over the fallen soldier and shook him gently. As the man regained his senses, he began to move and tried to roll over on his back. Shelby assisted only to find he had been a fool.

A cocked pistol appeared from nowhere and was now steered to a spot between his eyes. He froze. Unbelieving at first, but then he realized what the man was about to do. He watched the dirty, charred finger tighten and he knew there would be no miss at this distance. Yet, he could not move. A million things entered his mind and left. What remained was anger. He had often wondered how someone caught in a strategic moment of crisis could simply freeze. He had thought about that and knew it would never happen to him, yet here it was. He felt sweat trickle from his brow. Time seemed to have stopped and events he had not thought of in years were in the forefront of his mind. Why?

His eyes shifted from the muzzle to the man's eyes. He watched them change from hatred to puzzle and finally to recognition. How much time had passed? A second? A minute? He didn't know. The man's face... No, it was a boy's face... a young man's face, about his own age. It paled, and his hand trembled and began to drop. He whispered something foreign, but something with deep emotion.

In that brief moment, Kadian appeared. In a swift, graceful movement, he disarmed the young man and pulled Shelby behind him to safety. The soldier seemed not to care, he sat motionless with eyes locked on Shelby. Again, he almost reverently whispered his earlier words. He continued to talk, and with each sentence came more excitement.

As Shelby watched the young man, his own senses returned, and a shudder of fear caused a momentary tremble through his body. *Why wasn't I killed? The soldier surely intended that. Something had stopped him. But what?*

It was evident now that Kadian had things under control and the threat was gone. But the mystery remained in Shelby's mind. "Kadian. Why didn't he shoot me when he had the chance? What made him stop?"

Kadian turned toward Shelby, and his huge hand gently reached for the silver arrow point that hung from a rawhide thong around Shelby's neck. "This stopped him. And now for you, he has pledged his life in service."

"What? Is he crazy? This is just a trinket, given to me by a Cartokian girl! I am his enemy! I killed his comrades!" Then for a brief moment Shelby thought of the girl, Sinca. She had crossed his mind from time to time. *It would be nice to see her again,* he thought. *Very nice.*

"But he now knows who you are. He knows that you are the one that saved that girl's life. And she was pledged to be his wife. He had given the silver arrow point to her, and he knows full well why she gave it to you."

Shelby stood up, stunned by the coincidence but alert enough to kick his mind back in gear and grasp an idea. "Kadian, do you think we can really trust him?"

"Well, I don't know, but he's holding a lot of gratitude, and I really think he would do anything for you."

"Do you think he knows how to get us into Croseus' palace?"

"You cut right through the chaff, don't you, boy? That's a lot to ask of a soldier. You'd be askin' him to commit treason, you know."

"I know, but you just said…"

"I know what I just said. Maybe I spoke too quickly. Maybe we outta' think on this a bit."

"Come on, Kadian. Can he help us? We have to ask him."

"All right," he said seriously, and he began to interpret Shelby's request. The Texan watched the young soldier's expressions with expectant eyes. He saw surprise, but what did that really mean? *How could a man that Sinca loved and pledged to marry, be a part of this group of animals?* Shelby couldn't shake his thoughts of the girl.

Then the soldier responded, and Kadian translated. "He says you are mighty quick to trust him, and he wants to know why someone like you would place such confidence in an enemy? By the way, Shelby, he was also quick to add that he hated Croseus. He was forced into service and remained only out of loyalty to his friends… who are now dead."

Well now, the table is turned, Shelby thought. Then he walked right up to the soldier and looked him in the eye as though he could see right into his soul. "Remember, friend, I have held the warm hands of Sinca, the girl you love. I have looked into her enchanting eyes and seen strength. Who am I to doubt what a man would do for such a girl?"

Startled at hearing the name of his fiancée, the young man sat in silence and bewilderment as the translation unfolded. Then as realization settled in, a warm, broad smile took his face, and he reached for a handshake that began a powerful friendship.

Kadian leaned over and helped the wounded soldier to his feet. Then with Shelby on one side and Kadian on the other, they walked him into town.

The next day found Shelby, David and Sorek deep in a discussion with the young soldier, Anatol. From him they learned that Croseus' palace was impossible to enter by force. A dozen well-placed men could hold off an army.

David stood up. "I have read too many stories of places like that. They always had a way out, a secret passage or something. Are you telling us that Croseus has provided nothing?"

The answer was translated as a probable "Yes, he has provided nothing." The palace had been there long before Croseus, and nothing had ever been

153

mentioned about secret passages. The men sat in silence for a moment, knowing a solution was here someplace. They definitely would not give up.

"How long has Croseus been there, Anatol?" David asked.

"He was there when I came to duty. I guess I don't really remember exactly when it was. It is said that he came from the sky with the power of a god. He joined forces with the evil High Sorcerer, who was bad enough, but together, they overthrew our king and changed everything about our people. They joined their power and made war on all the people of this land."

"I remember a man that might be able to help us." Sorek said suddenly, as this line of thinking stirred his thoughts. "He was the caretaker of the palace when I was stationed there. If he is still alive and if there are any secret passages, he would know it."

"But would he help us?" David asked.

"You forget how much the common people hate Croseus. He moved in, killed their king, and took the palace. Anyone in that village would kill him if given the chance. If the man could be found and protected, he would gladly help."

"Well, let's go find him!" Shelby already was on his feet and headed for the door.

"I have to remember his name. That was a long time ago."

"Are you speaking of Etrusean, the old caretaker?" asked Anatol.

"Etrusean! Of course! Do you know where to find him?"

"No, but it can't be too hard. He would be known in the village."

Shelby waited for the translation to reach his ears and announced, "Let's go!" With that they all trailed out in a mad rush trying to catch up with Shelby.

It took the better part of the day to reach the Cartokian village near the palace. It only took a half an hour to find the old caretaker. He was easing past eighty but was very alert and absolutely afraid of nothing. The idea of helping against Croseus appealed to him and he smiled a toothless grin. "Ah, to get even with that butcher would let me die a happy man."

The same questions were asked and the two Texans grew impatient with the translation process. Again it was stated that there were no secret passages. The ground under the palace was solid rock... a fact that drew great disappointment. From a closet shelf, the old man took down a beautifully tanned buckskin map of the palace and its surrounding area. He spread it on the table, and they all gathered around asking questions.

David studied in silence for a long while before asking, "What are those little circles there? I see them in a couple of different rooms."

Etrusean scratched his jaw as he thought for a moment then said, "I think those were the cool air. Yes, that would be about where those things were."

David lit up. "What do you mean, 'cool air'?"

"Cool air just came from big holes in the floor, I don't know how."

Shelby looked at David and asked, "Are you thinking what I'm thinking?"

"Blowholes!"

"Right. And if they are blowholes then there must be a cavern under there someplace."

"What are blowholes, Shelby?" Sorek sensed the excitement but didn't understand the meaning.

"The Hopi of my world named them after the Yaapontsa, the Wind Spirit. They are small cracks or holes in the bedrock that penetrate down into a huge cavern. They act like vents. As the barometric pressure changes, air rushes in or out of a cave trying to equalize with the outside. It sort of breathes, only a breath might last for days or weeks. It's very strange to stand under the hot sun and feel cool air rush out of a hole in the ground. Here, they have used them to cool the palace. Pretty smart I'd say. I've only seen one before in Arizona near some Indian ruins. They were outside Flagstaff I think, they…"

"Ask a simple question…" David interrupted and turned away to hide his amusement.

"Well, he wanted to know, so I told him the best way I know how!" Shelby fired back, then he turned his own questioning back to Etrusean. "Are there any caves around here?"

The old man pointed to a place almost off the map. It was a mile northeast of the village and another quarter mile from the palace. The place was marked with a dragon head. "Takinacha, the Dragon hole. But you don't want to go there. It is very evil. Many have been curious and all have died. The dragon lives there, and sometimes at night when it is very quiet you can hear him scream and shake the ground."

To that, Shelby simply replied, "This has to be the cavern entrance, and it must run under the palace. That is the only explanation for the blowholes. If we can get in there, we can crawl right into the palace. What could be more perfect? How do you say that again?"

"Takinacha."

"Tak-i-na'-cha. Good. That's where we'll go."

"You missed the important part, Shelby," cautioned Sorek. "The dragon. And the fact that it has killed everyone that has entered the hole."

"Come on, Sorek, where's your adventure? Besides, I don't believe in dragons. But if they do exist here…wow! I'd love to see one."

"Because you don't believe in them doesn't change a thing, Shelby. Something has killed those people for as far back as stories go!"

It was late afternoon when they started back and Shelby wanted to have a look at Takinacha. Reluctantly, the little group followed Shelby and David as they followed the markings on the map. By dusk they stood in front of the Dragon hole. They argued about staying, but Shelby and David insisted that a reconnaissance was necessary. Finally it was decided that they would camp there and venture inside the following morning when the rising sun would illuminate the cave's entrance and provide better viewing.

Anxious for rest, Shelby gathered some tall prairie grass and fashioned a quick bed. He was careful to be well back from the glow of the fire, in the shadows of a clump of greasewood. His years of outdoor living on the ranch had taught him to be able to sleep anywhere, anytime and make the best of it.

He had the last watch, just after David. Sorek took the first and was walking out away from their small fire to take his post. Anatol was quietly but restlessly poking at the fire with a stick. He couldn't settle down, and for good reason. He had grown up in this area and knew all the stories of Takinacha. This would be a tough night for the young soldier. Superstition can be as real as life for those who concede to it.

All was quiet, but Shelby had stirred during the night, seeking a more comfortable position. He lay awake for a moment, admiring the dark velvet, star-flecked sky and noting familiar constellations. They seemed like old friends. No matter where he was, they were steady, they were always there, even in this strange place. And that brought peace of mind.

The coals were glowing red and he could see that Sorek had turned in. David was still asleep, so that meant Anatol was on watch. He thought about the young man and the strange way they had become friends. He thought, too, about the fact that had his shirt not been open enough for the silver arrowhead to be seen, he would be dead now. *Life is a delicate thing.* He thought. *How many times each day do we brush death and not even know it? How many decisions do we make that might have been fatal had we made a different choice or made it at a different time?* He reached up and fingered the silver arrowhead around his neck. He liked the feel of it there.

Suddenly, Shelby felt a low rumble deep within the earth. Was it an earthquake? Was it the beginning of a volcanic eruption? Whatever it was, it was distant and almost imperceptible, but it was real, and it lasted for almost a minute. It hadn't even disturbed the night creatures. Comforted by that, he filed it away and went back to sleep.

The dipper turned another quarter turn and he slept soundly until a boot crunched some of the small twigs he had scattered around his sleeping area. He was instantly awake with his hand around the handle of his knife. "Your turn, Shel." David noticed but didn't comment on the perimeter of dry twigs; he had done the same thing. They were in the land of their enemy, and every precaution was wise.

"One thing you should know, Shel. There is a rumble every now and then. And with it, a sound over by the mouth of the cave like an animal scream. It just happened not more than a minute ago, but I have heard it twice on my watch."

"Yeah, I felt it earlier during Anatol's watch. Does it seem the same every time?"

"Sure does. It lasts about a minute."

Shelby noted the time. Seven minutes past four, by his watch. He moved out away from camp and the breathing men where he could hear the night and discern its sounds. He knew every environment sounds different. Each creature in the habitat seeks out his own niche in the grand symphony of sounds. Every small voice performs his part in the animal orchestra…singing, croaking, or chirping in his own unique place on the animal orchestra staff. Each is careful to stay out of the other's vocal range. To intrude would keep another species from communicating or finding a mate. An intrusion into his own area on the staff for long periods of time could mean his demise or even extinction.

Some birds have the ability to move around on that musical staff if intrusions are made, but most do not. A casual listener simply hears the night as noise. To one that truly listens and respects the sounds, they become a beautiful symphony with rhythm, melody and harmony. One who hears that music will also hear the dissonance that occurs when danger approaches. For this, Shelby listened.

Twice before dawn, he felt the rumbling and heard the screams from the cave entrance as David had described. Since it was too dark to write, and too risky for a flashlight, he made a mental note of the time. Aside from the strange rumblings, the night was peaceful and uneventful.

At dawn everyone was up, and David and Shelby prepared to enter the cavern. Sorek and Anatol would remain outside, both for reasons of safety and because they, too, had heard the dragon screams during the night. They wanted no part of the evil hole.

The two explorers planned to examine only enough of the cave to confirm their suspicions and form a plan. They would return later with rope and other equipment. At that time they would seek to enter the palace and attempt the rescue.

As they entered the depths in the cavern, they noted the climbing humidity. They proceeded with caution, looking for watermarks, mineral deposits and evidence of fresh, loose rock. They traveled another half hour before they found all three, along with massive deposits of silica. Cautiously they backed off a safe distance and waited.

"What do you think, Shelby?"

"I think if we're right about this we should see our dragon in about six or seven minutes."

They turned off their flashlights and sat in the black stillness, waiting. Nothing seemed as dark as a cave. He had heard it said that a place could be 'so dark you couldn't see your hand in front of your face.' He didn't believe that. Even now he passed his hand in front of his face, and he could make out a peculiar image. He wasn't really seeing light reflected off his hand, but something was there. Was the mind so acute that it mentally placed the hand there, or was it something more extraordinary? He fascinated himself for the next few seconds by moving his hand in different ways, yet still seeing it. He tried the same experiment with his flashlight handle. It was undetectable. *Interesting*, he thought, and decided to look it up later when he got home.

The minutes passed, and finally the ground began to tremble. Gently at first, then more violently as the audible, distant rumble turned into a thunderous roar. Their flashlights could pick out nothing in the vast darkness before them. Fear mounted in them both, but neither spoke or moved. What if they were wrong? Or what if they had simply miscalculated? Suddenly, an explosion of steam and rock belched from a dark abyss some hundred yards away. It screamed and groaned as scalding water showered the cavern. Small rocks pelted all around them. By the time the scalding, spewing water had traveled to them it had atomized and settled as mist, but it left them just as wet as if it had hit them directly.

The spectacular event lasted for just over a minute and left the chasm before them full of bubbling hot water. "Well, there's Takinacha. The way I have him figured, he shows up about every sixty-eight to seventy minutes."

"Yeah," replied David. "But how long does it take the water to go down? We have to time our crossing this room between the time it's clear enough to walk around the pit and the next eruption."

They sat there for several more minutes and watched the foaming water disappear back into the black abyss where it would again be heated by the magma and build up enough force to spew to the top again. David took a compass bearing to determine the direction to the palace. At length, the water subsided and they carefully picked a route around the gurgling pit and to the deeper regions of the cavern in the direction of David's compass bearing.

They had barely worked their way passed the pit when Shelby again checked the time. "Hey, DC. We have about twenty-six minutes to get back out of here before that thing blows again. And if we don't get back across there we're gonna' be dragon meat."

They carefully negotiated the wet rocks and cleared the danger area with three minutes to spare. Again they stopped and watched the magnificent event. "It's no wonder the other explorers never got out of here alive." observed David. "It would take the better part of an hour to get beyond this one room. They would have no clue what this was and certainly no idea of timing it. To be caught anywhere in this chamber would spell certain death by boiling."

"Yeah, I know."

They headed out making their path over the steep slippery rocks to the entrance. When the emerged they were greeted by two very concerned friends.

"We heard the dragon, twice. What happened? How did you escape?" Their questions came in unison.

"Your dragon is simply a geyser...a nasty one, but still a geyser," replied David. "It is nothing to worry about."

"But you are unharmed...unconcerned!" cried Anatol. "Maybe you call it a geyser and I call it a dragon, but Takinacha is still deadly. Every other man to enter that dark hole found an even darker death! Do you indeed possess the strange power that my comrades attribute to Texans?"

"I guess you could say that we possess a great power," David said thoughtfully. "But it's not strange and it's not just ours, it's available to anyone. It's simply knowledge. You see, we know what that is in there. We know why and how it happens. More importantly, we know when it happens. That's not the power of magic, that's the power of knowledge, and knowledge is a protector of those who seek it. When you understand that, you can deal with anything."

"Do you mean to tell me that after generations of legend and who knows how many dead men, that what is in there is a natural thing like a...thunderstorm or a raging flood?" Anatol spoke almost indignantly. He had been raised on a lie and didn't seem to like it.

"I think for one raised on such superstitions," mused David, "you are in for a lot of surprises, my friend."

Chapter 19

Returning to Tekoa was uneventful, and as little time as possible was spent preparing for the rescue trip. Shelby and David were eager to be on with it and quickly accumulated the materials needed.

Deccan begged to go with them but was overruled by his friends and forbidden by the doctor. In spite of his energetic appearance, he remained too weak from his injury for such a stressful mission. That left Sorek, Kadian, Bob and Anatol to complete the rescue squad. There were six men, each with a specific skill to offer and each understanding his task and its related dangers.

The big "if" was: could they in fact enter through the blowholes? It could be that the holes penetrated the cavern at the top of a vaulted ceiling, hundreds of feet above them. They might also enter through small crevasses or cracks that no man could ever negotiate, or even find, for that matter. They placed a lot of confidence in something so dubious. The task was going to be difficult and not unlike finding a needle in a haystack.

With little fanfare, they were off, each carrying a heavy load of equipment and supplies. They had tried to prepare for the unknown and that left out efficiency and, naturally, everything having to do with comfort.

The small group reached Takinacha when the afternoon shadows were very long and the evening breeze was just cooling the rugged mountainside. They doubted they had been seen, but being cautious they moved immediately into the mouth of the cavern before removing their packs and resting.

In the dim, cool shade of the cave they broke down and stowed their equipment. Most of it would be hidden here in case it was later needed. The rest would be stowed further inside. They must travel light from here on.

Almost immediately the geyser erupted and rumbled deep within the cave, and David marked the time. The others, wary of such a strange event looked at each other uneasily. Yet, they had trusted these Texans so far. After all, they understood such things.

"We can't possibly be ready in time for the next eruption," Shelby said. "It will take forty minutes just to reach the pit. Let's hurry and try for the one after that."

The Texans barked orders and directed what would be taken and what would be stashed. Instructions were given on clothing and squad equipment. Food and water were checked, and the torches were lighted. They changed into their thick-soled moccasins especially made for the cave and took up their coiled ropes. Each man worked diligently and efficiently with a confidence that these Texans had done this stuff before.

Bob prepared base camp and stowed the emergency equipment. He was to stay near the entrance of the cave and stand guard day and night. His job included patrolling outside to warn against any Cartokian presence and standing ready with one of the radios in case of emergency.

Each man had been briefed on what to expect while living in the cavern. They had supplies enough to last a week inside the dragon hole. However, they could only be told of the predictable things…the dampness, the cooler, almost cold temperature, the quietness and the incredible darkness. And then there were the dangers: the slick rocks and slimy mud, getting lost, rock falls and deep pits and of course, the geyser. If respected, it posed no danger, but it was absolutely merciless and not to be toyed with.

With Shelby on point and David in the rear, the little group of rescuers filed cautiously into the dark mouth of Takinacha. They disturbed a phoebe from her perch high on a ledge, and she swooped around the room in graceful circles before returning to her well-made nest of moss and mud plastered to the wall.

"We're liable to run into anything from a skunk to a mountain lion in this region of the cave," Shelby said to the group. "They like the cool shaded entrance of caves and will venture back as far as they can see and find food."

Lacy ferns and clumps of moss huddled around the small stream that gently eased out of the cave. Curiously, Shelby stooped down to examine and finger the cold, clear water. A few rocks covered black-green with algae dotted a widened pool. It was a pretty spot touched only by the morning sun and shaded the rest of the day by the overhang of the entrance.

The stream came from a spot to their right and found higher ground in there someplace. They took a route to the left that led down into a gaping black mouth.

"I'm not sure I'm gonna' like this very much," grumbled Sorek.

"But you will, Sorek. It's enchanting," replied Shelby. "Notice the increasing coolness and humidity as we enter the cave's *twilight zone*. Listen to how quiet it gets and how disturbing a single small stone echoes in the chamber. The place is magic and it will get even better as we go deeper."

"What is this… *twilight zone*?"

"It's the region of the cave where the retina of your eye can still work. You notice that faint glow of light? Many nocturnal animals find refuge here where they can still see. I saw a horned owl in here yesterday. It's always damp and cool in this region, even if it's hot and dry outside. It's like a natural sanctuary for many animals trying to avoid the summer heat."

"Hey, look! What kind of strange thing is that?" commented Kadian as he pointed to the cave wall. It seemed to pulse and move as if alive.

Shelby swung his torch near the wall, and several thousand long-legged, lanky creatures stirred against the light and warmth of the flame. "Harvestmen. We just call them daddy long-legs. They're harmless enough, but it is kinda' creepy when there are so many."

For several minutes they descended a slide of loose rock. David paused to watch the others struggle for balance and to seek a safer route, then he announced the time remaining before the next eruption. Shelby slipped and fell under his load but was quickly up and going again. He reached the bottom and led the group through a ragged passage under an enormous fallen slab of limestone. They emerged in a room the size of a coliseum. Shelby paused just under the edge of the slab and said, "Now, we wait here for the dragon. How much time, DC?"

"Eight minutes."

"Better rest 'cause when the water clears there will be no stoppin' for the better part of an hour. If we get caught in here we'll be just like those poor critters." Shelby's flashlight stabbed the distant darkness and fell on the remains of what were obviously human bones. "We found them yesterday. There are more on the other side."

They sat quietly for a moment listening to the occasional monotonous dripping around the room. All was peaceful and deathly quiet. Shelby glanced at his watch. The stillness would be shattered momentarily by an earth-belch of magnificent proportions.

From the quietness, emerged a low rolling drone like that of a distant train. Subsonic tremblings came through the rocks where they sat and the air carried a hint of sulfur. A deep gurgling began and started to rise in pitch like a filling barrel. The trembling became more violent and jets of steam vented from fissures surprisingly close to them. Slowly, the dragon approached.

"No matter what happens, guys, stay right where you are. We'll be safe here," David said reassuringly. "Besides, this is gonna' be the neatest thing you ever laid eyes on!" That might have sounded good, but it was of no comfort to three men who weren't sure they would live through the next few minutes.

When the geyser erupted it was a grand sight and sound show. It lifted boiling water to the ceiling a hundred feet above them and blasted rock like a shotgun. Those rocks splattered like glass bottles against the cavern walls and ceiling, then rained down onto the protecting overhang above them. Rocks that hadn't moved since the beginning of time were violently ripped from their place and hurled by superheated steam and water out the mouth of the geyser. They ricocheted around the big room and came to an eternal rest, never to be moved again.

With the blast came a shockwave of air that shook their bones and a spray of ultra-fine mist that left them drenched. As the violence subsided, the boiling froth gurgled in a bubbling lake before them, and water trickled and dripped from the vaulted dome like rain.

Shelby turned and noticed the pale, white-faced men braced in a state of shock. "Now, wasn't that the neatest thing you ever saw?" No one spoke, they just stared. There were no words in their language to express what they felt, and if there were, it wouldn't include *neat*.

The lake quickly began to disappear as it was sucked back into the abyss, back into the bowels of the earth where it would prepare for another performance in a little more than an hour. That gave the little group barely enough time to cross the room.

"Let's go," announced David. "There will be no time to waste. In sixty-eight minutes this will happen again, and you can imagine what will happen if we get caught in here."

The men needed no prodding. They were eager to move on, and they were tense with the sense of danger. To this point, their biggest concern had been getting caught by Croseus. That now seemed like child's play compared to what lurked within this dragon hole.

Skirting the geyser pit proved difficult. They had packs, and their balance was impaired. The surface was very slick, as hot water flowed over the path and fell back into the hole. A fog, thick with the stench of the upheaval, stung their nostrils and watered their eyes. Had they tried to negotiate such as this anywhere else it would not have been so difficult, but the pit... the black hole without a bottom, was inches from their feet, and that affected the mind.

The light from their torches revealed little of the pit below about twenty feet. But David's flashlight followed the shaft down well over a hundred feet and chased the receding water as it gulped and gurgled like a giant toilet. The sight put a strange feeling of weakness in their knees and a strong desire to be away from there.

Twenty minutes passed and they had not gone twenty yards past the pit. Shelby began to show concern. They had so far to go, and forty-eight minutes in which to do it. The room was full of rubble, and finding a path was difficult. They had gone this way yesterday but without inexperienced men and without packs to slow them down.

At length they reached David's next bearing marker, a stack of rocks marking the direction to the palace and the extent of yesterday's travel. The previous marker had been placed back by the overhang where they sat earlier. It was within view of the flashlight beam, so they lined up the two markers and shot another bearing deeper into the cave. It was a large, plain stalagmite with an irregular top. It was safely beyond the danger zone of the geyser, and Shelby announced it as their next goal.

This method of travel would be the only way they could know where they were. Each marker along the compass bearing would be sighted, measured for distance with a piece of string, and marked with a number. That information was then transferred to the sketch map in David's journal.

Placing the knotted end of the string firmly under another rock, they set off in the direction of the stalagmite. David unrolled the spool as he walked. The plan would be to reach the string's measured distance, then pull it free from the rock and repeat the process. Even as danger clicked closer with every tick of the clock, their method had to be sound. A small mistake in a compass reading could mean missing a blowhole by a hundred feet and in this place, an error of ten feet would prove failure.

The minutes passed, and travel was slow and strenuous. This room had seen devastation every hour for eons, and the damage was evident and difficult to negotiate. Shelby looked at his watch. Twenty-one minutes. "How far from the last marker, DC?"

"Ninety yards, Shel. We're goin' too slow."

Shelby did his best to hurry the rescue team along without sounding absurd. They knew the danger and needed no pep talk. Besides, they were doing their best. He turned and scrambled onward toward the silent monolith that marked safety. He increased his speed, and they kept up. That was it then, he would say no more. He would simply tax their ability to keep up.

Eight minutes. Shelby looked back at David bringing up the rear and working with his string. He was a good man... one to ride the river with. They weren't made any more dependable than he. He knew his job and executed it with precision. He thought about Vishti. How could those two ever develop their relationship over such a barrier as living in different dimensions?

Shelby slipped, and a boulder slid loose. "Rock!" he yelled. The others stopped as if by command and moved aside, allowing the boulder to bounce past. Shelby was impressed. These men learned well and were quick. He enjoyed them and their wholesome view of life. It gave him a good feeling, and he knew they would be successful in this mission.

Shelby topped the last obstacle and looked at his watch. Three minutes remained, and the line of men had stretched out over about thirty yards. "Two minutes!" he yelled, knowing if he said three they would take three. Even as he yelled he felt the floor of the cavern shudder. It had started then, and he alone stood on safe ground. He heard himself screaming at them, but they knew. They had felt it themselves and were scrambling and clawing up the last pile of debris.

Sorek... Anatol... they came over the top and turned to watch as Kadian and David ran with all their might. Behind them the room exploded, and rock bombs landed nearby. They couldn't see the geyser. It was beyond the light of their torches, but its screaming roar told of its activity. Kadian had stopped and was reaching for David. Water and rocks showered down, and a white froth raged toward them as the basin filled with a scalding soup.

Kadian grabbed David and threw him up and over the top. He landed on the others, and they cushioned his impact. Then with the graceful move of a giant cat, the huge man lunged upward and jumped free of the basin.

"Let's get outta' here!" he yelled, and they ran to an opening that shielded them from the flying missiles. "I thought you said we had two minutes?"

"These things aren't always that predictable. They vary a couple of minutes either way. But now we know we can do it. Besides going back will be easier."

"Yeah, right. You young 'uns border on crazy, you know that?"

Shelby grinned and wiped the water from his face. "Boy, I love this stuff!" The others stood in disbelief for a moment, then broke into laughter. Behind them the room re-queued for another performance. And they made ready for the next bearing marker.

There were several passages leading in the general direction of the palace. Any or all of them could prove successful or turn out to be a blind end. David reached down and picked up a handful of dust. He proceeded to let it sift through his fingers and fall to the floor.

"Not much air movement here, Shel."

"Let's set up an air movement gauge in the mouth of the tunnel by that small pool over there. We can move it to the others and compare the air flow."

With that said, the two Texans unrolled a small sheet of thin plastic wrapped around several arm-length sticks. The others watched with interest as they lashed together two small tripods and rested a longer stick horizontally atop them. The plastic was then hung from the horizontal shaft and allowed to hang as a flat sheet.

"What is that?" Sorek quizzed.

"We're looking for any air movement that might lead us to one of the blowholes. Watch." David replied as Shelby placed a ruler beneath the contraption and aligned it with a plumb bob. Sure enough, the plastic sheet deflected past the plumb line a full half inch on the ruler.

"Well, we've got movement here," Shelby said. "Let's try the other passages." So in like manner they checked and found no movement in three of the remaining four. The fourth, however, had almost an inch of deflection.

"We go this way, guys. There's definitely an opening down there somewhere and if we're lucky it'll be in the palace." David spoke with an assurance that bred confidence in his companions.

The chosen path proved to be most difficult. They hadn't gone fifty yards before they were crawling on their bellies beneath a huge limestone breakdown. The passage had gone from an eight foot ceiling to a crawl space of no more than fourteen inches.

Shelby took the point and wormed a path beneath the limestone slab. Reluctantly, the others followed. Even though nothing seemed unstable, the small space was extremely claustrophobic and therefore disconcerting.

Kadian and David were the last to enter. The big man hesitated and turned back to David.

"Listen sprout, if I get stuck in there it could botch the whole mission."

"You gotta' at least try, Kadian. If it gets too bad…well, I reckon we could go on with out you. The trouble is, we're really gonna need you."

The big fella' took a breath and started under. David stayed close and kept a conversation going. He knew if this big guy panicked they might not get him out and the others certainly couldn't get back past him.

Several times the small tunnel got worse before it got better. Each time Kadian would try to make some joke to break the tension. Finally, they could see the others' torchlight.

"Just a little more Kadian. You're almost here," they called.

The exit from the breakdown was the worst and Shelby scraped the dirt down to solid rock. Even at that, the clearance was less than a foot. Shelby was worried. There would be no backing up for Kadian now. He had to come through.

As Kadian started through the last small hole he realized he couldn't make it and said as much. Shelby was thinking hard, seeking some possible solution and fearing he had made a fatal mistake that could cost a life. Sometimes his plans were just too optimistic. He himself was too optimistic, and that could sometimes cloud judgment.

"Guys, I'm stuck!" the big man said.

Then, from the darkness behind Kadian, David yelled. "Hey, Shelby. Remember what that crazy brother of yours did over at King Mountain? He was stuck worse than this!"

"You know, you're right! But, that was my crazy brother. Stuff like this is regular for him."

"It still might work."

Shelby laughed. "It sure might. Okay, Kadian, here's the plan according to one who would get into fixes like this just to have the fun of getting out.

"Back up about four feet where you have a little more room and take off your clothes. David, get his moccasins off so he can shed his pants."

Another time and they might have been laughing, but this was deadly serious and it had to work. Kadian didn't even question the idea. He and David struggled with his clothes in the tight space. Finally, he was barefoot to his chin and ready for a try at it. Carefully, he eased forward and into the hole again. He exhaled and wiggled through. David was pushing his feet and the others were pulling his arms. The rocks scraped him up a bit, but he made it and never groaned.

David tossed out Kadian's clothes and squirmed through behind him. "It sure would be nice to find another way back."

"I'd appreciate that," Kadian said cheerfully as he pulled on his trousers. "I surely would."

The new room was large… the size of a small house, and within minutes they had it explored and a route planned. Laboriously, they moved deeper into the cavern following air movement and compass bearings.

According to the map, they were still a quarter mile northeast of the palace and on a course that looked promising. A bat flew past them. Shelby switched on his flashlight. He had been conserving his batteries and using a torch, but he wanted a look at the ceiling which had now vaulted to well over fifty feet. Bats covered it, and they were beginning to stir.

"Let's watch where they go," said Shelby. "We need to find a better way out. It's not just Kadian I'm worried about. If we stir up much in the palace, we may have to move real fast. They sat down and listened, waiting as the bats began to bustle. It was a welcome rest for all.

From time to time Shelby turned his flashlight to the ceiling and watched as a few bats would drop and disappear faster than he could move his light. A few minutes later, as if by some general's command, thousands of the little creatures took wing and started their flight through the silent, twisting corridors to the surface. It was an awesome event...a battalion of creatures maneuvering as one in a maze of stone through total darkness. Their echolocation insured a flight path safe from the others and safe from the obstacles of the cave. Their chirps and squeaks filled the solitary hollow for most of ten minutes. To witness such an event and understand the magnitude of its complexity is a true testimony to the design of creation.

David had climbed up to the ledge behind them and was watching the bats from there. A moment later he was gone, hollering something about following them. When he returned he had mapped out a way back over the top of the limestone breakdown. He said it couldn't be seen or reached from the other side but with their rope they could easily make it back. Kadian signed in relief, knowing now that he wouldn't have to return through the difficult passage.

The cavern quickly turned from broken rubble to delicate speleothems and took on uncommon beauty. David and Shelby were duly fascinated with the rare formations; but the others, having never seen anything like them before, were spellbound.

They soon realized that the Texans had names for the beautiful formations and could explain how they were formed. An onslaught of questions followed. Here, in this quiet place, time meant nothing, yet it was measured by the drip of mineral-saturated water that over eons sculpted vast galleries of astonishing beauty. Here was nature's unique workshop, and on display were an endless variety of its wares.

The walls to one side were rippled like drapery. The other side fell away to a small, delicate wonderland. Jeweled crystals of calcium carbonate grew like frost on larger, older formations, indicating a fluctuating water level at some time in the past. Other, more delicate sculptures grew sideways and fashioned butterflies, tomahawks and Chinese fans. These bordered a clear, still pool that inverted and doubled their beautiful shapes.

The little wonderland huddled in a small dell sheltered by tiers of flowstone that cascaded like a frozen waterfall into the valley. Above, the stalactite-covered dome glistened in the torchlight, and in the distance their shadows danced against immense gypsum sheets.

As they moved beyond the little valley, they encountered large flower formations that had the appearance of being formed like a colossal cake decoration. Each petal seemed to have been squirted into shape by a large frosting syringe. David explained them and told the others they were gypsum flowers.

Beyond were hollow soda straws and small grape cluster formations along scalloped walls. The variety and beauty in this small section of the cavern was difficult to leave but they had a mission to accomplish and some place to be.

Each moment they delayed might spell torture or even death for the one they were to rescue. It was also possible that Aryan was already dead. After all, Anatol had been in the palace but had not seen him in over a week. Shelby considered the possibility that they might all be dead before this was over. But he also remembered their obligation to Bon. An obligation he didn't take lightly. Above all else, his dad had taught him to be a man of honor, regardless of the costs.

Again the walls closed in. Droplets of water on them indicated the air was completely saturated with moisture and could hold no more. As the pathway grew progressively confined they found themselves on their hands and knees in slimy muck.

"Why is this stuff so nasty?" Sorek asked in disgust. "It's not like mud, yet that's what it is."

Shelby pointed to some small tuffs of gray-white hairs an inch or so in length. They looked like mold. "Only bacteria and fungus can grow here. That's what gives caves a musty smell. They're the last link in the food chain, and as they work, they excrete by-products that are stinky and slimy. That's what we're crawlin' in."

"Well, I sure 'preciate you tellin' me that, son," Sorek replied. "I could've gone my whole life without that bit of wisdom."

The crawl space suddenly opened into a huge abyss. Shelby pulled back, weak-kneed. Before him was absolutely nothing. He switched on his light, but it failed to reach the bottom or the top.

"Hold it, guys!" he yelled over his shoulder. We've come to a domepit."

"A what?" asked Kadian.

"A vertical shaft in the middle of a large room. It goes straight up and straight down." Shelby rocked back on his heels and leaned against the wall as he answered.

"Well, can we get around it?" asked David.

"I'm not sure. I was so startled I didn't look. There's nothin' out there, David. It just drops off to the middle of the Earth." He looked into the large eyes of his companions. "I'll take a look, but hold on to my feet, Kadian. I think I'd feel better."

Shelby eased back toward the passage exit on his stomach. With his flashlight he surveyed the area around the pit. The crawl space they were in opened into the domepit over smooth, watermarked limestone. Water had passed this way and fallen in a never-ending waterfall. It would atomize long before it reached anything below. The wall to the right was flat and vertical. Below, there was nothing, and to the left the rock was undermined and fragmented. Shelby broke a piece off in his hand and let it fall. It never hit. He looked above. It could not be climbed, but he could see a landing about eight feet above, and from there stemmed a narrow ledge that skirted the shaft.

He pulled back in and ask David to backtrack, looking for anything that opened above their passage. "We're not goin' this way. Maybe DC can find a way up top. I saw a ledge above us that goes around this thing."

While they waited for David to return, each one had to take his turn at looking into the chasm. Each man pulled away a little weak. To fall into such a place would probably bring one to the devil's front door.

David's call sounded muffled and distant. "Back here!" And as one man they scampered toward his call, eager to be away from the pit. David was dangling upside down from a hole in the ceiling when they reached him. "Look, guys. I'm a bat."

"Are all Texans like you guys, or are you two just a special case?" mused Sorek.

"Oh, he's just funnin', Sorek. It breaks the tension," replied Shelby.

They climbed through the hole to the top only to again reach the edge of the domepit eight or ten feet above the original crawl space. There was a narrow ledge skirting the abyss that led to the large room on the other side. It was passable, but it would take nerve and mountain goat feet.

Sorek felt the need to release some of that tension Shelby spoke of. "Great, David. Now we have further to fall!"

"You reckon it'll make any difference?" David chuckled.

Strained laughter emitted from the others and they started to follow Shelby, who again took his post at the point. With great care he picked the route as David stopped the others. "Wait 'till he makes it. We don't want to be out there if he has to back up. Just watch what he does and where his feet go."

Unconsciously, each man held his breath until Shelby was safe. Then, in unison they all exhaled. Realizing what they had done brought on a bit of much needed humor, and one by one they timidly ventured out over the narrow trail.

Shelby used his flashlight to point out the best places to step. Encouragement and instructions came from the others as they watched, dreading their turn. If the ledge had been around a flowerbed outside, each man could have walked it with ease. But something happens in the human mind at great heights. Whatever it was, it certainly made this trip difficult.

Time and distance are misleading in a cavern. Nothing can be used as a reference, and there are no clues to follow. They had painstakingly marked their map and had confidence in that, but where were they, really? How far had they come? And how far must they go? These questions haunted them but were not expressed by such men. Shelby and David exhibited great confidence, and the others trusted their judgment. Each man knew what he was capable of and had confidence in that. But this was so unknown, the mission was so great, and the cost of failure was so high.

The path had been easy, and the measuring and marking had gone well for a good twenty minutes when Shelby pulled up short. He was examining the ceiling and caught the interest of the others.

"What ya got, Shel?" yelled David.

Shelby put his finger to his lips and motioned for the others to gather. He pointed to some small mosquito like creatures on the rock. "Midges," he said.

"So?" replied Sorek.

"It means we are near an opening. These can't live very far in. And keep your voice down. A blowhole could be anywhere close by, and we don't want 'em waiting for us."

They began to measure airflow again and check the map. They still

expected to be a fair distance away, but they could easily have made mistakes-
- many mistakes. Excitement was high as they watched the plastic sheet drift
in the low air current. Each knew what it meant, for it drifted more than it
ever had before.

After checking several locations they focused their search and found a
chimney. It was only about twelve feet high and narrow enough to be easy to
climb, but was it a blowhole?

"I'll climb it," David said as he started up. "Just in case, take those torches
back a good distance. We don't want 'em smellin' the smoke."

Shelby held a flashlight as David wormed his was up the chimney. He
pushed against one side with his back and walked up the other with his feet.
It was a slow process, but sure. At the top he rolled out of sight and a few
pebbles trickled down.

David found himself in a confined crawl space, but he could feel wind
rushing past. The wind had been increasing as he entered the chimney, but
now it was joined by other passages and cracks until it now felt like he had a
fan on him. Excitement grew and he switched off his light.

The remainder of the tunnel was washed in a pale blue-white glow like
moonlight. Eagerly he rushed on to its source. "Sunlight!" he whispered.
The last few feet required him to wedge into a tight opening, but he managed
it and could see outside.

Chapter 20

Not fifty yards away loomed the gray, stone walls of the palace. David strained for a better view of the area but was unable to move any closer. Giving up, he backed up enough to pull out his compass and take a reading. Once done, he scrambled back to the others.

"We're not inside, but we're sure close." he announced. Pulling out his compass he quickly shot a bearing. "Fifty yards right through there." he said as he pointed towards another passage.

The measuring procedures were duplicated and a new search point was converged upon. This time there was no chimney, only a narrow crevasse in the ceiling. Kadian hoisted Shelby up, and the Texan scurried into it with ease and disappeared from view. The others eagerly waited for word. *What if we can't make it? It could be as small as the opening David found. If that's the case, the entire venture is wasted.* Each man's thoughts focused and their brows furrowed.

Shelby crawled like he was born to it. The wind rushed past and howled in the cracks and holes. His heart pounded. So far, the passage was large and relatively easy to travel. Then before him he saw a faint glow. Instantly, he switched off his flashlight and moved cautiously forward.

He heard voices but could not get close enough to the opening to see anything. He felt around in the dim light but the space was too confined. They could never enter through here. The voices receded, and he heard footsteps on a hard, stone floor as two people walked away.

Switching on his light and carefully guarding the beam to avoid the opening, he studied the small chamber. The rocks here had been cemented in place. Hope leaped within him. The work of man! Mortar could be scratched away, and rocks could be pried loose. He looked around surveying all within view. There was plenty of room for his companions to work here. The only real problem was the noise they would make.

Quietly, Shelby took out his knife and scraped at the mortar. It proved to be a sandy mix and flaked easily under his blade. Within seconds he had removed two stones and was well on his way at dislodging another. He paused once when someone passed nearby, but they continued, so he did likewise.

Each stone he removed brought his view of the outside a little closer. He had to know where they were before committing the others and risking detection. Ten minutes passed, and he had removed four stones. He gently eased his head into the small hole he had made. In doing so, he disturbed a small avalanche of dirt. Dust fell into his eyes and he almost sneezed. He backed off and attempted to clear his eyes and get some tears flowing. Then, brushing the dirt from his face, he tried again.

He strained as far as possible and could just see into a room of some sort. It was lavish and dimly lit with oil lamps. There were large colored rugs and drapes. A red velvet bag rested within arm's reach outside the hole. It was much like a large beanbag and several large blankets were thrown over it. Try as he did, he could only see a small portion of the room but enough to make the effort worthwhile. They were inside!

He scrambled back to the others and reported his find. As he laid it out for them they discussed a plan. It was decided that Kadian would stay there and serve as a ladder. He could easily hoist the others up into the crevasse and back down again when the rush of escape was upon them.

They collected the few items they needed and were off. One by one they crawled into the hole in the ceiling like a bunch of ants. Once in the small chamber beneath the blowhole they began their assigned tasks. Working in shifts of five minutes then rotating jobs allowed for rest while insuring continued progress. One man listened and observed through the small hole while the others took their posts digging and removing debris.

Several times they stopped for activity in the outer room, but progress was being made. No man grumbled at the task; they were too close to success. Each heart beat with rekindled pride and each soul felt a renewed honor as they worked together, seeking to accomplish this noble task.

Shelby held his hand up for silence. They were ready to remove the last four stones that would allow entrance into the room. He reached out into the room and pulled the beanbag closer to hide their activity. Then carefully and ever so quietly they dislodged the last remaining stones. The entrance hole was scarcely eighteen inches in diameter, but it had to do.

Shelby was halfway into the room when he heard the footsteps. He pulled a blanket over him and lay still. Whoever it was came in and sat down nearby. He had no way to signal the others and he hoped they would lay low realizing that something was happening. The minutes ticked into an hour, but he lay motionless in a cramped position without so much as a twitch. Finally, someone else entered and talked for a moment before they both left and snuffed out the lamps.

The young Texan chanced a peek from under the blanket. The room was almost dark. Dim light entered through a narrow, slit window, but it was late evening light and wouldn't remain long. He crawled out. The others followed, then scattered like mice seeking hiding places around the room.

Shelby went to Anatol and motioned for Sorek. "Okay guys, where are we, and where do we go?"

"I think this is Croseus' quarters," replied the young soldier. "I have never been here of course, but I've heard it's like this." There were two doors in the large room. A small door was on the far side near the bed, and a huge massive door stood open on the opposite side. Beyond the door was a torch-lit hallway. Anatol pointed toward the hall. "That should take us where we want to go, but I don't know much about this wing of the palace. It was off limits to us."

"Where are the cells?" quizzed Shelby. "Where will Aryan be?"

"Down below," whispered Sorek. "Follow me."

The four rescuers moved out in single file, each following the other but allowing a good ten feet of maneuvering room between men. Corridors crisscrossed the dismal place, and all were dark and musty. This section of the palace was a confusing maze and very disquieting. Shelby had read somewhere about old castles being laid out like this. Not only were there secret passages, but the not-so-secret ones were as confusing as possible. Perhaps it was a form of security. He kept looking back, memorizing the return route. He had learned long ago that the way back never looks the same as the way in, and the best way to avoid getting lost is to stay found.

Sorek and Anatol found a narrow, winding stairway, and they descended. It was scarcely wide enough for their shoulders, and they had to walk hunched over to avoid the ceiling. *Kadian would be miserable here*. Shelby thought. *But he would sure be a comfort to have around if we get cornered in this place.*

The stairway opened into a small room. Rough-cut, wooden benches and shelves lined two walls like a locker room. A large iron rack, apparently for weapons, leaned against another wall. There was a table in the center and two benches nearby. A blackened fireplace covered much of the remaining wall.

"The guardhouse," whispered Sorek.

The place looked unused and Shelby worried about what they might find. Anatol had said that the few remaining prisoners were being neglected for days at a time because so few soldiers remained, and they seldom came down here or thought of the prisoners.

There were two doorways exiting the room. The first they tried led to the sleeping quarters for the guards. It was a small room, less than ten feet square, lined with unused, wooden bunks. The room had long been without occupancy.

They lifted the heavy bolt on the second door—a thick, solid, wooden door laced with iron and meant to be impassable if locked. It opened defiantly onto a long, damp hallway with cell doors along its sides. Almost reluctantly they entered the small passage. It stunk of death... human death. It is a distinct smell that is never forgotten. Each man knew what they would find in these cells. They only hoped that some still survived. They passed a water barrel, alive with tiny, swimming creatures in it. Disgusting, to be sure, but if anyone still lived in this wretched place they would crave even this water.

David reached up and lighted a wall lantern. The action brought a moan from one of the cells. Shelby and David switched on their flashlights and quickly examined each cell. The first three had occupants beyond the look of humans. They had been dead for several days at least. The next eight were empty.

They came to the last cell. More sounds emerged. A man-beast appeared and clung to the iron bars. His eyes were wide and wild and his hair was long and shaggy. Dried blood caked his face from beatings. "Water! Water! Please give me water," he said hoarsely.

David passed his canteen through the bars and the man drank greedily. Sorek moved up to the door and spoke gently. "Aryan? Is that you old friend?" The man lowered the canteen from his lips and turned. He had thought these men were simply soldiers. He moved back to the door and squinted against the light.

"Who calls me friend?" David turned his light on Sorek's face. "Sorek! Is it really you?" Aryan said.

"It is. And I bring help. Can you walk?"

"Yes! Yes, of course. I am a little weak. The guards have not been here in three days, so there has been no food. But seeing you gives me strength...much strength."

Sorek passed what few rations they had through the small, iron bar window in the door while the others tried to find the cell key. Through the door he could just make out a slit of sunset color through the cell's outside window. *Strange,* Sorek thought. *Such a beautiful, vertical line of rich color, framed by such cold, sad dullness.*

He held his light higher and noticed the wall scratches. "I knew you would never give up, Aryan. Your courage and driving will are to be commended."

"Don't think too highly of me, Sorek. I gave up for a time. Now tell me...please. What of Bon? What of my family?"

"The only pain in their life is not having you, Aryan. Bon is fine. He is a strong lad who grows up like his father. A brave one too. You know, that boy tried to rescue you himself. Got in a little over his head and was pulled out by a couple of Texans."

"Texans?"

"Shelby and David. They organized this. It was a promise they made to Bon."

"Then they are friends to my children?"

"Oh yes. You could definitely say that. In fact, one of 'em's sweet on Vishti. You're gonna' like these boys. I had a little run in with them at first, but they started to grow on me."

"Sweet on Vishti, you say. Well, we'll see about that...I've yet to meet anyone good enough for her."

"Well, you're about to. Here they come."

"Can't find any keys, Sorek," Shelby said. "Guess we're gonna to have to blow the lock."

"Shel. Meet Aryan."

"Howdy, Sir. I sure am glad you're okay. I was beginning to sweat a little over a promise we made to Bon. Now that you're fine...well, we'll just blow this door and go home. How 'bout it?"

"You make it sound so easy, young man. What of the soldiers?" His voice trailed off a moment as realization set in. "Say, how did you ever get into this place anyway? How'd you get past the guards?"

Shelby was busy with the lock. From his possibles kit he pulled out a folded package of toilet paper. Tearing several sheets, he placed them into his mouth and chewed. A moment later he removed the wet paper, shoved it into the lock and wedged it in place with his knife. He then tore several more sheets and placed them within the lock.

The others watched with interest but also without a clue as to what he was doing. "So, Shelby is it? Sorek tells me you two know my daughter. There was… trouble?" Aryan probed like a suspicious father.

"Oh that. You must be talkin' about the fight we had with Sorek when we first met her. That's kinda' hard to explain...not to mention embarrassing."

Shelby poured gunpowder from a small container he had in his bag onto the paper he had placed in the keyhole. Then laying a foot-long piece of toilet paper on the floor, he sprinkled powder into it as well.

"Sorek had to fight you regarding my daughter? What were you doing to her?"

"Well, it's really more complicated than that," Shelby said as he carefully twisted the toilet paper into a tight string. "There. This should work just fine."

He placed the newly formed fuse into the lock and chewed more paper. Finally, he sealed the lock with the soggy mess. "Sir, do you have a mattress or something you can get behind in there?"

"No. There is nothing in here but rats and roaches."

"Then move up against this forward wall and get as far to the side as possible. And protect your face." Shelby said as he motioned the others back with his hand.

David was just approaching from the guardroom. "No key, Shel. I looked everywhere."

"We don't need one. I've got it picked," he said as he placed a flame to the fuse. It sputtered and went silent for a moment before exploding with a dull, muffled whump. Shelby pulled the door open. "Let's get outta' here before we attract any attention."

Sorek was fascinated. "What in the world is that stuff?"

"Just toilet paper."

"Is it for blowin' stuff up," asked Aryan. "or did you just use it for that?"

"Actually it's for cleaning stuff up," grinned David in amusement.

"Impressive," Sorek said as he scratched his rough chin in thought. "I could think of a hundred uses for it."

"A hundred and one, Sorek," mused Shelby. "I'd say when you need the stuff, it's about as valuable as gold."

Sorek reached for the folded paper inquisitively. "What do you use it for...besides blowing up door locks?"

Well, now he had Shelby over a barrel with no graceful way out. The young man looked over at his companion seeking help. David stepped right in with both feet. He took the roll and unrolled a few sheets. Wrapping it around his hand he stated matter-of -factly. "We use it instead of leaves or rocks. Then we just bury it."

For a long moment, Sorek twisted his face in confusion, then understanding began to settle in and change his color a bit. He grinned sheepishly. "I'll be switched. Instead of leaves, you say?"

The small group took off the way they had come. This time David took the point, and Shelby brought up the rear. Sorek and Anatol held Aryan's arms and helped him in his weakness. As it turned out, most of his problem was simply stiffness, and he was soon on his own. He was a little wobbly, but running on his own two feet.

Shelby looked at his watch. "DC, we'd better get Bob on the radio before we go back underground. He needs to be ready for us."

"Right." David replied as he pulled his radio. Bob was supposed to climb to the hilltop with his radio every hour on the hour in case they should call. Being in the cave, they had not tried to notify him before this and now found Bob alert and sounding relieved. They all listened as David relayed Aryan's condition as well as their possible arrival time to Bob.

Suddenly, David ended his transmission and motioned the others into a darkened corner. At the top of the stairway they heard approaching soldiers. Quickly, they squatted in the corner to wait. The soldiers passed. They seemed alert and were checking the palace, but it was unlikely that they had heard the small explosion through the thick, stone walls.

After the passage was clear they continued, but the alerted soldiers stuck in Shelby's mind. *What if they had found the opened blowhole already? What if they waited for them even now? What if they entered the hole and waited in the cave? No. Kadian and Bob would deal with that.* He expressed his concerns to the others, and they agreed that it was very likely.

"The only other way out is the main entrance, and it is surely guarded," Sorek said. "We must at least try to go back. Maybe they didn't find it."

The rest agreed and they moved on. From time to time they heard soldiers but saw none, so they quietly retraced their steps to the blowhole. The fact that they encountered no one indicated that the palace was practically empty. Once it had housed hundreds of men. Now fewer than two dozen remained within its walls.

Thousands across his command had deserted Croseus. And the common people were on the verge of revolt. The desertions were common knowledge among them and the talk in every tavern. Any day now their courage would flourish enough to attack the palace and retake it for themselves.

Most all of the Cartokians, except for the children, remembered when they had had a good king in the palace. They had been welcome there then. Peace and prosperity had been abundant. But then Croseus came. He had killed their king and taken over the land. They had been slaves to him and the High Sorcerer since that day. Now the sorcerer was dead and Croseus' army was dwindling.

The tavern talk and village gossip spoke of strange and powerful men among the Tekoans…noble men who walked with the God of the Tekoans. These men possessed power beyond that of their gods. No matter. The Cartokian people had no quarrel with the Tekoans and had never feared them. The Tekoans were a gentle, resourceful people. If the God of Tekoa was fair and just, and these men could call on His power and protection, then the Cartokians might someday again welcome the Tekoans as friends.

As the rescue team approached Croseus' room, Aryan was beginning to grow more steady. It was very quiet, almost too quiet. Each man had an augury feeling and these were men that paid attention to such feelings. Sorek motioned each man into a hidden position. Anatol then walked briskly into the room, and started for the blowhole. He removed the blanket with a flourish and started to enter.

There was a rush of activity as three men attacked him. But the ambushers' movement was simply a queue the rescue squad waited for, and instantly they were upon the soldiers. Within seconds the soldiers were unconscious, and the rescue team started to squirm back through the blowhole.

Shelby restlessly awaited his turn in the darkened room. Other soldiers might come, or these could wake up and he would be left to fend for himself. His friends would not know for several minutes that he was in trouble. *Hurry, please hurry.* Finally, the last man disappeared through the dark hole and Shelby started forward. Something hit him in the head. A wicked blow and he was out.

Chapter 21

Croseus stood in the dark room with a brass lamp stand in his hand. As he wondered about the intruder, he kicked his men into awareness and they began to stir. "Get up you fools!" he yelled angrily in Cartokian. "Your blundering allowed the others to escape. Someone light the lamp and let's see what we have here."

He kicked curiously at the blowhole. "Does anyone know where this goes?"

"No, Master," came a soldier's timid reply. "They are simply air vents. There are others in the palace, but how they blow air or where they begin is not known to us."

"Quickly then, fill this in with dirt and rock. And place guards at the other vents." He barked quick and decisive orders, and the soldiers moved into action. He then turned back to the man on the floor and rolled him over. Instantly, he recognized the young Texan and his hatred mounted. He would never forget the humiliation this young man had caused the day of the ceremony. And he would certainly never forget the damage he had done to his command.

Now, after weeks of tracking and scouring the countryside, after the desertion of almost a thousand men and the death of so many more, his hated enemy lay at his feet. How had he come to be here and for what purpose? Who were the others that had escaped? He had a dozen questions for this Texan and he would get his answers. And, oh, how he would enjoy getting those answers.

"Tie his hands behind him, and pour water on him. I need answers…now!"

Startled, Shelby rolled over slowly. He looked up through clouded vision at several dark figures standing over him. He started to speak but was splashed with water again and gasped for air. He got to his feet only to be knocked down again. They kicked him and spat on him as they yelled their curses.

His thinking was not yet clear, but he possessed enough discipline to avoid crying out. Again he got to his feet, and again they were kicked from under him. Without hesitation he got up again. A soldier started to kick his leg once more, and Shelby raised his foot, caught the man in the shin and sent him to the floor in pain.

He was seeing clearly now and recognized Croseus. A wicked smile broke his lips, and his figure straightened. "We meet again, great evil one." The comment brought a lash from Croseus' scourge. *Perhaps that was a bit smart aleck,* he thought.

"Why are you here, Texan?" He spoke perfect English.

Instantly, the picture was clear for Shelby. *Then he doesn't know about the rescue. He probably forgot he even had Aryan down there. I must keep it that way.* "It's well known that your army has dwindled. How far, we didn't know and had to find out. We were here to defeat you once and for all."

Croseus laughed. "But your companions...they ran like rats."

"No. They hurried for the others when we saw how few men you have. We were just a recon team. By tomorrow they will return and overrun this place. It was only a matter of time anyway. Surely you knew that."

Croseus may not have believed, him but he couldn't afford not to be warned and ready. He leaned over and laid a knife against Shelby's face. "Where do they exit the air vent? Tell me now, or I will slowly cut out your heart."

"I have no way of knowing that! There are dozens of other air vents in the woods by the village...surely you must know that. We entered one of them, but they could leave by any of them. It would be impossible to know, so I do no harm to them by telling you."

It was a bluff. Shelby had no way of knowing about any other blowholes by the village, but if he could get Croseus to waste his few resources in the woods west of the village, his companions could get away. The dragon hole was over a mile away to the northeast, and surely they would never imagine that to be where they were.

Croseus took the bait. "Assemble the men, but leave me one squad to guard the palace and, of course, our new prisoner. Scour those woods, and don't come back without them. They must not get word back to their army."

The men scrambled into action. In moments they stood alone together, listening to receding footfalls on the stone corridors. "Now, Texan. Let's talk. Just you and me." Croseus was calm now, and his tone was conversational. "I am a very wealthy man, and I could also make you a wealthy man. Working together, we could be rich beyond measure. Work with me, and you will want for nothing as long as you live."

"What are you getting at? What can I offer that you don't already have?"

"The way back! You came from the other side. I know. I have heard the talk, and I must go there."

"Why? If you are rich, as you say you are, why leave?"

"To be richer. Don't you see? My gold, on the other side... in that world..."

"You must be crazy. I wouldn't betray my world and subject it to your kind of vermin."

Croseus flared with anger, and wanted to lash out at this insubordinate youth, but he restrained his temper. "What would it take? Name your price. You could take it back, and you would have everything."

"I wouldn't have my self-respect. No deal. We are as opposite as the poles of a magnet, and I don't sell out my values."

"You idiot!" Croseus screamed and hit Shelby with his scourge. The Texan flinched but took it without a whimper. That seemed to drive Croseus insane, and he beat him again and again until he had to stop from exhaustion.

He called out, and an evil looking little man resembling the earlier sorcerer entered the room. He was dressed much the same in a flowing robe that sparkled like a Las Vegas cowboy outfit and dragged along the floor. A gold medallion, similar to the one Croseus boasted, hung from his neck, and each finger blustered a ring.

He bowed and spoke from a kneeling position as he kissed Croseus' hand. "I am at your service, Master Croseus." Shelby didn't understand his words, but some things are clear in any language. He was plainly a bootlicking, sniveling little creep. Every culture had them and every decent man despised them.

His beady eyes studied Shelby past thick, bushy eyebrows that carried a perpetual scowl. Obviously, he considered the Texan a mere dog. His pitted face twisted beneath a coal black mustache as though he had just had a long drink of sour milk.

Shelby looked at the shriveled up wanna-be man with greasy, slicked down, black hair, and almost laughed. If he had not been in so much pain from the whip lashings, he might have.

Croseus gloated. "Meet Soron, my new sorcerer. He is young but eager and needs a lot of practice." As he spoke his figure straightened, and a gleam of pride washed over him. "I am his mentor. Before he finishes, you will tell me everything I want to know. Tomorrow, I believe I will show him some of my more unique skills. I think I shall first teach him to skin your right arm. Yes, that will be a good place to start. From there we can be more… creative. You will talk. Oh yes, you will beg me to let you talk. Think about that in your dark cell tonight. Take him away, Soron."

The sorcerer put a razor sharp sword point against Shelby's neck and said something in a squeaky voice that resembled fingernails on a chalkboard. He flicked the blade and laughed. Blood trickled from Shelby's throat. Then, with another nudge of the sword he urged him back down a stairway that Shelby knew well by now. He opened the first cell and pushed him in.

The only light was Soron's lantern, and it didn't reach inside the cell. He didn't need to see. He could smell, and he remembered the hideous corpse there from before. The stench almost made him vomit, and he knew he could not endure the night here, nor did he intend to.

The cell door had no sooner slammed shut than he was working out his plan. For a second time the Cartoks had failed to search him. He still retained his possibles bag and in it was all he needed to repeat his earlier door lock trick…toilet paper and all.

Croseus had ordered a squad to remain behind. *Well then, at least a half dozen men were still here somewhere.* He knew he must be out of the dungeon before the men retired to the guardhouse. Once they were there, he would never get past them. Worse yet, he would still be there when Soron returned the next morning. He knew he couldn't let that happen.

He found it even easier to perform his escape trick the second time. Within twenty minutes he was upstairs trying to locate the palace entrance. He worked quickly, mapping the passages in his mind and noting markings on the walls, anything that might offer direction clues later. He knew he had until the soldiers went to the guardhouse downstairs to move about freely and make his escape. Once they discovered that he was missing, the search would be on and the palace sealed tight.

He remembered that the main entrance was on the south wall. His route took him through a maze of passages and rooms in that general direction. Once more he passed the familiar hallway to Croseus' wing. He made a mental note, for he planned another visit.

Now he made his own markings on the walls. They would not attract the attention of the palace occupants, but his simple scratches would be his road map if he had to move back through in a hurry.

He heard the soldiers before he saw them. They were eating and drinking in a drab, torchlit dining hall. He watched them through the crack in the door and counted six. Croseus and Soron were there too, and that would make eight. Someone had to cook and others were on duty at the entrance, so the count probably went to about a dozen.

He turned around and found himself in a grand gallery. It was a very large room decorated with thick drapery and fine paintings. At one end gaped a huge, open hearth... the biggest fireplace Shelby had ever seen. A full size man could walk directly into it and take six steps from end to end. He looked up at a carved and painted ceiling twenty feet above the floor. Old as it was, it had the mark of a master. Two dozen lanterns lit the space, and several hallways, including his, converged here.

As he walked to the center, he could see eight hallways emitting from where he stood. It was like the hub of a giant wheel, and from here a direct route led to every wing in the palace. He noticed a larger hall lined with flags leading off to the south and decided that it would be the main entrance.

With great care, he made his way along the lengthy hall. There would be soldiers, he knew, but he had no idea where they might be. The corridor had too many darkened places where a man might lay in wait...darkened places that he could also use to his advantage. Quiet as a shadow, he moved from one cove of darkness to another.

After several minutes, he began to hear low, conversational voices. At their distance they were just a wash of echoing mumble, but as he approached they became more clear. The echoing sound in the hallway was deceiving, but it gave him some idea of the soldier's distance. Only when he began to detect some direct sound did he stop, carefully listen, and try to determine exactly where they were.

Two soldiers talked lazily, and he soon had their location. He also determined that he had gone as far as he could go. They had most excellent guard positions, and he certainly couldn't expect to get past them. Shelby sat down to think beside an elaborately carved trunk. It was in a shadow, and its bulk would somewhat conceal his outline against the gray, hallway wall.

Before a plan developed, a clattering of a triangle sounded an alarm. At home such a bell was a call to dinner, but here it was sure to be an alarm announcing his escape. Indeed, mere moments later he heard soldiers running toward him from the direction of the dining hall. From the entrance, the other two guards started down from their posts to see what the commotion was. He was exposed and trapped between them. No place to run and no apparent place to hide, just an empty hallway with soldiers approaching from both ends.

Croseus led the small group in a mad rush toward the entrance. Each had a torch and a musket, and they did a quick, running search of every nook in the corridor. Later, if necessary, they would be more thorough, but what was needed now was to quickly cover as much territory as possible.

David eased down from the cleft, and Kadian took his feet. They all worked to get Aryan down. He had quickly exhausted and needed rest and nourishment. They laid him on the ground, and for the first several minutes they gathered cheerfully around him.

Kadian had warmly greeted his old friend but now stood looking up into the black crevasse. He was growing concerned. Minutes had passed, and nothing stirred in the black notch above him.

He turned to the others. "Hey, guys. Where's Shelby?"

The cheerful little group fell suddenly silent trying to piece together the events of the past few minutes. There had been the attack, the scuffle, and every man was on his own. Each looked at the other hoping for a clue. One didn't exist.

David jumped up. "Get me in that hole, Kadian!" The big man caught him in mid-air and shoved him upward. David clawed and kicked for traction, then was gone. A few pebbles and loosened dirt trickled down, then everything went quiet.

David made it to the blowhole in record time only to find it being systematically filled in. The voices outside were muffled by the growing dirt barrier, and finally they went silent. David went helplessly limp for a moment, then hit the dirt with his fist as frightened anger took hold of his emotions.

Later, in the corridors of the dark cavern, a heated debate began. David and Anatol wanted to go back for Shelby immediately, but the others feared a blundering attempt would only make things worse. Sorek finally took command and started the reluctant group out of the cavern. They had accomplished their mission and couldn't begin another without a well thought out plan. Shelby was obviously a prisoner, and Croseus would want to get as much mileage out of that fact as possible. That would give them some time to get back and plan another way into the palace, even if it meant going through the front gate.

Shelby gently lifted the lid of the trunk and peeked out. The soldiers had moved their search elsewhere for the moment, so he must move on before a more thorough search unveiled his hiding place. He quietly stepped out and closed the lid.

More soldiers had reinforced the guard posts at the entrance so his chances of going that way, for now, were slim. He chose the shadows of the corridor back toward the hub and turned off at the first opportunity.

He found a storage room stocked against lean times. It wanted for little, everything from barrels of whiskey to block and tackle. Shelby made a quick survey and selected some small rope, a dozen candles, timber nails or spikes, and a couple of apples. That done, he looked for another way out of the room and found a passage on the far side that led outside.

It opened onto a courtyard that was empty for the moment, but six other doorways opened onto it. The quadrant was large…a half acre would be a modest estimate. Every inch of it cobblestone, except for a twenty foot square near the center that was dirt. Lush vines covered the north-facing walls and shadowed a dribbling fountain.

The trickling water looked inviting, but the six doors offered no warning to the approach of his enemy. Shelby thought about that for a moment as he looked at the rope and spikes he held. They were indeed his enemy and must be treated as such. They were after him, and they meant to kill him in the end. Whatever he had to do to slow them down, or stop them completely, was fair play.

As he looked on, two men emerged, one to throw out a bucket of water and the other to get firewood stacked nearby. Shelby deduced their door to be that of the kitchen. As he watched from the shadows he heard the soldiers enter the room behind him. The search was too near.

He slipped outside just as the two cooks went back in. Then, in broad daylight, he walked to the thick vines. He wanted to run with all his speed, but that would attract attention. He walked calmly, hoping that if anyone happened to catch him out of the corner of his eye, he would not be alerted.

The vines covered him completely and were sturdy enough to climb, so he started upward. The new location on top offered nothing. The roof was too steep to traverse, and it was encircled with a sentry walk. Soldiers were searching there too. He eased back into the vines to hide and plan.

This cat and mouse game would not get him out of the palace. It would simply go on until they prevailed. He must make them leery of him…less careful and less thorough. Only in their carelessness could he hope for escape.

An hour later he rolled a barrel of whiskey into the main hall and hid it behind a huge drape. With his knife he made a small hole and let the wicked beverage drip out and soak the floor and wick up the drapes. Then in the shelter of the drapery, he lit a small, well positioned candle and left. He repeated his task in two other well chosen locations down the hall.

Soon he heard them coming again, working their way toward him. Quickly, he chose a darkened section of passage and stretched a trip line just off the floor. Then, cringing with guilt, he broke several glass bottles and scattered them about.

When the soldiers made the corner he stepped out of the shadows at the other end of the corridor. He stood watching them in a torchlit pool of light. "You lookin' for me?"

As one man they ran in attack. As one man they tripped and fell into the broken glass. Shelby winced at their screams. *It's your own fault. You shouldn't be trying to kill me, guys.*

In the main hallway another group of four men searched. They discovered the almost empty trunk, where Shelby had intentionally gone back and placed a half-eaten apple core. The discovery brought on a concerned discussion. Not only was this Texan slippery, he was now taunting them, and that was unsettling. They had all heard the stories of the past weeks, and, even though they were brave men, they were weak with superstition.

The soldiers were checking behind the hallway drapes when suddenly they burst into flame. The curtains went to the ceiling, as did the fire. Within minutes, as they fought to bring the fire under control, two more broke into flame down the hall. Shelby had sent his first message, and it was well received.

The evening brought serious talk among the guards in the guardhouse. On their bunks lay companions already willing to give up the search. Several booby traps had left all but two in serious condition. They had encountered a dozen traps in all, and each had taken its toll. Most had only caused injury, but two of their number lay dead, impaled on timber spikes.

The Texan was playing for keeps now, and several times during the night he awoke from short spurts of rest to stir their fears even more. At one point before sunrise, he rolled a keg of whiskey down the stairwell to the guardhouse and set it aflame. They retreated against the back wall to escape the heat and wait for the flame to die. One barrel posed no real physical threat, but, the possibility of more...emotionally, it was a disaster.

By morning, no one ventured out to search. The Texan could have the whole palace if he wanted it. Their allegiance to Croseus was going the way of their many, smarter companions who had already left.

Soron awoke with a start. Shelby stood over him, tickling his nose with a feather. He lay petrified, as Shelby knew such a man would. He was a coward who could only show strength over men whom others had already rendered harmless.

As he started to jerk away, Shelby held up his hand, and in a quickly made up sign language, he pointed to the many strings tied to the man's toes and fingers. They were almost taut and connected to a small, carved, wooden trigger mechanism. Shelby ran his finger along the string and up to Soron's sharp sword, which hung suspended four feet above his chest and poised to drop at the slightest move.

The man went pale and whimpered a plea. Shelby couldn't understand his words, but their meaning was clear enough. He replied in disgust, "Why is it that men who beg for mercy never give it?" He picked up the sorcerer's medallion from the nightstand and meticulously rolled up the gold chain. As he turned to leave, he noticed the magician's robe and wondered if it was as flammable as an earlier one he had set afire. He tossed it in the fireplace that had been banked against the night. It smoldered a moment and burst into flames.

Shelby tossed the medallion in the air and caught it with a flourish. "I wouldn't move if I was you. Maybe for…about a week."

Soron blinked his eyes as he strained to make his dry mouth swallow, and like a ghost, the Texan was gone. He looked up at his poised sword and caught the glint of the sharpened point he had so carefully honed. Sweat beaded up on his pale brow, and it was a cool morning.

Shelby moved cautiously down the hall toward the main gate. He had plans of attempting it once again. After all, he had given them a rough night, and they might be less alert, allowing him to slip passed. On the other hand, the palace was quiet, and he had seen or heard no one in almost an hour. Perhaps they lay in wait. It would be safer for them than moving about among his traps.

He passed the burned drapes and blackened walls, still stamped with the smell of smoke. The damage he had done to such a beautiful place grieved him, but survival justifies things in a man that are otherwise wanton. He thought of the men he had hurt or killed and wondered if it could have been any other way. *No! They chose their path. They made me a fugitive. They hunted an innocent man. The guilt of this is not mine.*

A moment of anger swept over him… anger at what he had become and who had driven him to it. He was justified in it, he knew, but what would his poor mamma think. She had taught him kindness and respect for all living things. She had taught him to avoid violence, yet he had become violent. Knowing it wasn't his fault didn't matter… it still shamed him.

He passed a familiar corridor, and after a long moment of angry thought, he turned into it. He had something he needed to do.

An hour later he was nearing the main gate once again. The guard rounded the corner before he could react. He froze. The man held a musket and awkwardly leveled it on Shelby's chest. A moment of fear was in the guard's eyes as he tried to decide what to do. He had caught the dreaded Texan. He held his musket on the man who had made fools of his gods.

Shelby remained still, showing no emotion. He stared into the man's unsure eyes. Mere seconds passed, but they seemed eternal. The soldier cautiously dropped the muzzle of his musket and spoke something quiet and friendly. His words meant nothing to the Texan, but his purpose was clear. He gestured and turned, indicating for Shelby to follow. The soldier led him to the main gate and pushed open one of the huge doors. He stood there grinning and motioned for Shelby to open the other.

Together they walked outside and could see curious villagers, paused from their morning duties, watching them. Then, in plain view, and for them all to see, the soldier smashed his musket against the stone wall and walked off toward the village. Shelby stepped over to the flagpole and retreated the ugly black dragon head flag that Croseus flew. He ripped it in half and threw it to the ground.

Within minutes, scores of shouting villagers ran toward the palace. Hope leaped in their hearts, and questions occupied their minds. Could they retake their palace once again and put their own king on its throne? And what of Croseus? Was he finally destroyed or gone?

Croseus awoke to the sound of a yelling mob and broke a cold sweat. He leaped from bed and opened his door. Men from the village approached from the long hallway. They were inside the palace! He slammed his door shut and turned back to his quarters. *What has happened?* His mind raced for a plan of action, a way out. He must escape!

As his tortured mind raced, his eyes unconsciously scanned the room and fell on a sight that chilled his soul. A dagger, stuck deep into his paneled wall. It had been stabbed through a note. And hanging from it was a medallion on a gold chain. Instinctively, he grabbed for his own medallion and discovered it was still around his neck. He held it and looked at its jeweled dragon head and realized that the medallion on the dagger belonged to his sorcerer, for it had no such jewels. In disbelief he walked over to it and withdrew the dagger. His veins ran cold as he read the note.

Mornin', Captain Crawford,
Yes, I know who you are. I suspected it when I found your plane, but I needed more to go on. Now, after finding your dog tags and flight suit among your collectibles, I know for certain.
How can an officer of the United States military stoop so low and become so corrupt? You are a disgrace, and I will make that fact known when I return home.
By the time you read this I will have left this palace and again be free. You, sir, have been defeated and left with nothing.
May you live many miserable years.
Shelby Ferris, Texan.

Croseus crumpled the note in disbelief. His enemy, the impudent young Texan, had been in his quarters and played around like it was some game. His mind was in a rage, but panic drove his actions. He ran to his gold chest and flung it open. It was empty! He screamed at the top of his lungs. "I will kill you, Shelby Ferris!" But even as he said it, he didn't know how he would do it. If he couldn't do it with a thousand men, how could he do it alone?

He sat still for a moment, lost in a swirling, clouded mind and trembling in a wicked rage. His pulse beat with such force that he imagined he could hear it, and fury commanded his every action. Then, like a wild man, he tore through his quarters, destroying everything that would break and overturning everything that wouldn't. The pounding in his head grew louder and louder. Suddenly, his senses returned enough for him to realize the pounding to be an angry mob bashing at his door. He turned in time to see a heavy, timber battering ram splinter its way through the huge, oak door and retreat for another blow.

Shelby walked around the side of the palace to six large sacks of gold he had dropped over the wall. He took three of them into the woods and temporarily covered them before returning for the others. These he brought back to the entrance and scattered along the road for the women and children who had gathered as their men went into the palace. Then, gallantly tipping his hat, he walked back into the woods. He shouldered the remainder of the heavy gold and headed for Tekoa.

Chapter 22

There was a party in Tekoa that night… a grand party with lanterns lining the street and dancing, singing, sovereign people loose from the bonds of domination. After over twenty years, they once more had their freedom and their pride. This day had marked their new independence, something they intended to guard as precious with each coming moment. On this day each father stood a little taller before his family. Each mother would tuck her children into bed with a new hope in her heart and a different prayer on her lips. It was a good day in the shadow of the great mountain.

Aryan was the center of attention. Tired as he was when they pulled him into town on a travois, he now seemed to have a new strength. Bon refused to leave his side, and he seemed to draw a great power from that.

Shelby had arrived to a cheering crowd several hours after the others and had immediately gone to see Sardisai. The old gentleman's eyes sparkled at the sight of him.

"When they came back without you, Son, we all took it pretty hard. The whole town was ready to head for that palace in the morning, men and women alike. Now, just listen to them out there in the night. There hasn't been this kind of happiness here in…. well, too long, Son, much too long."

"I brought something back for your people. It isn't much, but it should make up for some of the bad times." Shelby hefted one of the gold sacks to the table and let some of the gold spill out. "Maybe this will help get this town back on its feet again."

Sardisai was speechless, but after a few awkward moments, managed a few simple words. "Shelby, where'd you get this?"

"From the palace. Croseus sends his regards. Yonder's two more sacks," he said as he pointed over his shoulder with an upturned thumb.

"You must tell me about Croseus... but not now. There's a party out there, and you are one of the honored guests. Go. Enjoy the gratitude of my people."

Shelby went out to the celebration, but there was a melancholy mood working him over. He chose to stand off by himself in the shadows. He felt good about how everything had turned out, and he liked these people, but something was wrong. He finally decided he must be a little homesick. A restless feeling stirred him, and he yearned to start back. It was a natural feeling a man gets when his job is finished and done well. Besides, he never enjoyed sitting around with nothing to do, and he certainly didn't like crowds.

A girl emerged from the herd of high-spirited folks and urged him to join in the fun. Reluctantly, he followed her into the crowd and offered his howdy to those that initiated talk. In short, concise statements, he answered their questions in a way that wouldn't encourage further conversation. He was pleasant enough to them, but with each moment came an added degree of crowd claustrophobia.

Someone slapped him on the back. "Shelby, you old sidewinder, when do we go home?" He turned to see Bob. And then there was Deccan, jug in hand, grinnin' from ear to ear and staggering to keep vertical.

"Real soon, Bob. I've gotta'... Never mind. I'll tell you later. You better get him home and into bed before he does something stupid."

"He already did."

Shelby realized another reason he hated social functions. People he liked and respected would get a little tipsy or sometimes all out smashed. He hated seeing his friends that way and could never imagine allowing anything to tarnish one's judgment. What if there were some kind of an emergency and a clear mind was needed? Most of the fools at the party would just add to the problem.

The corner of his eye caught an exaggerated movement. It was Vishti waving at him. He walked over. She was holding to David with a prominently possessive grip, but he looked to be enjoying it. Grinning, he said, "What happened back there, Shel?"

"Me an' Croseus had a run-in but it's all settled now." He was short and to the point. He wanted to talk to David and tell him everything, but this wasn't the time nor the place.

David understood his friend and knew he must feel like a treed 'coon. David was much the same way, but Vishti was taking care of that. He was absorbed in her gentle nature, and nothing could rile him now. Still, he felt for his kindred companion and reached out for something he might enjoy.

"Shel, they're servin' the sweetest melon over under that tree. It's almost like a Black Diamond, and I know how you love those. Better get some before its gone."

"Thanks, DC, I'll do that." He reached up and touched the brim of his hat in a gesture of courtesy. "Ma'am."

"I'm glad you're safe, Shelby. You certainly have an uncommon way of keeping folks on the edge of their seat."

With that said, David and Vishti walked off arm in arm, and Shelby headed for the watermelon. He did turn back long enough to see if Sorek was following them. He grinned as he realized that he wasn't.

Shelby sat under that tree and put away a whole melon before he patted his tight stomach and walked off into the night. The road out of town was quiet, as were the houses he passed. Behind him, the party clamored on… it was the only disturbance in the entire valley. Before him, the night creatures went about their nightly duties, unaware that this day was any different from the one before it.

In the distance, silhouetted above the trees and marked faintly by the moon, stood the copper dome of Wardenclyffe. It drew Shelby as surely as a magnet draws iron. It took twenty minutes to walk the distance but he soon stood in the doorway of the once buzzing and humming power station. It rested now. He had never rewired it since the night he recreated Tesla's great experiment. They didn't need it right away. There were fewer than two dozen lights in the whole town. Reverently, he ran his fingers along the hand-written door sign and wondered who had printed it. Had it been the great inventor himself?

The scant light of a waning moon lit the doorway but not the interior. It didn't matter… he didn't desire to go stumbling around in there anyway. He looked up at the tower and decided to climb it. He had no reason other than it was something to do on this lonely night.

From the top he had a grand view of the peaceful valley. Long fingers of silver mist hung low to the ground and probed the deeper canyons and depressions. He sat, awestruck, under a canopy of a million stars that served to decorate his own private theater. From his spot the village was a mere golden glow a mile or so across the pasture. Tekoa Mountain raised dominant above the horizon as though it guarded the land. The moon washed it silvery-blue, and a gray ghostly wisp drifted upward from its peak. In the opposite direction loomed the great tabletop with its silent city in the sky that he would always remember.

Frogs sang in a pond somewhere to the south and encircling him was a chorus of night creatures unrivaled by any music man might compose. Blue shadows marked the trail he had walked, and a coyote's wail drifted on the soft breeze. The landscape was marked with such grand beauty it gave him the feeling that God had just touched this spot.

An hour passed, then two. Shelby remained, reluctant to leave the evening's performance. He had counted nineteen meteors, seven bats, a dozen coyotes, a horned owl and a loon.

Suddenly, in the distance he noticed seven bright lights much like very intense stars. They began as white but soon evolved in color as they drifted upward. On occasion they would dart sideways in a straight line then resume their wandering and color changing. Some would disappear, and others would take their place. At their peak, Shelby counted fourteen.

He had been so intent on the brighter points of light that he almost failed to notice the backdrop curtain of pastel color that washed the sky behind them. It was a small version of aurora, which he knew to be caused by magnetic forces. They moved and changed color gently, almost imperceptibly, then violently, but remained very dim. Then, as quickly as they had appeared, they were gone, both the points and the curtain.

He had never seen anything like it and knew of no phenomenon that might account for it. Unless…. He played it back over and over in his mind as he walked back to town. *Could those be the Tekoan version of the Marfa Lights?* Later he would ask Sardisai. The old chief seemed to have seen so much in his time here in this strange land.

The next two days were spent in preparation to leave. Sardisai had consulted the Nephilim and they said the Texans had just missed an opening of the gateway the night before and the next would occur in two days. There would be two window opportunities; each twelve hours apart, starting at 11:00AM. They would last about twenty minutes each. If they missed those they were stuck for another two weeks.

Bob and Shelby were restless, but David spent every waking moment with Vishti. He was somber, and she cried a lot. One evening David showed up wearing Vishti's amber tear drop pendant.

"As nice as that is, DC, you wear it back in Texas and you might get a real ribbing."

"I'm not sure I'm goin' back, Shel. What do you think about me stayin' behind?"

"Are you crazy, DC?"

"I could work with these these folks, just like I've been doin', Shel. They're eager to learn about new agriculture. Do you realize what I could do in this valley?"

Shelby looked thoughtfully at his friend and noticed a thin, white strip around his otherwise tan finger. That spot had belonged to his class ring. *This is not about agriculture. This is a lot more serious.* Shelby looked at his own A & M ring with its crossed sabers, cannon and shield. No girl was worth such a ring. To give it away, after what it took to get it, bordered on unthinkable.

Shelby tried to talk some sense into his companion but found it an uphill trek. "Maybe later DC, but not now. What about your family? Your lettin' your heart do your thinkin', and that's not good." After a quiet moment he added, "DC, don't forget, we know how to come back."

The two days went slowly for Bob. While David was being tortured over leaving his girl, Bob was equally tortured as he endured the wait to see his. Shelby, on the other hand, spent his time with Sardisai. He had a passion for knowledge, and the old man was an athenaeum.

Shelby had always sought the company of older folks as long as he could remember. He longed to sit at their feet as they told of times past and of places they had been. He loved to hear history unfold in their wonderful stories. He thought he understood death and knew why it was necessary, but each time an elderly person died it was like someone had burned a library. Their stories were gone, forever, and at such a loss to those that never thought to ask, until it was too late.

Shelby had grown up on those stories, both from his grandfather and an uncle. His grandfather had ignited his young life with stories of trail drives and big cities like Fort Worth and Abilene, when they were still just railhead stockyards. He told of traveling across Texas in a covered wagon as a young boy and peeking out from under the canvas to see the Alamo for the first time.

Shelby's Uncle Jack had kept that interest alive. He was one of the last real cowboys and could spin a good story like a master artisan. In the evenings after the chores were done he would sit back next to a crackling fire and recount events that would make all the kids bristle with excitement. A twinkle would come to his eye, and the golden firelight turned magic. The flickering shadows played out the lowing cattle, and one could almost hear his old saddle creak.

The television had replaced that for most kids, and as much as Shelby loved technology, he loathed much of what it had done and how it had impoverished people's minds.

Finally, the days passed, and they were off. The sad farewells had been said, and three Texas boys were headed home. The others would have gone with them to the cave but for the danger. Sardisai had been warned that Croseus had escaped the palace. The man was said to have a dozen loyal followers, and revenge burned his soul. Sardisai also warned against their being followed through the gateway. At all cost, Croseus must not discover the way.

They moved with caution, keeping to the low ground and moving quickly. They could not afford to miss the opening time. David checked his compass and compared it to the crude map he had drawn in his journal. They felt sure they would remember the route to Bon's cave, but they couldn't afford to wander even a bit.

Bob pointed to David's journal. "You guard that thing like its gold or somethin'."

"It is, Bob." replied Shelby. "To an explorer a journal is priceless. David writes everything in that notebook, and if something happens to us… well, someone can read about it and learn from it."

"Anything in there 'bout me?"

David grinned. "Maybe I'll read that part to your wife."

Sure enough, like seasoned troops they walked directly to the cave. Shelby looked at his watch…the gateway should open in about fifteen minutes. That was too close… they had spent too much time with goodbyes. They should still have time, but who was to say these things were that predictable?

Shelby turned up a goatskin for a drink, and Bob did likewise before passing the waterbag on to David. "Better drink this, DC." Bob said grinning. "You're gonna' need your mind sharp and your urine clear."

David laughed. "I see you got the lecture."

A bullet splattered the rock wall of the cave, and broken flakes stung David's face.

"Inside!" yelled Bob. As one man they tumbled into the opening and to the floor.

Shelby growled through clinched teeth. "Croseus!"

"You should've fixed his wagon when you had the chance, Shel," Bob said. Shelby made no reply. The comment didn't warrant one.

David voiced a concerned comment. "We can't forget how dangerous that man is and our promise to those people back there."

"What are you gettin' at, DC?" quizzed Shelby.

"Just that he now knows where the gateway is, and that leaves us with only one choice. For the sake of all those folks back there and all the folks in our world, we can't let him leave this place."

Bob joined in, alarmed, "Just hold on there! I don't know what you guys are thinking, but I'm goin' home, and don't even think of tryin' to stop me. You can play hero if you want, but leave me out of it!"

"Easy, Bob. I got a hunch we can pull this off and still take care of the Devil's angel out there." As Shelby spoke, several bullets ricocheted off the back wall and cut the air dangerously close to them.

"Well, think hard, cowboy, 'cause they got guns, and we ain't got nothin'!" Bob's voice was starting to crack with the excitement.

David pulled out the flare gun. "This won't stop anybody, but it might slow them down."

Shelby turned. "How many flares are left?"

"Two."

"Good! Let's go!" Shelby said as he took off in a run toward the dark corridors of the cave. David and Shelby switched on their flashlights, and with Bob running between them, they made the dimension warp in ten minutes.

Shelby stopped short of the thunderous rumble to communicate instructions. "I'm going to set a trap for them and ignite this methane."

"With what Shel?" David asked. "I don't think a match or a candle will set off firedamp… the flash point is too high. You'd have to be here to create some kind of spark or something. You don't plan to do that do you? 'Cause when this stuff goes, it's liable to take the whole top off this cave."

"I'm gonna' use a flare. I know for a fact that phosphorous will set off anything. Now, you two run ahead, and if the gateway is open, get out of here. Whatever you do don't stay too long in the firedamp. Sardisai told me it has a strange effect on your mind and makes you forget stuff."

"Can you be a little more… specific about that, Shel?" David asked.

"He explained it as nature's way of protecting this gateway. He said long exposure to the gas would make us forget most everything that has recently happened to us. It would all seem like a dream and not real. Say, maybe we ought to leave Bob down here a while."

"Real funny, Shel." Bob was not amused.

"When we came through before, we moved pretty fast so it didn't bother us. We need to do the same goin' back. Now, you guys git! I'll see you on the other side."

David and Bob took off through the warp, and Shelby went to work with his booby trap. Remembering Sardisai's warning, he held his breath and chose a spot that he was sure was well within the firedamp. Using dental floss, he strung a trip line across the floor and arranged it to trigger the drop of the flare. He used duct tape to attach rocks to the flare for added weight and positioned it to fall on its primer cap. Several times he had to go back down the tunnel for a fresh breath of air. But, at last, the deadly trap was set.

He stood up carefully and stepped over the trip line. He heard them coming, then saw their torches. *Torches! They could possibly set off the firedamp. If they waved them around a bit, they would burn hotter. It was at least a possibility.* The thought eased his soul somewhat. It was a little like having one member of a firing squad fire blanks. You never knew who fired the fatal bullet. And Shelby would prefer living with the possibility that their torches set off the explosion.

He crossed the warp, still holding his breath and caught up to the others. "Why haven't you gone out?"

David pointed to the ceiling and said quietly. "It's not open yet, Shel. We're trapped."

Horror stricken, all eyes turned helplessly down the dark tunnel toward the warp. True, it was a good hundred yards away, but such an explosion would offer no mercy.

As if on queue, a dull, deep whump sounded and was followed by a growing roar. The tunnel glowed orange and suddenly a wall of flame rounded the bend. The boys dropped to the floor with their back ends toward the approaching flame and covered their heads. The last sound that was understood was Shelby's yell. "Cover your ears!"

The flame didn't make it to the boys, but the shock wave did, and it hit with the force of a train. They were picked up and slammed against the back wall before falling like rag dolls to the floor. David tried to stand but blacked out and fell once more. The concussion echoed into the distance, leaving behind the trickle of pebbles and sifting sand. That, too, came to rest, and all fell silent and black... so very black.

Chapter 23

I remember coughing against the foul air and the pain it caused in my ribs. That stabbing pain woke me, and I lay on my back in the darkness. Dirt had settled on my face, and I brushed it away. It was then that I noticed the warm moist blood on my head. My mind tried to retrace the last few minutes but found nothing. Where was I? What was I doing on my back in this dark, dismal place?

A subtle grinding rock sound emerged from the stillness, and a strange tingling went through me. The small dark space seemed electrified and began to glow faintly with a near violet color. Above me I noticed the pattern of the rock change, an eerie metamorphosis that resulted in a window above me that opened to the outside. I shook my head for clarity and brought on a searing pain.

I lay dazed for a moment, hanging between dream and reality. Above, through the jagged hole in the rock, I could see stars. I recognized them readily enough as those of Cygnas, the swan, also called the Northern Cross. As the moments passed, bright, colored points of light emerged from around the cavity and danced just above the hole. They looked strangely familiar, and I felt I had watched such unusual, changing lights before... in a dream! They first moved with the grace of a ballerina, then shot straight up out of the hole and veered out of sight. As they streaked out of view they were replaced by others that seemed to be born within a colored haze, an aurora curtain that hung just above me.

Lost in the spectacle, I no longer attempted to move until something stirred beneath my foot. I jerked away and heard a moan. Suddenly, I remembered my flashlight and found it in its place on my belt. Switching it on I discovered two other people in the cavity with me. Then I remembered. I had been walking around and had fallen into a hole. David had come to my rescue... but I thought he got me out.

The presence of my light brought them both to stir, and I recognized David. The other man looked confused and vaguely familiar, but I couldn't place him. "David, look! They're beautiful!"

"The Marfa lights," he whispered in wonder as we gazed upward. "They're comin' out of this hole we're in." The three of us sat spellbound for a good twenty minutes as the light show ebbed and surged, keeping pace with the glowing energy within the cave.

Suddenly it stopped like a switch had been pulled, and with it, the tingling left as well. The third man said, "What in the world was that?" He drew the questioning attention of both of us. Who was he? I sensed that I should know him, and somehow felt I did... but I wasn't sure.

Suddenly, rocks began to crunch and groan, and the opening above us started to change. "Let's get out of here!" David yelled, and we all scrambled out through the closing hole above us.

Puzzled, we looked around. It seemed like any other normal night in West Texas. The sky was clear, and the stars were sparkling bright in the dry skies. A few crickets chirped nearby, and there was no breeze.

"I'm Bob Remes. Who are you guys, anyway?"

"Robby? I'm Shelby Ferris, yonder's David Carson. We came out here hopin' to find you. How'd you get in that hole? Where'd you come from?"

Still bewildered, I removed my bandanna and tied it to a mesquite branch to mark the hole, then we walked back to camp. We were quiet at first, each confused about the strange turn of events but not willing to be the first to reveal a lack of understanding to the others.

"Sure is warm," Bob awkwardly remarked, attempting to break the silent stalemate."

"Seventy-four," David stated, without expression, and peeled off to his tent.

Bob twisted his face in puzzlement. "Now, how'd he know that? Ain't no thermometer that I saw."

"A cricket told him," I remarked and headed for my tent.

"Just wait a cotton-pickin' minute. It's bad enough that I can't figure out what's just happened around here without you guys layin' somethin' like that on me. Now just how did a cricket tell him such a thing?"

"It's nothin' really. You count his chirps in fifteen seconds and add thirty-nine. His metabolism is tied to the temperature. Actually, as the temperature changes it affects all the creatures, even you. Did you know…"

"Hold it! I didn't ask for no lecture, I…" Suddenly, Bob stopped his comment. His head took an inquisitive tilt as he looked curiously at Shelby. "There's somethin' about you, cowboy, somethin' mighty strange." Then, regaining his original composure, he said matter-of-factly, "Now, where can I bed down 'til daylight?"

"Use my tent. I can't sleep anyway." I lifted the flap of my tent and gestured for him to enter. He seemed grateful and said as much.

My curiosity stood off sleep, and I walked back out into the night to think. It was quiet, except for the usual creatures of the night, and conducive to thought. Still, my mind whirled with images and events that I couldn't explain. At times they seemed so real, but then I would dismiss them as merely contrived images from my mind… characters that simply danced upon my dreams. After all, dreams and reality are recorded in much the same manner, and when later retrieved, what label is there to absolutely distinguish one from the other?

At one point, an hour later, I thought I heard the movement of something large, and I caught a strange, familiar odor on the night breeze… a disgusting, filthy odor that I felt sure I should know. I finally dismissed it and gave the credit to a stray steer, although I'd never smelled one like that. There were a couple hundred of them in this pasture, and it wouldn't be unlikely for one to be off by himself. Maybe it was sick or something. That might account for the smell.

Vague thoughts haunted me. Images of dreams, vivid dreams and strange places stirred my mind. Patches of it seemed so real, but they were laced together with so much that did not make any sense at all. The mystery was just too great, and I was still turning it in my mind when the eastern horizon began to take on color.

I was sitting atop a small knoll watching golden, crepuscular rays emanate from a rising sun when David walked up. "Nothing like a prairie sunrise to settle a soul, is there?"

I turned to greet him. "No, I can't say that there is. I've always savored mornings like this." Suddenly, the sunlight glistened off an object around his neck. "DC. Where'd you get that?"

As he looked down, his hand naturally moved to touch the amber teardrop, and he noticed his finger. "Shel! Where's my Aggie ring?" I almost replied that he had given it away, but how would I know that? And who would he give it to? Yet I sensed, ever so slightly, that I did know.

At that point we began to compare thoughts and concerns. Something strange had happened to us. Time had passed, although we didn't know how much, and we both felt as if we had done something that was worth remembering and yet we couldn't. And how did Bob end up in that hole with us? And how did we get so banged up? We could see that we were both a bloody mess, but we couldn't remember how we got that way.

After several confusing minutes, I did remember something and said excitedly, "DC, where's your journal? You keep that notebook like a diary. It should explain some of this."

He instinctively slapped his shirt pocket, then cocked his head in thought. "It must still be in the hole with everything else. We crawled out so fast I must have left my pack down there."

I looked over the pasture where my bandanna waved in the breeze and marked the hole. "We'd better get it." And we both took off at a brisk walk. Our pace quickened as we approached, and apprehension grew. Something in the back of my mind told me we wouldn't find the hole, but what? It was an absurd idea. Why would I think such a thing? Where could a hole in the ground go?

We stopped cold. The opening *was* gone! Moccasin tracks were everywhere, but the cave we had fallen into and climbed out of was nowhere to be found. My bandanna still waved from the branch where I had placed it while standing over the hole.

David looked around and pointed, "Look!"

Beneath my bandanna, and stacked neatly under the mesquite, were our packs and water bags. And hanging from one of the thorns was a gold medallion, blackened with soot. We had not done that. We had not been in any condition to even think about our stuff, much less stack it neatly under a mesquite. I picked up the medallion in wonder and turned it slowly in my hand. With my thumb I wiped off the black residue and revealed a jeweled dragon head.

"Strange, I've seen this before, DC. I'm sure I have. Did you ever do or see something and think you had dreamed it before? That's the way I feel about this. Dig out that journal!"

For the next hour we sat there in the tall prairie grass, against a backdrop of blue Chinati Mountains, excitedly turning through the worn pages of David's journal, and unraveling a mystery that no one was likely to believe. David finally asked, "How could all this have happened to us and we don't remember it?"

"I don't know, but I'd give a new saddle for the answer."

In the distance we heard the rattle of an approaching vehicle and turned to see Mr. Remes' old pickup leading a tail of dust and bouncing across the pasture road. Bob had heard the commotion and had come out of my tent. He was waving wildly to a pretty girl in a blue gingham dress who held on for dear life in the back of that old bouncing truck.

David broke a warm smile at the sight and said quietly. "Wanna go back, Shel?"

"I sure do! I've got to figure out where I left my boots."

The End

Glossary of terms

Anasazi- "Anasazi" is a Navajo word meaning "Ancient Ones." They are thought to be ancestors of the modern Pueblo Indians.

Athenaeum- An institution for the promotion of learning.

Aurora- Bands or streamers of light that appear in the sky at night in areas around the magnetic poles, caused by solar particles striking atoms in the outer part of the earth's atmosphere.

Big Medicine- A rare white Bison bull calf with ice-blue eyes and brown horns was born in 1933 on the National Bison Range in western Montana. He was named "Big Medicine" after the Native Indian legends about white bison. He soon became quite a tourist attraction

Black Diamond- A variety of large, sweet watermelon.

Blowhole- A small opening to the surface from a large cavern. Atmospheric pressure causes air to pass through it with considerable velocity.

Calcium carbonate- Calcite. Common cave material forming most cave features.

Calcium flowers- A Speleothem with crystal petals radiating from a central point usually composed of gypsum, epsomite or halite. Due to changes in flow rate, the flower petals tend to curve.

Chaparral- A low, dense growth of shrubby oaks and brush in the American Southwest.

Concho Ridge- Part of the Edwards Plateau running through the Permian Basin in West Texas. The ancient Permian sea left this ridge rich with fossils.

Copse- A dense, small wooded area or thicket.

Corona- A glowing electrical discharge at the surface of a high voltage conductor or between two electrodes.

Cradleboard- The cradleboards were used to protect the child from the cold and it was handy to hang in a tree or lean against something. The cradleboard could also be hung from a saddle horn for a long days ride.

Drainwires- A net of wires connected to an earth ground for draining off electrical energy.

Eddy -An area behind rocks where the current flows in a different direction.

Equinox- Either of the two times during the year when the sun crosses the earth's equator so that day and night are of equal duration worldwide, occurring in March and September.

Ether - A theoretical, universal substance believed during the 19th century to act as the medium for transmission of electromagnetic waves.

Exegesis- A critical explanation or interpretive analysis.

Firedamp- A gas that occurs naturally in mine tunnels. The gas is nearly always methane (CH_4) and is highly explosive.

Fissure- A narrow crevice or other opening, esp. one caused by splitting.

Flowstone- General term for deposits formed by dripping and flowing water on walls and floors of caves. Flowing films of water move along floors or walls and build up layers of calcium carbonate (calcite), gypsum, or other cave minerals.

Geothermal- Originating heat produced internally by the earth.

Geyser- A spring that erupts periodically, spewing up a stream of hot water, steam, or mud.

Goatskin- A container for water or wine, made of goatskin.

Greasewood- North American weedy shrub. Greasewood is a characteristic plant of the desert plains of the American West. It is a spiny shrub, up to three meters high with small, fleshy, toothless leaves.

Gunwale- The upper edge of a boat's side or bulwark.

Gypsum sheets- A speleothem in the form of a wavy or folded sheet or curtain hanging from the roof or wall of a cave, often translucent and resonant.

Hopi- The westernmost group of Pueblo Indians, situated in northeastern Arizona in the midst of the Navajo Reservation and on the edge of the Painted Desert. Formerly known also as the Moki, or Moqui, they speak a Shoshonean language.

Kachina- Ancestral spirit of the Pueblo Indians. They are more than 500 of these spirits, who they believe act as intermediaries between humans and the gods.

Kiva- A large, often underground room used by Pueblo Indians for ceremonies and councils.

Lava tube- Lava tubes are natural conduits through which lava travels beneath the surface of a lava flow. They often appear as long, smooth tunnels. The nature of the hardened lava can act like a thermos. Many of these tubes have ice flows in them even during the summer months.

Mano - Hand held stone used to grind grain in a Metate.

Manzanita- Low evergreen shrubs of the western United States, bearing clusters of edible berries. The trunk is red and smooth.

Marfa Lights- These dancing lights actually exist along a mountain range outside the West Texas town of Marfa. They have been a mystery for many years and authorities still quibble over their origin.

Mesquite- A shrub or small tree of the legume family, found in the southwestern United States and Mexico, which bear pods rich in sugar that are used as fodder for livestock.

Metate- A stone bowl where grain was placed to be ground with the mano stone.

Nephilim- "Nephilim" is a Hebrew word that means "fallen ones". In the Bible, in Genesis 6, we meet these people for the first time. What became of them?

Niche- The part of an ecological system occupied by a particular organism, or the functions of that organism in the system.

Nikola Tesla- The Serbian-American inventor, electrical engineer, and scientist born in 1856 in Smiljan, Lika (Austria-Hungary) Died on January 7, 1943 in New York City. His inventions included a telephone repeater, rotating magnetic field principle, polyphase alternating-current system, induction motor, alternating-current power transmission, Tesla coil transformer, wireless communication, radio, fluorescent lights, and more than 700 other patents.

Obsidian- Natural glass of volcanic origin that is formed by the rapid cooling of viscous lava. Obsidian has a glassy luster and is slightly harder than window glass. It is typically jet-black in color.

Ollas- Indian water containers of clay

Palo Duro canyon- An erosion canyon in the Texas Panhandle.

Pedagogues- A learned teacher.

Phoebe- Small plain gray bird. Being a flycatcher, they are always watching for a juicy flying insect to catch. Their song resembles their name - fee-bee.

Potato cannon- A pipe with a closed end that can be filled with gas vapor and air, then ignited so as to launch an object (often a potato) that has been stuffed into the pipe.

Poultice- A soft, usually heated mass of moist meal, leaves, or the like that is spread on a cloth and applied to a sore or inflamed area of the body as a therapy.

Prickly Pear Tuna- The fruit of the prickly pear cactus. It is edible and sold in stores under the name "tuna." Prickly pear branches (the pads) are also cooked and eaten as a vegetable.

Recon team- Short for reconnaissance. A team sent ahead to survey conditions prior to the movement of the main body.

Rhytons- Ceremonial jars or containers usually made of clay.

Scourge - Whip

Shale- A soft, multilayered rock that can easily be split into sheets.

Sheathing splints- A protective covering of wood splints inside the birch bark canoe.

Shield volcano- Large, dome-shaped mountains built of lava flows. The name comes from their similarity in shape to a warrior's shield lying face up on the ground. They are usually composed of basalt.

Sipapu- Pueblo histories and religion recognize two kinds of sipapus: The first is the original sipapu, through which First People entered the current world from the Third or Lower World. The second kind is a current passage to the Third World, which can be found as small holes or even more elaborate structures in kivas. Special bodies of water or even special places in the landscape are also often considered to be sipapus.

Slate- A fine-grained rock that tends to split in smooth layers.

Soda straws- Hollow, elongate, generally translucent tube of calcite representing the earliest growth of stalactites. They are equal in diameter to the water drops conducted along their length.

Soogan – A blanket roll like a sleeping bag

Speleothem- Cave features created after the underground chamber has been formed. They are a result of slow-moving water, usually containing calcium carbonate, which has been dissolved from the limestone where the cave was formed. When this water enters the cave, a chemical change causes the calcium carbonate to harden, creating all manner of cave formations and features called speleothems.

Stalactite- A stalactite hangs like an icicle from the ceiling or sides of a cavern.

Stalagmite- A stalagmite appears like an inverted stalactite, rising from the floor of a cavern. They form from various minerals in slowly dripping water.

Yaapontsa- Indian wind spirit

Printed in the United States
17115LVS00004B/295